DEADLY
Satisfaction

Also by Trice Hickman

Dangerous Love Series
Secret Indiscretions

Unexpected Love Series
Unexpected Interruptions
Keeping Secrets & Telling Lies
Looking for Trouble
Troublemaker

Playing the Hand You're Dealt
Breaking All My Rules

Published by Dafina Books

DEADLY
Satisfaction

TRICE HICKMAN

A Dangerous Love Novel

KENSINGTON PUBLISHING CORP.
www.kensingtonbooks.com

DAFINA BOOKS are published by

Kensington Publishing Corp.
119 West 40th Street
New York, NY 10018

All Kensington Titles, Imprints, and Distributed Lines are available at special quantity discounts for bulk purchases for sales promotions, premiums, fund-raising, and educational or institutional use. Special book excerpts or customized printings can also be created to fit specific needs. For details, write or phone the office of the Kensington special sales manager: Kensington Publishing Corp., 119 West 40th Street, New York, NY 10018, attn: Special Sales Department, Phone: 1-800-221-2647.

Dafina and the Dafina logo Reg. U.S. Pat. & TM Off.

ISBN-13: 978-1-61773-749-7
ISBN-10: 1-61773-749-6
First Kensington Trade Edition: February 2016
First Kensington Mass Market Edition: August 2018

eISBN-13: 978-1-61773-748-0
eISBN-10: 1-61773-748-8
First Kensington Electronic Edition: February 2016

10 9 8 7 6 5 4 3 2 1

Printed in the United States of America

Acknowledgments

Writing this portion of the book is always one of the most gratifying for me because I get the opportunity to give thanks for the many blessings in my life. I thank God for His grace and mercy. He is always faithful and He always gives me what I need, when I need it. To God be the glory!

Thank you to my parents, Reverend Irvin and Alma Hickman. You have always been in my corner, no matter the situation, with love, guidance, encouragement, and great advice. I love you to the moon and back! Thank you to my brother and sister, Marcus and Melody, whom I love dearly. Thank you to my many aunts, uncles, cousins, and family friends for loving and supporting me.

Thank you to the Hayes crew; Todd Sr., Todd Jr., Eboni, Mary, and sweet Gabriella. I couldn't ask for a more loving, supportive, and kind group of people to be in my life. I love you all!

Thank you to my girlfriends who always have my back and support me in everything I do. You are the definition of "I am my sister's keeper." I love each of you: Vickie Lindsay, Sherraine Mclean, Terri Chandler, Kimberla Lawson Roby, Barbara Marie Downy, Tiffany Dove, China Ball, Lutishia Lovely, Tammi Johnson, Cerece Rennie Murphy, and Yolanda Trollinger. Thank you for being my sisters and friends!

Thank you to my phenomenal agent, Janell Walden Agyeman. Your expert guidance, professional integrity, and genuinely kind spirit have been a blessing to me, and I'm proud to call you a dear friend.

Thank you to my amazing editor, Mercedes Fernandez. You push me to go deeper with each book and your keen eye and suggestions make it all come together. Thank you to the entire Kensington staff for all that you do to bring my books from words on paper to a published book.

Thank you to the super talented book publicists Ella D. Curry, of EDC Creations, and Yolanda Gore, the Literary Guru. I appreciate the work and dedication you put into helping to spread the word about my books. Thank you to the librarians, bookstore managers and employees, vendors, and online retailers who sell my books to your customers. Thank you to the Book Referees, Urban Reviews, AALBC, and the many bloggers and reviewers who support my work and help spread the word.

Thank you a million times over to the readers and book clubs who support my work! I'm honored that you make the investment in time to read my work, book after book. I can't tell you how much that means to me and how much I appreciate you! I hope you all will enjoy this book!

Happy Reading and Continued Blessings,

When we stop to think, we often miss our opportunity.

—Publilius Syrus, Maxim 185

Chapter 1

DROPPED THE BOMB

The elegantly sleek interior of G&D Hair Design was alive with chatter, laughter, and gossip. Even though G&D was a high-end salon situated in the trendy Arts District section of town, the owners, Geneva Owens and Donetta Pierce, made sure their establishment was as down home and welcoming as sweet potato pie, which they often served their clients as treats. And on this particular Tuesday morning, the salon was unusually busy. It was two days before Thanksgiving, and as Donetta had said, "Every woman in town is tryin' to get their style on for the holiday."

From one side of the salon to the other, each stylist's chair, shampoo bowl, and hooded dryer was occupied, and even more women were patiently waiting in the lobby, sipping coffee and tea from the complimentary beverage station. From blowouts to twist-outs, to full sew-ins, roller sets, and everything in between, the ladies of Amber, Alabama were primed and ready for the royal treatment that had become G&D's trademark. Geneva and Donetta had worked hard to overcome many obstacles to open their salon, and now they were reaping the rewards with their thriving business.

"I've been doing hair for as long as I can remember, and this is the busiest holiday turnout I've ever seen," Donetta said. "You'd think we were giving away weaves up in here."

"Everyone wants to look good when they visit with their families," Geneva said with a smile as she reached for her flat iron.

"Speak for yourself and these other women," Shartell Brown huffed as she sat in Donetta's chair. "As for me, I'm gettin' fly for me, myself, and I. My family is on my last nerve right now, and I'm glad I only have to tolerate them once or twice a year during the holidays."

Donetta made a *tsk*ing sound as she measured a track of hair for what would become part of Shartell's full sew-in weave. "Girl, why're you stressing about your family?"

"'Cause ever since I blew up, they're always coming to me with their hands out and a whole lotta foolishness."

"Shoot, if they know you like I know you, they'll leave you alone before they end up in one of your columns, or maybe even that new book you're writing."

Shartell smiled slyly. "You know, Donetta, that's

not a bad idea. I can write a juicy story from all the shenanigans that go on in my family. Real life is much more scandalous than fiction."

Donetta pursed her lips. "I was just joking."

"Girl, that's not a joke, that's a good idea."

"Shartell, that would be flat-out wrong to put your family members' business on front street. That's cold."

"Honey, please. That's business, and it's called being shrewd."

"How 'bout it's called being coldhearted." Donetta quipped in return. "Where the hell are your morals, Shartell? Don't you have a conscience anymore?"

"Of course I do. But if I'm telling the truth, what's wrong with that? Even the Good Book says the truth shall set you free."

"Don't use the Bible to justify your mess."

"I stand behind the things I say, that's why no one can ever accuse me of a being a liar, and that's the truth."

Geneva chimed in. "Just because something is true, that doesn't mean you have to say it."

"You better listen to Geneva," Donetta said as she parted Shartell's hair with her comb. "And don't think about putting anyone in this salon in your book because if you do, you'll end up having to do your hair your damn self, 'cause you know I won't touch your head again."

"Whatever," Shartell said.

"Heffa, you know I barely like you anyway," Donetta teased.

Geneva shook her head and laughed. "You two talk so much junk."

"Donetta knows she loves me," Shartell said with a chuckle. "And hey, I might be a heffa, and I might even be coldhearted, at times, but I'm one of the realest chicks you ever gonna meet, and there ain't a phony bone in my body."

Everyone within earshot nodded in agreement with what Shartell had just said. Shartell Brown, who had once worked as a stylist with Geneva and Donetta a few years ago, at Heavenly Hair Salon, had been nicknamed Ms. CIA, because she was a known gossip with intel on everyone in town. Now she was a respected news and entertainment reporter for Entertainment Scoop, a wildly popular online website that was giving TMZ a run for their money. Shartell had risen to prominence thanks to the most salacious and talked about murder case the town of Amber had ever seen.

Two years ago, Johnny Mayfield, who had been Geneva's ex-husband, had been murdered inside his home. Johnny had been a charismatic but nefarious man who'd amassed a legion of enemies, both male and female. The list of suspects had been as long as a hot summer day, but thanks to Shartell's contacts, inside information, and her uncanny ability to find out the word on the street before it ever hit the pavement, she'd provided the authorities with useful tips that helped them solve Johnny's murder and had cemented a new career for herself in the process.

Geneva shook her head. "Shartell, try to go easy on your family. You should count yourself blessed that you have relatives to spend the holidays with. I'd give anything to share a meal with my mother again, God rest her soul."

"That's because your mother was probably just as nice as you are, Ms. Pollyanna," Shartell teased. "My mama, on the other hand, could drive Jesus to drink hard liquor. And my four siblings . . . let's just say that if the devil needed extra disciples he'd come looking for them, and their badass kids."

"Shartell!" Geneva chided. "That's an awful thing to say."

Donetta threaded her needle and nodded her head. "That's the kind of truth telling she probably shouldn't have said, but you have to admit, it was funny as hell."

"Thank you," Shartell said, reaching up to give Donetta a high five. "My aunt is coming in town for the holidays and I have to pick her up from the train station tonight, but once I drop her off at my mama's house I'm gonna be in the wind and they won't see me again until Thanksgiving dinner, which I plan to cut short."

"You're seriously not going to spend time with your family?" Geneva asked.

"I'm gonna try my best not to. Besides, I have work to do. I'm writing an article about finding love during the holidays, and it's due tomorrow afternoon so it can run on Thanksgiving Day, and I know none of my knuckle head, backwards-ass relatives can help me with that subject matter."

Geneva adjusted her smock as she spoke. "You two are the most jaded human beings I know. Where is your optimism? Where's your hope?"

Donetta sighed. "Oh Lord, we've gotten her started."

"I'm serious." Geneva put down her flat iron and reached for a hair clip as she continued to speak. "Try not to be so pessimistic about everything."

"We're not pessimists, we're realists," Donetta said, hand on her slim hip. "Hell, I know exactly what Shartell's talkin' about when it comes to family. Every time I spend the holidays with mine I end up needing a double dose of therapy. They're just way too much, and that's why I'm not foolin' with them this year."

"Donetta, you know you're more than welcome to spend Thanksgiving at my house," Geneva said, "but your aunt is going to have a fit if you don't stop by and visit with her and your cousins."

Donetta smirked. "She'll just have to have one because my backstabbing relatives won't see my face this Turkey Day. I refuse to go over to my Aunt May May's and listen to the bullshit that I know she's gonna be serving. I got my life to live and I'm doin' just fine without them."

"I'm truly sorry to hear that," Councilwoman Harris spoke up from Geneva's chair. "Donetta, I'm going to say a prayer for you, and you too, Shartell, that you and your families will find peace."

Charlene Harris was one of Geneva's favorite and most loyal clients, and over the last two years she had become a close friend and confidant. Charlene was a pillar of the community, and much like Geneva, she was a woman who'd mastered the art of reinventing herself. Two years ago, after putting up with years of infidelity from her husband, she'd ended her long-suffering marriage and had started a new life. She'd updated her look and style from classic conservative to contemporary chic, but she'd kept the same elegant grace and comportment that she'd become known and respected for, along with her humility.

Geneva smiled at Charlene. "You understand what family is all about, and I know you can't wait to see your children when they come to town."

"Yes, I can't wait to see Phillip and Lauren. We

haven't all been together since last Christmas, so I'm certainly looking forward to it."

"That's a blessing," Geneva said as she worked her flat iron through Charlene's razor-cut, chin-length bob, putting the finishing touches on her chic hairdo.

Although no one else listening to Charlene speak could recognize the catch in her voice when she'd mentioned her children, Geneva had. And that was because Charlene had omitted any reference to her eldest child, Brad. Brad had moved to Los Angeles over ten years ago, married a tall blonde from the Valley, and hadn't spoken to his family since. It had hurt Charlene to her core, knowing that her firstborn had basically disowned his entire family, but she'd learned to make peace with it over the years through prayer, and the hope that someday her son would come to his senses. But until then, she poured all her love and care into the two who still remained close in her life.

"Yes, it is," Charlene said with a nod. "Lauren's doing well in med school at Johns Hopkins, and Phillip was just named senior associate at his law firm."

"That's impressive," Donetta said. "You did a great job raising them."

"Thank you, Donetta. But I have to say they made it easy because both of them have always been very focused, self-directed kids who never followed the crowd. They stayed true to who they are, and that's why I'm so proud of them. They're good, kindhearted human beings who care about people, and that's what's most important in my book."

Geneva nodded. "Yes, it certainly is."

"Amen to that," Donetta chimed in, along with Shartell. "Not everybody has the opportunity to pursue their dreams and still remain true to themselves while they're doing it. That takes a lot of effort and sacrifice."

Geneva looked at her co-owner and best friend and smiled. She knew that it was a topic near to Donetta's heart. It had been a little over a year since she'd undergone gender reassignment surgery, commonly known as SRS; or as the trans community called it, bottom surgery, so that her outward physical appearance reflected who she was inside. It had taken Donetta many years, tremendous sacrifice, and at times, painful heartache, to pursue her long-held dream of living life the way she'd always felt she was meant to.

"Your words speak so much truth, Donetta," Councilwoman Harris said with a nod. "Life is a journey filled with many paths we can take to arrive at our intended destination. The key is knowing how to navigate your course, regardless of what anyone else thinks, and then master how to stay on it."

"And the best way to reach any destination is in a pair of Jimmy Choos," Donetta replied with a wink.

They all laughed at Donetta's joke, but suddenly the room fell silent when Shartell looked up at the fifty-inch television screen hanging on the wall and let out a loud gasp. Every eye was glued to the face on the screen that put panic in each of their hearts, for very different reasons.

Geneva stood frozen in place while Donetta reached over her, grabbed the remote, and turned up the volume. The "*Breaking News*" caption rolled across the screen with a photo of Vivana Jackson above it. A hush came over the entire salon as they listened to news that left everyone's mouth hanging open with questions.

Vivana Jackson—formally known as Vivana

Owens—had been convicted of murdering her ex-lover, Johnny Mayfield, in cold blood, and was serving a twenty-five-to-life sentence for second-degree murder in the Alabama state penitentiary. But according to the information coming out of the reporter's mouth, Vivana was now being represented by a prominent local attorney who'd taken her case pro bono, and had found compelling evidence that suggested Vivana was innocent of the crime for which she'd been convicted. A murder committed impulsively, and without premeditation.

"I've uncovered evidence that corroborates my client's claim that she is innocent of killing Jonathan Mayfield," Leslie Sachs, Vivana's attorney, said. "I can't go into detail now, but when I present the evidence to the judge next week, it will be clear that Ms. Jackson, formerly known as Mrs. Owens, was not only framed, but the real killer is still at large, and is quite possibly watching this interview right now."

The reporter ended the clip by telling viewers that an exclusive jailhouse interview with Vivana would air tonight on the evening news.

Everyone remained silent while their eyes fell on Geneva, who was still frozen in place.

Donetta looked at Geneva. "Honey . . . you okay?"

Geneva shook her head from side to side. "No, I'm not. I need to go home."

From that moment forward, the salon was filled with voracious gossip, wild speculation, and unfounded theories about the murder case that had rocked Amber. Johnny Mayfield had done so many people wrong that a different suspect had popped up each week after his death. Mostly everyone in town believed that his scorned ex-lover, Vivana, had done it, while there were a select few who believed Vivana's claim that she'd been framed. But there were only four people who knew without a doubt that Vivana was innocent. One of them was dead, one was sitting in jail, one was Johnny's real killer—the honorable and well-respected councilwoman, Charlene Harris—and the last person who knew the identity of Johnny's real killer was the person who'd sent Councilwoman Harris a mysterious text, telling her that they had proof that she'd done it.

Later that night, nearly everyone in Amber was held captive in front of their televisions as they watched Vivana's defiant face and listened to her lawyer's self-assured words. People from one end of town to the other were abuzz with chatter and speculation, and there were a few who were more than a little concerned, namely Geneva, Donetta, and especially Charlene Harris. Each one of the women knew that in the days to come, this would be a holiday they'd never forget.

Chapter 2

GENEVA

The two loves of Geneva Owens's life were her loving husband, Samuel, and their adorable ten-month-old daughter, Gabrielle. They added meaning and purpose to everything she did, and she looked forward to coming home to them at the end of each day. But this afternoon wasn't one of those days, and as Geneva drove home—ten miles above the speed limit—she prayed that Samuel and Gabrielle wouldn't be there when she arrived.

Geneva breathed a heavy sigh of relief when she opened the garage door and saw the empty space where Samuel's SUV was usually parked. "Thank goodness Samuel's already on his way to the airport," she whispered to herself.

A small twinge of guilt pulled at Geneva's stomach for feeling that way, but she couldn't help it. She didn't want her husband or daughter there because she needed to be alone so she could sort out her thoughts in peace. She'd been stressed and anxious ever since she'd seen Vivana's face flash across the television screen at her salon this afternoon. From that moment forward, Geneva had not been able to shake the feeling that something bad was about to happen.

After she removed her clothes and changed into her comfortable lounge pants and matching shirt, Geneva went into her den. She curled her feet under her hips as she leaned back into the comfort of her brown chenille sofa. She looked to her right and picked up a beautifully framed picture of Samuel, Gabrielle, and herself, and let out a sigh. "I've got to keep them safe," she said. "Nothing else matters."

Geneva didn't know what Vivana was cooking up, but there was one thing she was certain of, and that was the fact that nothing good could come of anything Vivana Jackson was involved in. The thought was nearly too much for her to process, and again, she was glad the house was empty. She looked at her watch and noted the time. "They probably won't be back home for at least another hour or two."

With Thanksgiving only two days away, Samuel's parents were coming to town to celebrate the holidays and he'd taken Gabrielle with him to pick them up from the airport. Geneva had been excited about her in-laws' visit. She loved Samuel's mother and father as if they were her own parents, and their love for her was equally sincere. But at the moment, Herbert and Sarah Owens were pushed to the back of Geneva's mind, thanks to her new worries surrounding Vivana.

Geneva picked up the TV remote control and flipped to the local news station that was set to air Vivana's interview. "Whatever craziness that woman is scheming, I know it has trouble written all over it," she whispered as she sat on the edge of her couch, as stiff as a park statue. She stared at the TV in disbelief. "This can't be happening," she whispered again, bringing her hand to her mouth at the sight of Vivana's face on the screen. "What in the world is that psychopath up to?"

Geneva was struck by the change in Vivana's appearance. Vivana had once been a full-figured beauty who had been meticulous about her appearance. But in the span of the two years that she'd been incarcerated, the woman looked as though she'd aged a decade. Her smooth skin had become wrinkled, her vibrant eyes had lost their sparkle, and the apples of her cheeks had begun to sag. She fidgeted back and forth, constantly tucking and retucking her salt-and-pepper strands behind her ear. Geneva knew that was the nervous habit of someone who had something to hide.

Geneva watched without blinking as a haggard but defiant-looking Vivana Jackson spoke freely, proclaiming her innocence. Geneva paid close attention to Vivana's every word and movement, and she noticed that the woman's eyes, now weathered with tiny crow's-feet on each side, still harbored a wild emptiness that was almost frightening. She had the look of someone whose burdens ran deep and whose capacity for ruthlessness flowed even deeper.

"My story has never changed and it never will," Vivana said resolutely.

Geneva gasped because Vivana looked into the camera as if she was speaking directly to her, and it sent chills up her arm.

"I said it two years ago, and I'll say it again," Vivana continued, "I didn't kill Johnny. He wronged a whole lot of people, and that's where the focus should've always been . . . on those other people, not me. I've been locked up for a crime that I didn't commit while the real killer is still out there. But believe me," she said as a menacing smirk overtook her lips, "what's done in the dark always comes to the light, and that light's about to shine real bright because—"

"Yes," her attorney said, cutting Vivana off in mid-sentence. "Ms. Jackson is innocent of the murder of Johnny Mayfield. She was framed and was wrongly convicted and incarcerated while the real killer is still at large. Once I present the judge with the new evidence next week, I'm confident that my client will be vindicated."

The news reporter launched question after question, aimed at both Vivana and her attorney, hoping to get more detailed information about what type of new evidence was going to be introduced that would prove Vivana's innocence. Although it was clear to see that Vivana wanted to say more, as was evidenced by her edgy behavior and shifting eyes, she remained silent under the advice of her attorney. Finally, after several minutes of unsuccessful probing, the reporter gave up and went to commercial break.

"I don't know what to think," Geneva whispered aloud as she shook her head. She knew from firsthand experience what Vivana was capable of, and that knowledge made her feel a little afraid. "I've got to shake this off. I can't let this get to me."

Not since Johnny's death had she felt so many conflicting emotions. But oddly, her anxiety and heavy heart hadn't come from the grief or sadness that most people experienced when losing someone; rather, Geneva had been unnerved because she felt an overwhelming amount of guilt.

Geneva hadn't been completely surprised on the fateful morning she'd learned that Johnny had been murdered. At the time, she and Johnny had been estranged. Geneva had left him, and they'd been separated for several months pending divorce. In that time she'd moved on, met and fallen in love with Samuel, and had been more than ready to start a new life after the hell Johnny had put her through during their five and a half years of marriage. He'd been a dishonest, deceitful, womanizing dog whom Geneva had grown to detest toward the end of their turbulent union. And even though Johnny had been the guilty party in their relationship, he had contested the divorce and had vowed to fight her to the bitter end.

The week before Johnny was killed, he had come by the salon where Geneva worked and begged for her forgiveness. He'd told her that he was remorseful about the way he'd mistreated her and taken her for granted for so many years. But in the process of his apology he'd caused a scene in front of her clients, and Geneva had no patience for him or his drama. All she'd wanted to do was remove him from the salon and from her life. She told him to leave and she even walked him to the front steps, and that's when things turned from bad to worse.

Geneva and Johnny had exchanged heated words before Geneva made the misstep of telling him that she was in love with another man. Hearing that news sent Johnny over the edge. He'd impulsively grabbed her arm, and as she pulled away, she'd lost her balance, and caused them both to tumble down the salon's steep steps and hit the hard concrete one story below. That single fall cemented both their fates. Geneva had ended up in the hospital, where the doctors revealed that she'd been pregnant and had lost the baby. Her grief had been heavy, and was made worse by the fact that Johnny came out of the accident without so much as a scratch.

That night, as Geneva lay in her hospital bed, she'd prayed for Johnny's death. She'd prayed that he would befall a slow and painful demise, and that he would suffer greatly. A week later her plea was answered. Johnny was shot in the chest at point-blank range, and he'd died slowly, suffocating on his own blood as a result of his fatal wound. When Geneva had heard the news, guilt had crept in.

Geneva shivered at the thought. She turned off the TV and slowly rose from the couch. She walked into her spacious gourmet kitchen, filled her stainless steel teakettle with water, and reached into the cabinet for a box of her favorite herbal tea. "I need this to calm my nerves," she said aloud. She shook her head when she thought about the fact that there was a time not too long ago when a glass of wine would have been her drink of choice to calm her anxiety. But during her pregnancy, Donetta had persuaded her to start drinking herbal tea. "Honey, folks sleep on tea, thinking it's weak. They just don't know that it's the liquid of the gods."

Geneva had to admit that Donetta had been right. Orange hibiscus had become her favorite lately, but as she stood by the stove waiting for the water in her kettle to whistle, the anticipation of the flavorful taste was overshadowed by whatever scheme she knew Vivana was plotting.

Geneva hadn't been shocked that Vivana had killed Johnny; after all, she was the same woman who had deceived Geneva for months. Vivana had walked into the salon where Geneva had been working and said her name was Cheryl, and that she was newly divorced and had just moved to Amber for a fresh start. She'd struck a chord with Geneva, who'd been on that same path and had just filed paperwork to divorce Johnny.

But as time went on, Geneva, as well as everyone else at the salon, quickly realized that Cheryl was unstable and had major problems. She was moody, attitudinal, arrogant, and obnoxiously rude. Geneva eventually found out that Cheryl's real name was Vivana, and that she'd assumed that identity so she could find out everything there was to know about her, and then kill her. During Johnny's murder trial Vivana had even confessed that her plan had been to kill Geneva first, and then do away with Johnny as payback for all the pain they'd both caused her. But she'd said that someone had gotten to Johnny first, foiling her plans.

Geneva's mind kept replaying the look she'd seen in Vivana's eyes when the disturbed woman had been on the witness stand. It was the same look Vivana had during the interview tonight, and Geneva knew that meant that if Vivana got free, she'd come looking for her to finish what she'd started.

As Geneva poured her tea and waited for her husband, daughter, and in-laws to arrive, she knew she had to do what she'd been putting off for the last two years. Tomorrow, while she was out running errands and getting food for her family's holiday feast, one of the top things on her list was going to include paying a visit to Rusty's Pawn Shop so she could buy a gun.

Chapter 3

CHARLENE

Councilwoman Charlene Harris was a responsible woman who always followed the rules of proper order and conduct. She'd never been arrested, had never been late with a mortgage payment, and had never bounced a check. She always treated people with kindness and was generous to a fault. Yet with all her glowing attributes she was a cold-blooded murderer.

Charlene was normally calm and rational, but right now she felt out of control and reckless as she pressed her cream-colored Valentino heel against the pedal of her luxury sedan, sending her car flying down the highway. She couldn't care less about the fact that she was driving twenty-five miles over the posted speed limit, because all she could concentrate on was getting home so she could plan what her next move was going to be.

"I've got to find out what's going on," Charlene said aloud. Her slender fingers were tightly gripped around her steering wheel as she continued to drive at breakneck speed. "I need to know what Vivana's up to and what kind of evidence she has."

Charlene took a quick glance into her rearview mirror and barely recognized the tired-looking eyes of the woman staring back at her. In just a few hours she'd gone from feeling on top of the world with the anticipation of seeing her children for the holidays, to worrying about her future, and more specifically, her freedom. "I wish I'd never laid eyes on him," she said with a heavy sigh as she thought about Johnny Mayfield. "If I'd just gone back to my office that day, none of this would've ever happened."

Charlene's mind flashed back to the day she met Johnny Mayfield. She'd just filed for divorce and had been looking for a new home to start a new life. A young couple she knew had highly recommended their Realtor, who happened to be Johnny. Charlene had agreed to meet him at a coffee shop to discuss what type of property she was looking for, and when she'd walked in and seen him, it had been lust at first sight. Johnny had been well-dressed, charming, and so sexy that she couldn't help but be flattered when he'd started flirting with her. He'd made her feel young, beautiful, and desired, and she'd basked in the attention. They'd exchanged heated glances as they sipped their coffee, and before Charlene had known it, an hour later she was having unbridled sex with Johnny in one of the vacant units inside a small apartment building he'd managed. But what Charlene hadn't known was that Johnny had a video camera set up in the room that had recorded every detail of their wild sexcapade.

Johnny had blackmailed Charlene and had threatened to send copies to her colleagues, who held her in high esteem, to her neighbors, who respected her, to her children, who looked up to her, and to her husband's divorce attorney, who would surely use the evidence against her. Charlene had gone along with his scheme for months until one fateful Saturday morning, when she learned just how despicable Johnny really was.

Charlene had been at the hair salon when Johnny came walking in, pleading for his estranged wife's forgiveness. Charlene had sat in the lobby with a towel over her head, looking on in shock as she realized that her hairstylist, Geneva, was Johnny's wife. And added to that, Vivana had shown up, caused a scene, and then stomped out, but not before telling Johnny that he was a dead man who would regret ever meeting her. But what happened next pushed Charlene over the edge.

When Charlene found out that Johnny's reckless behavior had caused Geneva to miscarry, she'd decided to make sure Johnny would never harm another woman, and she got busy devising a plan to kill him. A week later Johnny was dead.

"I should've known it was only a matter of time before what I did caught up with me," Charlene said, shaking her head as she zipped in and out of lanes amidst the heavy rush hour traffic. Over the last two years Charlene had tried not to think about what would happen if the truth was ever discovered. But one very clear reminder that was always in the back of her mind was a cryptic text message she'd received from a blocked number a few months after Vivana had been convicted. The anonymous sender had called Charlene a murderer, and when Charlene had responded by asking who they were, their simple reply had been, *"I'm the person who has proof that you murdered Johnny Mayfield."* She'd immediately deleted the text exchange and prayed it wasn't the beginning of the end.

But not since that day had Charlene heard so much as a peep from the anonymous person. She knew if she obsessed about the text, who'd sent it, and what evidence they had, she would eventually lose her mind. So she worked hard to live life as normally as she could, and there were times when the thought of being a murderer was a distant memory. But now everything was coming to the surface again, and she didn't know what was going to happen next.

Charlene ignored the honking horn accompanied by a middle finger from a motorist whom she'd just cut in front of because the only thing her mind could focus on was the trouble she was in. She thought about the deceitful things she'd had to do over the last two years—lying, stealing, falsifying documents, and manipulating people to her advantage—all to cover up the murder she'd committed. "What have I allowed myself to become?" she whispered to herself. "I don't even know who I am anymore."

Charlene shook her head from side to side as she thought about Vivana Jackson—the woman behind the cause of her worries. Charlene had been in Geneva's chair at G&D Salon getting the finishing touches on her freshly styled hairdo, when *"Breaking News"* flashed across the large TV screen on the wall, causing Charlene to nearly jump out of her seat. When she saw Vivana's face appear with a caption running below it that read, *New Evidence in the Mayfield Murder Case*

To Be Revealed, her mouth ran dry and her head began to pound. Even though her heart had been thumping as if she'd just run a marathon, she'd managed to remain calm, because the last thing she'd wanted to do was draw attention to herself.

As Charlene barreled onto the exit that would lead her to the affluent, picturesque neighborhood she'd called home for the last two years, she was pulled from her thoughts by her car's Bluetooth alerting her of an incoming call. A small smile came to her face when she saw that it was her son, Phillip, who was traveling home for the holidays.

To say that Charlene was proud of her children was an understatement. Philip and Lauren brought her great joy and happiness, and they'd seen her through dark days that she hoped to never experience again. She was glad that even though they were both adults with lives of their own, they'd still remained close, and they'd always be her babies. She thanked God every day that they'd inherited her kindhearted nature and temperament instead of her ex-husband's deceitful, conniving ways. Charlene took a deep breath, calmed herself, and answered the call. "Hey, Phillip," she said in a cheery voice that belied her true mood. "Are you getting ready to board your flight?"

"No, I'm getting ready to go to the grocery store because there's nothing here in this fridge."

Charlene was confused. "Wait a minute, are you at the house?"

"Yeah, I took an earlier flight and got here about two hours ago."

"Two hours . . . why didn't you call me and let me know you were home?"

Phillip chuckled. "I wanted to surprise you. After I

got here I took a quick nap and then I showered. I was going to cook dinner for you, but when I came down to the kitchen I couldn't find any food. That's not like you, Mom. This place is usually loaded with food during the holidays. What's up?"

Charlene gulped, knowing her son was right. She'd had every intention of going to Whole Foods straight from the salon with her Thanksgiving food list in hand, and she had planned to make a quick meal for her and Phillip tonight, and then cook all day tomorrow for their holiday meal once Lauren arrived. But it had taken her much longer at the salon after hearing the breaking news about Vivana Jackson, because Geneva had experienced a mild panic attack and she'd stayed there to help calm her. Over the last two years Geneva had become more than her stylist, she'd become her friend, and Charlene felt she owed the woman that much to offset the guilt of killing her husband.

After staying at the salon for much longer than she'd planned to, Charlene had left with her nerves in an uproar. She was flummoxed, and shopping for food had been the last thing on her mind. "Sorry, baby," she said to Phillip as she came up to a stoplight. "It's been a long week, and I've had a very, very long day. I'd planned to go grocery shopping this afternoon but—"

"I was just kidding, Mom. I know how busy you are. Just come home and relax. I'll go out and pick up something for dinner tonight."

Charlene smiled as she rounded the corner and turned onto her street. She knew that not every parent could say their child was as responsible and thoughtful as Phillip. She knew that one day he was going to make some young woman a fine husband, but sadly, she didn't think that day would come anytime soon.

In addition to his physical size, the other attribute Phillip had inherited from his father was that he loved women. He'd been a ladies' man since kindergarten, sharing his snacks with the pretty girls in his class and then charming the rest with his Play-Doh skills during recess. By the time he was in college he had co-eds and professors alike swooning over him. And now, as a successful, handsome bachelor with a good job at a prestigious law firm, he was a highly sought-after commodity.

Charlene smiled when she saw Phillip's rental car parked in the driveway. "I'm home now," she said as she drove around the side of her Tudor-style home and pushed the button on her garage door opener. "I'll see you in a sec."

When Charlene walked through her back door and into her large eat-in kitchen, she smiled widely at the site of Phillip standing in front of the sink, washing off an apple.

"Here, eat this. It'll give you a little boost."

Charlene shook her head. "Son, after the day I've had, I need that apple to be sitting inside a martini glass." Her joke made both of them laugh.

"You might be tired, but you look great, Mom," Phillip said. He reached for her briefcase, set it on the kitchen counter, and gave Charlene a hug.

For the first time in hours, Charlene felt a semblance of calm return to her mind. "I'll take that compliment any day. Especially from a good-looking, good-smelling man. What are you wearing, son?"

Phillip smiled. "It's the Versace cologne you got me for my birthday."

"I have good taste."

They both laughed again and walked into the family room. Charlene sank her tired body into the comfort of her custom-made, oversized couch and kicked off her designer heels as Phillip took a seat beside her. "How was your flight?"

"It was full to capacity. I'm glad I was able to get out of DC early because the airport was a zoo, and it's probably a madhouse right now. You know how it is during the holidays."

"Yes, I'm just glad you made it here safely. I hope Lauren won't have problems tomorrow."

"Me too. I talked to her this afternoon, and she's still scheduled to get here in the morning. I told her I'd pick her up from the airport."

Charlene sighed with relief. She'd forgotten what it was like to have someone around to help her with things. "Thank you, baby. I appreciate you going to pick up your sister because that will free me up to start cooking early in preparation for Thanksgiving dinner."

"And speaking of food, like I said, I'd planned to make dinner tonight, but now I can do one better; I can get dinner for us from our favorite place."

"Sebastian's!"

"You got it."

"I haven't been there in a few months."

"Well you're in luck tonight." Phillip stood to his feet. "You want your usual?"

Charlene nodded. "Yes, chicken marsala with extra wine sauce on the side. And ask them to put the sauce in a medium container, not those tiny condiment cups that only hold a teaspoon."

Phillip shook his head and laughed. "I know the drill."

"At least I'm consistent," Charlene said with a laugh. "And after the day I've had, I need something steady like my favorite dish. Food truly is comfort for the soul."

"Sure is. I'll place our order on my way there. Text me the grocery list and I'll pick up what we need on my way back."

"Grocery list?"

Phillip nodded. "While I'm out I might as well pick up groceries for Thanksgiving dinner, that way you won't have to leave the house tomorrow unless you just want to. You need the rest."

Once again, Charlene was grateful to have a child as thoughtful and unselfish as Phillip. Unlike a lot of men she knew, including her ex-husband Reginald, Phillip didn't go overboard with fancy words or expensive gifts to show his love. Instead, he demonstrated it through the little things he did that added up in big ways. Getting her dinner and picking up groceries meant more to Charlene than any holiday gift he could buy her. And what made his gesture even sweeter was that even though she knew Phillip liked to cook, he detested having to actually shop for food. He was a regular with Peapod, and had groceries delivered to his house once a week.

"Phillip, are you sure? You hate going to the supermarket, and you barely know where anything is located once you get there."

Phillip laughed. "True, but if I can write an interrogatory, I think I can figure out what aisle the ketchup is on."

"Well, I know you've got to be tired from going in to the office this morning and then taking the early flight home."

"Mom, I remember growing up you used to work

all day, take Lauren and me to piano lessons and soccer practice, and still manage to cook dinner, help us with our homework, and whatever else we needed. I don't do half that, so I think I can handle dinner and a walk down the grocery aisle."

Charlene smiled. "I've said it before and I'll say it again. You're gonna make some woman a very happy lady one day, and I hope that day comes soon."

"I know you're determined to drag me out of bachelorhood, but believe it or not, I'm doing just fine."

"I'm not saying you have to get married right now, but . . ."

"Here it comes."

"Don't you think it's time for you to start considering the idea of having a committed relationship? You date so many random girls who fly in and out of your life that I can't keep up with them all."

Phillip rose to his feet, clearly not wanting to have this conversation. "I'm having fun, and I'm honest with all the women I see. I don't lead anyone on, and I'm straight up about where I am as far as a committed relationship goes."

"So they're all fine with being one of many?"

"You make it sound like I have a harem or something," Phillip joked.

Charlene raised her brow. "You said it, not me."

"I'm being careful, and above all, I'm being honest. I thought that's what women want."

"We do . . . but trust me, no woman wants to be one of many. If you date a woman who doesn't mind being placed on a list, she's not wife material."

"That's my point, Mom. I'm not looking for wife material. I'm dating and I'm having fun, and the only list I'm thinking about right now is that grocery list you need to text me." Phillip smiled and leaned over to plant a kiss on Charlene's cheek. "I'll be back in a little while."

Charlene shook her head as she watched her son walk out of the room. She used to stay out of her children's business when it came to their relationships. But ever since the fiasco two years ago involving Lauren's ex-boyfriend, which ultimately led to the unraveling of Charlene's marriage, she'd been very concerned about who her children dated. When Lauren had brought her college boyfriend home to meet the family, they learned that the young man was actually her half brother, the result of an illicit affair that Charlene's husband had carried on years ago.

She sighed. "I hope that boy settles down." Charlene knew she shouldn't worry so much because Phillip was a grown man who was capable of making his own decisions, and so far he'd made good ones. But there was something that she knew she needed to worry about, and that was the breaking news interview with Vivana. She picked up the remote control and turned on her television.

She looked at her watch and noted she had five minutes before the interview was set to air. She quickly sprang to her feet and headed into the kitchen. "I'm going to need this," Charlene said as she reached into her refrigerator for a bottle of chardonnay, and then pulled a wineglass from the cabinet above her head.

With her wineglass and chilled bottle in hand, Charlene returned to her place on the couch just in time to hear the evening anchorwoman's voice as she began the broadcast with the breaking news segment. This was the moment Charlene had been stressing over all afternoon. As soon as Vivana's face appeared on the screen, Charlene's breathing became shallow. Unlike when she was in the salon earlier today, she didn't have to curtail her reactions, and she could take more time to fully digest what was being said.

Charlene listened closely, paying careful attention to every word coming out of Vivana's mouth, but more important, her lawyer's. Charlene knew from firsthand experience that Vivana was a loose cannon who was subject to say and do just about anything. The woman had no impulse control, which had made it very easy to frame her. But Vivana's attorney was a different matter, because she was the complete antithesis of her client. Leslie Sachs was composed, direct, purposeful, and above all, she was very smart and extremely careful. Leslie was so smooth in her approach that people never felt her bite until after they were bleeding. She was skilled and ruthless, and she never took a case unless she knew she could win. This knowledge made Charlene more afraid than ever.

Charlene had first met Leslie more than thirty years ago when the two of them had worked together at a prestigious, good ol' boy law firm in downtown Birmingham. Leslie had been a mousy, timid young woman who didn't seem to fit in with the rest of the rising stars at the firm. Charlene had been the only first-year associate who'd befriended Leslie, partly because she felt sorry for the woman, and partly because being the only African American associate on staff, Charlene knew what it was like to feel like an outsider. The two women formed a bond and they looked out for each other.

Leslie's timid streak came to a halt on a hot summer night that ended in murder. She'd been working late with one of the senior partners, and he'd invited her into his large corner office for a drink to ease the tension of their long workday. One drink turned into five, and friendliness turned into unwanted advances. By the end of the night the senior associate was dead, and Leslie had blood on her hands.

Leslie had made what everyone had thought was the colossal mistake of representing herself in the murder case. But it turned out to be the best move the timid young woman could have ever crafted. She successfully argued her case, was acquitted of all charges, and became a legal star. She'd been successfully representing accused killers ever since.

By the time the five-minute interview was over, Charlene had drunk half the bottle of wine and her nerves were even more frayed than before. Neither Vivana nor Leslie had said much, and that was what made Charlene's heart race. She knew this was Leslie's strategy—bait the hook and then reel in the fish. Leslie knew her client was innocent; otherwise she wouldn't have taken Vivana's case, and that meant she knew that the real killer was still out there, and that they were probably watching the interview for clues—just as Charlene was doing.

Charlene pressed the power button on the TV, turning it into a black slate of silence so she could think. "I need another drink," she said as her unsteady hand struggled to pour more wine into her glass. She was about to guzzle the chardonnay when she was startled by her ringing cell phone. She looked at the caller ID and nearly dropped her glass when she saw Leslie Sachs's name flash across the screen.

Charlene temporarily stopped breathing as her lungs filled with panic instead of air. A million thoughts raced through her mind, but the one thing she knew she had do to was snap out of her haze and answer Leslie's call. She took a deep breath and pressed the Answer button. "Hello, Leslie," Charlene said in a voice so calm it surprised even her. "To what do I owe the pleasure of your call?"

"How are you, Charlene?" Leslie asked, sounding as polite as a concierge.

Over the years Charlene and Leslie had drifted apart as their lifestyles and careers changed. The high respect they had for each other still remained, and they kept each other's number in their phones, but these days the only contact the two women had was when they briefly saw each other at political functions or women's networking events. They would chitchat and catch up on each other's lives in polite but quick conversation. Now Leslie was calling her in the early evening on the eve of a holiday, out of the blue. But Charlene knew this wasn't really out of the blue, that there was a purpose attached to Leslie's call. She responded with caution. "I'm well, Leslie. And you?"

"I can't complain."

Charlene didn't follow up on Leslie's response. She'd already asked the woman why she was calling, so the ball was in Leslie's court. Charlene decided not to say another word. She took a quick sip of wine as five seconds of silence passed before Leslie spoke.

"Did you see the breaking news tonight?"

"Yes, I did."

"What did you think?"

Even though Charlene was shaking inside, she kept her composure. She didn't want to say too much, but she also didn't want to beat around the bush trying to figure out Leslie's angle. Charlene prided herself on being a woman of purpose, and she liked to confront

?hings head-on. "Leslie, do you need my assistance with anything?"

Leslie paused for a moment, and Charlene knew it was intentional. "As a matter of fact, I do," she finally said. "I need your help on the Mayfield murder case. Both the victim and my client were your constituents."

Charlene gulped. "Yes, they were, but I'm not exactly clear how I can help you."

"I'll fill you in when we meet. How does coffee next Monday morning sound?"

Charlene bit her bottom lip. That was five long days away, but she knew she had no choice. "Sure, where and when do you want to meet?"

Leslie hesitated again. "The Whole Bean Café, at ten."

Charlene's heart began to race again. The Whole Bean Café was where she'd first met Johnny. She nearly gasped, but instead she smiled into the phone. "Sounds good. I'll see you there."

"Oh, and Charlene . . . have a happy Thanksgiving with your family."

"You too, Leslie."

Charlene leaned back into the couch and drank the rest of the wine in her glass. She wanted to run and hide, but she knew that was out of the question. She wondered what Leslie had up her sleeve, and intuition told her that whatever it was, it couldn't be good. "Calm down, calm down," she whispered to herself.

Charlene breathed in deeply. She wasn't sure what her next move was going to be, but she knew that whatever she did, she had to use her head, just as she'd been doing ever since she'd killed Johnny Mayfield and framed Vivana for the crime.

Chapter 4

DONETTA

Donetta picked up the remote control and turned off her TV in pure disgust. "That crazy-ass woman is nothing but trouble, and she looks even more deranged now than she did on the witness stand during her trial."

Donetta had just finished watching Vivana Jackson's prerecorded jailhouse interview. Every time she thought about the woman, her blood boiled and then ran as cold as ice. She knew from direct experience that Vivana was the type of person who could make you mad enough to slap her, but also make you think twice about doing it because she was more dangerous than poison.

"Geneva has finally gotten her life back together, and now this heffa has to come along and turn it upside down again." Donetta shook her head as she thought about the sheer havoc that Vivana used to wreak upon everything and everyone she came into contact with. She was a devious, conniving snake, and although Donetta was one of the very few people who'd never been fully convinced that Vivana had killed Johnny, she knew the woman was very capable of murder and much more.

"I wonder what kind of evidence they have?" she said with curiosity. Donetta knew that if Vivana was truly innocent, and the real killer was still out there, justice needed to be served. But at the same time, the thought of Vivana roaming free was a scary proposition.

Donetta sucked her teeth and frowned as her mind drifted to the past with the memory of how she had first met Vivana at Heavenly Hair Salon, where she and Geneva used to work. The way Vivana had made up a false identity so she could openly stalk Geneva had been more eyebrow raising than any work of fiction a novelist could write.

Donetta remembered seeing the gleam in Vivana's eyes when she'd sit in Geneva's chair and say things to intentionally piss Geneva off. But she didn't stop there; she would spread her venom across the entire salon, upsetting and irritating stylists and customers alike. No one liked her, but Vivana hadn't cared because she'd been on a mission.

"There's something about that woman that ain't right," Donetta had told Geneva. "Watch her, because I have a feeling she's up to no damn good."

Donetta shuddered when she thought about how close Geneva had come to sharing Johnny's fate. During the murder trial, Vivana had testified in open court that she'd wanted to kill Geneva first, and then do away with Johnny. But someone had gotten to Johnny before she could carry out her plan, causing her to forgo it entirely.

"What a psychopath," Donetta said aloud, shaking her head. "I hope she rots in jail, because even if she didn't kill Johnny, I'm sure her deranged ass has done something that justifies keeping her behind bars."

Thinking about Vivana, along with her hectic day at the salon, had made Donetta's head hurt. And it didn't help that she'd just started taking a new dosage of hormone replacement therapy. Her new prescription, combined with her daily dose of anti-androgens—meant to further suppress what little testosterone she had left in her body—had left her feeling tired and a little light-headed. "Maybe if I eat something I'll feel better."

Donetta walked into her kitchen and rummaged through her pantry in search of something she could throw together for a quick meal. But she came up short, so she searched her refrigerator and then let out a frustrated sigh. "This is the only part of my life that's just like a damn man," she said jokingly, and then paused. "Yep, that's definitely the only part." Donetta looked down at her flat crotch and leaned against her gray quartz countertop. She ran her hand over the area between her legs where until a year ago, a bulge had been. Thanks to her gender reassignment surgery, she no longer had to worry about binding the penis and testicles that had never felt like they'd belonged on her body.

Over the past ten years, and particularly the last two, Donetta had embarked upon what she could only describe as an odyssey. She'd completed male-to-female transformation, or MTF, as it was commonly referred to in the transgender community. At times she'd felt anxious, excited, frustrated, and scared. But more than anything, she was grateful to finally be able to live comfortably as the woman she'd always known she was meant to be.

For as far back as Donetta could remember, she'd felt as if she'd been living in a body she was never meant to inhabit.

She'd been born Donald Eric Pierce, named after her maternal grandfather, who had been the epitome of an overtly masculine alpha male. But instead of little Donald inheriting his grandfather's qualities, he'd leaned toward the exact opposite, acting dainty and more feminine than the girls in his neighborhood. When he was a child he'd gravitated toward Barbie instead of G.I. Joe, and he favored jump rope over stickball. He loved reading his grandmother's *Redbook* magazine, and secretly longed to wear the green uniforms the Girl Scouts proudly sported to school, instead of their counterpart's blue one that his mother had forced him into.

Donald was five years old the first time he realized with absolute knowing that, despite the fact that he looked like a boy on the outside, he was 100 percent female on the inside. It had been his first day of kindergarten, and his teacher announced that the class was going to take a bathroom break. She asked everyone to line up according to gender—girls on one side and boys on the other. Young Donald instinctively walked over to the side where the girls were standing.

"Donald," the teacher had said, "I don't think you heard me correctly. The boys are on the other side."

The children giggled, and they all thought, along with their teacher, that Donald had misunderstood the directions. What they didn't know was that Donald fully comprehended what the teacher had said, and that, in fact, he'd gone to the line that he believed he was meant to be in. After a moment, Donald complied and walked over to join the boys because he didn't understand, let alone know how to articulate his position at such a young age.

As Donald grew older, he learned how to hide who he was, not wanting to bring embarrassment to his hardworking but insensitive single mother, or physical harm to himself. His father had checked out of the picture the day before his seventh birthday, and his mother had blamed him. "Your daddy didn't want to raise no sissy, and that's why he left," Donald's mother had told him. Donald had never gotten along with his mother, and she, too, eventually abandoned him at the start of his sixth-grade year. "Your daddy didn't want to raise a sissy, and I'll be damned if I'ma raise a punk," she'd said. One day when he came home from school, all her clothes and furniture was gone, and that was how he came to live with his grandma Winnie.

Junior high school was miserable for Donald, and high school was torturous. *Gay*, *queer*, *fag*, *fairy*, *freak*, and *homo* were all words he'd become used to hearing associated with his name. If it hadn't been for his beloved grandma Winnie, whose husband Donald he had been named after, he wouldn't have survived. She was the only person who showed him unconditional love. "Baby, you a part of me, and I'm a part of you, so we both gon' make it, you hear?" she'd often tell him. He knew if he had a part of her goodness inside him, he could do anything, and that's what helped *him* become *her*.

Donetta ran her hand across her soft, curvaceous C cups, and smiled. It had been a year and a half since she'd had her breast implant surgery, and she still couldn't get over how much she loved the difference it made in her appearance. "Real boobs!" she'd said to Geneva when she showed her best friend the amazing results of her perfectly-shaped breasts.

Although Donetta had always been effeminate when she'd lived as a man, she'd tried as hard as she could to repress her feminine side for years, which helped protect her from retaliation in the rural South Carolina town where she'd grown up. But once she moved to Amber several years ago to enroll in cosmetology school after earning a degree in business from Florida A&M, she'd finally felt comfortable enough to break out of her shell. Little by little she took baby steps toward her dream to live fully as a woman.

She had always been slender, with narrow shoulders and lean muscles, which made looking female slightly less challenging than it was for many trans women she knew. She'd started off slowly, dressing androgynously in women's blouses, low-rise jeans, and flat sandals. Then she stepped it up with accessories by wearing chandelier earrings that highlighted her long, slim neck, styling bold bangles that clanked at her slender wrists, and rocking a midlength weave that gave her a fresh look. She accentuated her feline-shaped eyes with black liner, smoky shadows, and perfectly arched brows. Her cheeks looked rose-kissed after applying the perfect shade of blush, and she played up the contours of her near-perfect bone structure with strategically applied bronzer.

But no matter how much estrogen she took, clothes she wore, or makeup she applied, Donetta knew she would never look the way she wanted without taking more drastic measures.

She smiled to herself as she remembered the day her late grandma Winnie and Geneva had sat by her side in the waiting room of the Gender Wellness Center, where she'd gone for her first hormone replacement therapy. She'd known that HRT was going to be a permanent part of her life from that point forward, and the thought had been a little daunting. She was glad she'd taken her primary care doctor's advice years ago to not only seek clinical therapy, but to join a good support group to help her deal with the multitude of physical and emotional changes that were ahead.

During her first few months of HRT, Donetta had been sorely disappointed that the only noticeable results she'd experienced had been bloating, mood swings, and hot flashes. But slowly, the estrogen and anti-androgren drugs kicked in and began to transform her body. Her skin's slightly rough texture started to soften and become smooth. Her flat chest began to morph into small breasts. The hard muscles in her arms, thighs, and legs seemed to melt away. Her weight slightly increased, and her body fat began to redistribute to her butt, hips, thighs, and legs, giving her a more womanly shape. But even with all those transformations, there were a few things the hormones couldn't come close to touching, and her voice and facial features were two of them.

Donetta enlisted the help of a voice coach whom she trained with for six months to learn how to control the inflection in her tone and pitch when she spoke. Each morning on her drive to work, instead of listening to the radio, she practiced out loud, as if she was giving a speech to a room full of people. By the end of the summer, her voice mimicked the sound of a perfect Southern belle.

The next thing Donetta knew she had to address was her facial features, and although it had been costly, after much research she'd decided to undergo facial feminization surgery to further soften and enhance her good looks. Her first step had been to get her trachea shaved. She'd been nervous the day of the procedure, but the end result had made her jump with joy and forget she'd ever had a single worry. After she healed, she and Geneva had flown to Brazil, where medical procedures were much cheaper, to have her forehead, chin, jawline, and hairline cosmetically reshaped and repositioned, and after she recuperated from that, her once androgynous features now looked undeniably feminine.

Her transformation had come at just the right time, shortly before she and Geneva opened G&D Salon on the other side of town. Many of the clients and a few of the newer stylists at the salon had no idea that Donetta had once been a tall, good-looking, girlish-looking guy, because now she looked like a diva straight from the pages of *Essence* magazine. She turned heads wherever she went, and she felt confident and beautiful for the first time in her life.

Donetta knew all the sacrifices she'd made were well worth it, along with all the ups and downs she'd experienced. However, just like everything, there was a price to be paid, and she was experiencing a big one now as she looked around her gourmet kitchen that didn't contain anything of substance she could cook. "All I have is a can of cream of chicken soup and some expired milk," Donetta said with a sigh, shaking her head. "This is a damn shame."

There had been a time when her pantry and refrigerator were always stocked, even with her busy days and long hours at the salon. But ironically, ever since she'd been living full-time as a woman, her kitchen had turned into a wasteland. "I'm tired, I'm hungry, and my damn hormones are raging," she said in frustration. "I need a good meal." She picked up the to-go menu from her favorite restaurant and placed her take-out order.

Five minutes later, after changing into a pair of light gray leggings and an oversized gray sweatshirt, Donetta slipped on her hot pink Uggs and walked out her door, headed to Sebastian's.

Chapter 5

PHILLIP

Normally when Phillip was in his car, he listened to talk radio, orchestral jazz from his iPod playlist, or his favorite old school hip-hop station. But right now, as he navigated his black rental car around the quiet streets of Amber, he was driving in complete silence. He was in deep thought from the conversation he'd just had with his mother about his love life.

Phillip was a ladies' man, and he'd inherited his love of women from his father, whom he was now estranged from—mainly because of his father's philandering ways. Phillip had known since he was a teenager that his father cheated on his mother on a regular basis, and it had angered him. During his senior year of high school, he'd been at a wild party one Saturday night at a hotel in downtown Birmingham, when he saw his father and a strange woman coming out of one of the hotel rooms. He and his father had gotten into a heated argument about that incident that nearly turned to blows.

Phillip had felt tormented, caught in a tug-of-war between loving his father in spite of his scandalous ways and protecting his mother from inevitable hurt. He didn't want to insert himself into his parents' marital affairs, but at the same time it bothered him to helplessly sit on the sidelines as he watched their marriage implode.

By the time Phillip had graduated from law school, his relationship with his father was strained at best. Their rift was noticeable to everyone, especially his mother. Phillip was glad she'd thought their distance was a result of a falling-out the two of them had had over a legal matter during Phillip's last year of law school. He and his father were both stubborn men, and neither one of them budged once their mind was made up. Even though his mother's feelings were temporarily spared, Phillip knew that she would eventually find out about his father's cheating ways.

And sure enough, one hot summer night two years ago, the Honorable Charlene Harris made the discovery of her life. Phillip still shook his head to this day when he thought about the drama-filled night his family had learned just how trifling his father was. When mild-mannered, play-by-the-rules Lauren found out she'd been dating her half brother, she'd been crushed. She'd cursed out her father and vowed never to speak to him again. But her actions had come nowhere close to their mother's.

Charlene had been so hurt and angry that she'd turned violent. That very night, after Lauren, her boyfriend, and Phillip had all stormed out of the house in disgust, Charlene remained behind, exacting her revenge with a baseball bat that had landed her husband in the emergency room.

Phillip had been angry too, but not because his father had suffered a black eye, broken arm, severe bruising, and was later kicked out of the house. He was upset because he'd never seen his mother so distraught, or his normally reserved sister so emotionally devastated and vulnerable. The pain of that night still lingered with all of them, and Phillip knew that neither his sister nor his mother had ever been the same. They rarely spoke of what happened, but the weight of it was always present.

"Damn, I'm hungry," Phillip said as he pulled around to the designated take-out parking area of Sebastian's restaurant. His mouth started watering as soon as he walked inside and smelled the delicious aroma of food and spices wafting through the air. He was actually glad that he'd had to get takeout tonight because, truth be told, after the stressful week he'd been having, and the rush of packing and traveling after working a half day, he really didn't feel like cooking.

Phillip strolled up to the counter and smiled to himself when he saw that not only was the cashier checking him out, a woman who was sitting on one of the two long benches in the small to-go space was eyeing him too. Even though he resented his father in many ways for many things, he was thankful that he'd inherited the man's impressive height, killer smile, handsome face, and muscular physique.

Phillip wasn't conceited, nor was he stuck on himself like some of his friends who hung in the circle of well-heeled, successful professionals he was a part of.

But he knew without a doubt that he was well above average when it came to looks, and he was confident in knowing that he could have just about any woman he wanted. Young, old, tall, short, slim, full-figured, short hair or long, Phillip loved them all. But he did have certain standards that he refused to compromise. Kindness, intelligence, and compassion were musts for him, and above all, he valued honesty.

If there was one great lesson he could say he'd learned from his father's many mistakes, it was that honesty was truly the best way to operate within any type of relationship. His father had covered up, lied, and outright schemed about so many things that it was hard to believe anything he said or did. Phillip believed that as long as there was honesty, everything else, like respect, love, compassion, and understanding, would fall into place.

The cashier looked him up and down with an expression that Phillip could now see wasn't the admiration he'd originally thought. She hesitated and then greeted him in a flat tone. "Welcome to Sebastian's. Do you need a menu, or do you already know what you want?"

Phillip could see that the woman was obviously having a bad night, so he tried to disarm her. "You're perceptive." He smiled. "Yes, I know what I want."

"A man who knows what he wants . . . now that's a trip."

"Is it?" He wasn't surprised by the woman's remark because it went along with her salty attitude. He glanced down at her ring finger and saw a wedding band. If he had to wager, he'd bet her ring was a symbol of disappointment, not love.

"Yeah," she answered. "Half the time y'all men

don't know what you want, and then when you finally figure it out and get it, you don't know what to do with it or how to appreciate it."

Phillip raised his brow, but instead of giving attitude right back to her, he looked at the woman's name badge and smiled even wider. "Well, Angela, I have to agree with you, and it's a real shame. But fortunately for me, my mother raised me to know exactly what I want, how to get it," he said, pausing for emphasis, "and more important, how to keep it. And with that in mind I'm going to order the chicken marsala for my mother, and the T-bone entrée for myself."

Phillip could see that not only had he broken Angela's grumpy attitude, he'd just won over the woman sitting on the bench, too. Now both women were smiling.

Angela nodded. "All right, sir. Do you want any dessert with that?"

"You know, I think I will. What do you recommend?"

Angela's smile grew. "Our cheesecake is delicious. And I'm not just sayin' that. It tastes like what your mama would make."

"Then cheesecake it is."

"All right. That'll be fifteen to twenty minutes."

Phillip took a seat while Angela and the woman sitting on the bench across from him continued to check him out. He felt good knowing he'd been able to ease the woman into a good mood, so he leaned back and began to scroll through the e-mails on his phone to pass the time. He was busy reading messages when the side door opened and brought in a rush of cold wind along with a woman who made him look away from his phone. To say that she was beautiful wasn't enough, and he didn't know if there were words for her.

Phillip watched as the tall woman gracefully sauntered in, surveying the waiting area as she walked up to the counter. Their eyes locked and he gave her a smile that she didn't return. *What is it with the women in this town?* he thought to himself. But he wasn't deterred.

"Hey, girl," Angela greeted the beautiful woman. "How you doin' tonight?"

The beautiful woman gave a small smile, but it was big enough to light up the room. Phillip watched her carefully, and even though she was dressed casually in leggings and a sweatshirt so big he could wear it himself, he could tell she was stylish—her colorful pink boots told him that. The chrome watch on her wrist was large and gleamed with glitzy embellishments around the face, and her fingers were well-manicured, and best of all, ring-free. He'd been around enough women to know that the black handbag hanging from the crook of her arm was well-made and expensive. Phillip also appreciated that her makeup was flawless and just enough, not overdone.

"I'm tired, hungry, and ready to eat," the beautiful woman said. "I sure hope my order is ready."

"I'll go check for you," Angela said.

Phillip could tell by the way the woman interacted with Angela that she was a regular customer. He watched as the beautiful woman stood at the counter. He wanted her to take a seat on the bench while she waited, or at least turn around, which would give him an opportunity to strike up a conversation with her. But she remained standing with her back to him.

"Sorry, girl," Angela said as she came from the back. "It's gonna be another ten minutes or so."

The beautiful woman looked at the glitzy watch on her wrist and let out a loud sigh. "But I called my order in more than twenty minutes ago."

"It's been extra-busy today, and that's the way it usually is right around the holidays. But if you wait, I promise when you get it it's gonna be delicious."

"All right. I guess I'll just have to wait."

Phillip watched as the woman finally turned around—actually, she looked as if she twirled—and then walked over to the bench across from him and sat down. She nodded to the woman sitting a few feet from her and then crossed her long legs. He could tell that she was purposely ignoring him, but he didn't care because he couldn't take his eyes off her. He made it so obvious he was staring that the woman beside her glanced back and forth between them, with an expression that begged to ask if they knew each other.

"Ma'am, your order is ready," Angela said to the woman sitting on the bench.

The woman stood and smiled as she walked to the counter to get her food. She stacked her bags on top of each other and smiled. "Y'all have a happy Thanksgiving," she said on her way out the door.

Just then Phillip's phone chirped, alerting him that he had an incoming text message. He looked down and saw that his mother had sent him a laundry list of items to pick up from the grocery store. He shook his head and smiled because his mother was so meticulous that she'd grouped each item on the list by category. As he looked at the list he startled himself because in that moment a question came to him that he'd never thought about until now. But he didn't have a chance to fully explore what it meant, because his thoughts were interrupted.

"I'm gonna go check on your order," Angela said to the beautiful woman, then turned around and headed back to the kitchen.

This was Phillip's opening and he took it. "Do you have plans for the holidays?" he asked.

The woman looked at him without answering as she pulled her ringing phone from her handbag. He thought she could've given him a head nod—at the very least—as she'd done to the woman who had been sitting beside her. Yes, the beautiful woman was definitely ignoring him on purpose, and it served to make him even more interested in her.

"Hey, girl, I tried calling you after the interview went off but I got your voice mail," the woman said. The concern in her voice was so strong that a worry line appeared across her forehead. "Are you okay?"

Phillip watched as the woman slowly recrossed her legs and leaned against the back of the bench. She was consumed in her conversation, oblivious to the fact that he was watching her every move. He thought she was sexy without trying to be, and that made her even hotter. She shook her head and looked up at the ceiling as she listened with what appeared to be pain on her face to whomever was on the other end of the phone.

"I wish I knew, too," the beautiful woman said. She let out a deep breath as she ran her fingers through her long, silky hair. Phillip noted that although her fingers were slender, her hands were large. But then again, she was very tall, so it stood to reason that the rest of her body would be in proportion. He looked down at her pink boots and could see that her feet were large, as well. He thought it was ironic that such features could be found on a woman as slight and as delicate as she was, and he thought it made her even more unique.

"Yes, and I wanted to reach through the damn screen and choke the hell outta that heffa until her lyin' tongue hung out . . . uh-huh . . . I know, girl . . . uh-huh . . . 'cause it's probably some ol' bullshit . . . that psychopath is crazy . . . Yes, and that's why I'm worried about you."

Phillip was startled by how bold and rough the stylish woman was talking, unfiltered and without a care. If it had been any other woman talking the way she'd just done, it would've turned him off completely, but it did just the opposite coming from her.

"When will Samuel and his parents be home?" she asked. "Uh-huh . . . okay . . . Do you want me to come over and keep you company until they get back? Are you sure? I'm at Sebastian's waiting for my take-out order, but I should be leaving soon and I can come straight over."

Not only was Phillip physically attracted to her, he liked her. Her caring and sincere manner was endearing, and it melted the hard shield she'd put up when she sat down and ignored him just moments ago.

"Your order is ready," Angela said, coming out of the back.

The beautiful woman nodded. "My order is ready," she said to the person on the other end. "I'll call you back after I get out to my car." She hung up, shook her head, and exhaled deeper than she had when she'd started her conversation, which Phillip could see hadn't been a good one. It was obvious that her friend was in distress and now she was, too. She looked up at the ceiling again, uncrossed her long legs, and rose slowly. Phillip wanted to ask her what was wrong, but he knew that would be way out of line, and judging by the way she'd been acting toward him she might even tell him that it was none of his business.

"You okay?" Angela asked.

"Yeah, you know me. I'll be fine."

"All right, girl. Go home and enjoy your meal. I threw in a complimentary dessert for you since you had to wait so long."

The beautiful woman smiled, but it wasn't the same happy expression she'd had on her face when she'd first walked in. "Thanks, I really appreciate that, Angela. Dessert always brightens a girl's day."

She paid for her food and thanked Angela again. She was about to walk out the door when Phillip decided he had to say something to her. "Have a happy Thanksgiving."

She stopped in her tracks and slowly turned around. Her eyes seemed to glow as she zeroed in on him. She leaned against the door and nodded her head. "Thanks . . . you too."

The moment the door closed behind her, Phillip knew something special had just happened. And when the same question he'd had moments ago popped back into his head, he knew the feeling was real.

Chapter 6

GENEVA

Geneva's hands were shaking so badly she could barely hold her cup of tea. Normally, the soothing blend of chamomile and natural honey calmed her, but this was her second cup and she was still on edge. She jumped when her cell phone rang, but she was relieved to see it was Donetta.

"Thanks for calling me back," Geneva said. She moved from her couch in the family room and perched herself atop one of the high-back bar stools at her large kitchen island.

"I can still come over there if you want me to. We can split my dinner, 'cause you know Sebastian's portions are huge."

"That's okay. Like I said, Samuel and his parents will be back in a little while and he's bringing me something to eat." Geneva said as she walked over to the sink and poured her tea down the drain. "What did you order?"

"Do you have to ask?"

"Chicken marsala."

Donetta laughed. "Hell, yeah, and I'm gonna devour it, too."

"I know you are. They have the best food in town. We'll probably take Samuel's parents there before they leave."

"You're blessed to have such great in-laws."

"Yes, I am. They're wonderful people, and they raised a good man. I don't know what I'd do without him. When I got home this afternoon I was relieved that he and Gabrielle weren't here, because I needed some time alone, you know? But now I can't wait till they get home."

Donetta sighed into the phone. "Girl, cherish that feeling."

"I will, and enough about me. I haven't asked you how you're doing tonight. You okay?"

"I'm good, just worried about you."

Geneva smiled. Other than Samuel, Donetta was the one person she could count on, rain or shine. Donetta was always supportive and ready to lend a hand in any way she could. She was a friend, counselor, babysitter, business partner, comedian, and style expert all rolled into one. And even though she'd gone through a lot over the last two years, she'd found a way to remain positive and encouraging in her own way. "Don't worry about me. I'll be fine." Geneva returned to the couch and wrapped her chenille throw around her body.

"You know I can't help but be concerned. Especially after how wild and crazy Vivana looked on TV. The thought of her getting out is like a nightmare."

"Tell me about it. She's a very disturbed person, that's for sure." Geneva heard Donetta's car door open and close. "Are you home already?"

"No, I'm walking into the grocery store."

"I thought you just picked up dinner."

"I did. But I don't have anything in my cabinets or my fridge, so after this meal I'm up shit creek. I'm gonna pick up enough food to tide me over through the beginning of next week when I'll be home."

She could hear the noise of Donetta's shopping cart, and she imagined her friend perusing the aisles, probably decked out in a casually stylish outfit. "I hope you have a list with you. If I don't have a list I pick up everything except the things I really need."

"I don't have list the first. But I need practically everything, so . . . hey, what ingredients do I need to make that chicken and mushroom dish you brought to work a few weeks ago?"

Geneva began to rattle off the ingredients for the delicious chicken casserole that was always a hit with everyone who tasted it. Samuel had raved about it, and when she'd brought leftovers to work the next day, Donetta had eaten nearly all of it. Geneva stretched her legs, realizing how good it felt to do something as mundane as talk about groceries and recipes instead of thinking about Vivana, murder, and danger. She was finally calm.

"Oh shit!" Donetta whispered into the phone. "You've gotta be freakin' kidding me."

"What's wrong?"

"He's here. Damn it! I hope this guy isn't following me."

Geneva's back stiffened, and she immediately became concerned. Donetta was forever having some kind of drama with men. But ever since she'd stopped dating last year in order to concentrate on her final stages of transition, she'd been worry-free. Geneva hoped it wasn't one of her crazy exes from the past. "Who's following you?"

Donetta lowered her voice, and Geneva could barely hear her. "There was this guy at Sebastian's, and . . ."

The line went silent. "Donetta? Donetta?" Geneva listened carefully, trying to make out the voice in the background. Her ears perked up at the sound of a man's deep baritone. Even through the phone, Geneva could tell the voice belonged to what had to be a handsome specimen attached to it.

Donetta cleared her throat. "Geneva, I'll call you back later, okay?"

"But you said someone's following you. Are you sure you're all right?"

"Um, yes. I'll explain later."

Geneva heard a particular lilt in Donetta's voice that let her know that her instincts had been correct—whomever Donetta was talking to was undoubtedly handsome. Geneva had been friends with Donetta long enough to know that even though she was cynical when it came to men, she loved them almost as much as she did her high-end clothes and shoes. Geneva shook her head. "Okay, Donetta, but call me when you get home so I'll know you made it there safely."

The moment she hung up the phone, Geneva heard the garage door open, and the sound was like music to her ears. She practically jumped off the couch and made

her way back to the kitchen as the door to the mud-
room opened.

Samuel walked in with a big smile on his face and his
parents in tow. And an added surprise was that his older
brother, Joe, whom they hadn't seen since Gabrielle had
been born, was there for the holidays, as well.

"Mom and Dad knew Joe was coming," Samuel
said, "but they kept it a secret so we'd be surprised."

It was the first time all evening that Geneva truly
felt like it was the holiday season. They shared warm
hugs, happy smiles, and laughter, and the joyous moment temporarily took Geneva's mind off of Vivana
and the horrible memory of her ex-husband that she
couldn't seem to shake.

While Samuel showed his parents and Joe to their
rooms, Geneva fed Gabrielle her bottle and then put
her down for the night. The sight of her precious baby
girl sleeping peacefully in her crib gave Geneva a
sense of joy she couldn't explain. But unfortunately,
the feeling was short-lived, because when she walked
back downstairs she found Samuel and her in-laws
gathered around the television watching a repeat of Vivana's breaking news interview that had aired earlier
that evening.

Geneva walked in quietly and sat beside Samuel
on the couch. She leaned into his waiting arms just as
Vivana's attorney assured the reporter and viewers that
justice would be served, and that her client would be
exonerated of the murder she'd been wrongly convicted of. When the reporter asked if there had been
misconduct on the part of the police department that
investigated the crime, Vivana's attorney declined to
comment, and became vague on details. Once the interview was over, Joe immediately spoke up.

"I knew from the minute I laid eyes on Vivana that she was nothing but trouble. She didn't have a genuine bone in her body. But hey, I tried to warn you." He stared at Samuel with an *I told you so* look on his face.

"I can't believe you just went there," Samuel said incredulously.

Joe hunched his shoulders. "Why not? It's true, isn't it? I'm just sorry you didn't listen to me, is all I'm saying."

Samuel shot his brother a hard look. "You've been in my house for less than an hour and you're already starting."

"Starting what?" Joe asked, as if he had no idea what Samuel was talking about.

"Right now I don't need to hear *I told you so*. And of all people, I definitely don't need to hear it from you." Samuel looked at his brother as if he wanted to strangle him, and his reaction worried Geneva.

Geneva and her in-laws each took deep breaths and braced themselves for what they knew was about to come. Samuel and Joe had never seen eye to eye about anything, and they'd bickered back and forth ever since they'd been little boys. Everyone who knew the two brothers understood that their sibling rivalry was fueled by Joe's insecurities and his less-than-impressive attempts to compete with Samuel.

Joe was the oldest, but he'd always felt second to his younger brother's achievements. Samuel was more handsome, unquestionably smarter, more industrious, more popular, and the more successful of the two. He had a beautiful wife, a precious daughter, a huge house, and a thriving career. Conversely, Joe had always fumbled his way through life feeling unfulfilled because of poor decisions and a quirky, oftentimes abrasive personality that rubbed people the wrong way. He'd been married three times, and each divorce left him more broke and bitter than the last.

Marrying Vivana was one of the few mistakes Samuel had made, but Joe felt his brother's one faux pas had equaled all of his three marriages combined, and he loved throwing it up in Samuel's face. But their relationship had seemed to get better for a brief time two years ago when Joe had come for a visit. He'd been in Birmingham for a convention through his job with a manufacturing company, and had driven to Amber to see Samuel. Ironically, it had been the same week Johnny had been killed. Samuel had been stressed because of the heavy scrutiny that he and Geneva had been under, and Joe had been sympathetic.

Joe had put their childhood issues aside and came through for Samuel during a time when Samuel had needed him. They'd even kept up a steady flow of conversation for several months. Geneva had been happy to see that Samuel and his brother had gotten closer. But almost without warning, Joe stopped calling and the relationship between the two brothers had gone back to the way it had always been.

Geneva wished Samuel and his brother could overcome their contempt for each other and get along. She liked Joe because he'd always been nice to her, but she didn't like the way he treated Samuel, and she knew that kind of behavior couldn't continue, especially not now that Joe was in their house, on Samuel's turf, even if it was only for a few days.

"I don't want to hear anything from you right now," Samuel said to Joe. "We all know that I made a mistake. You don't have to state the obvious, or rub it in."

"All I was trying to say is that if you had listened

to me and called off the wedding when I told you to, you wouldn't be going through this stress right now."

"Let's not point fingers," Samuel's mother chimed in.

Samuel nodded. "Mom's right. When you start pointing fingers, you'd better be ready to stand up to the same scrutiny you dish out. And if anyone shouldn't want any fingers pointing in their direction, it should be you."

"What's that supposed to mean?" Joe balked.

"Exactly what you think it does." Samuel sighed and rubbed his chin. "Let's drop it because this isn't helping anyone, especially not Geneva."

When Samuel said her name, all eyes landed on Geneva, and she was sure they could see the melancholy resting in them. She didn't want her mood to dampen what was supposed to be a time of celebration and thanks, but she also couldn't hide the fact that she was scared, and for good reason. Vivana had testified in front of a standing-room-only courtroom that she'd wanted to murder Geneva. Now there was a possibility that the crazy woman might be released, and Geneva feared Vivana might try to finish what she'd started.

"I didn't mean to upset you, Geneva," Joe said with sincerity. "I apologize if my comments made you feel uncomfortable."

Geneva nodded. "Honestly, I was on edge before you all got here. When I saw the interview earlier this evening, I had flashbacks of how Vivana used to come into the salon where I once worked, sit in my chair, and pretend to be a woman named Cheryl. She did that just so she could get close to me with the intention of killing me. It takes a very troubled person to go to those lengths."

Sarah shuddered. "I'm so sorry you had to go through that, dear. Just the thought of it . . ."

Everyone nodded solemnly, thinking about how stressful that time had been for the entire family. At one point, both Geneva and Samuel had been under heavy scrutiny and had risen to the top of the list of possible suspects in Geneva's ex-husband's murder. Johnny Mayfield was a man of duplicitous character and unscrupulous morals. Both Geneva and Samuel had had good reason to want him dead. But neither of them had let their emotions lead them to commit murder.

Geneva let out a deep breath. "I had hoped that after Vivana was convicted, I'd never have to see her again. Now there's a possibility that she may be released, and Lord only knows what she might do."

Herbert shook his head. "Surely she wouldn't do anything that would land her back in jail?" He looked directly at Samuel. "Would she?"

Geneva looked into Samuel's eyes, and she could see that he was thinking the same thing that was running through her mind.

"I don't know, Dad," Samuel replied in a solemn voice. "All I can say is that I wouldn't put anything past her, and if she does get out . . . I'll do whatever it takes to protect my family."

Joe spoke up. "Maybe we're getting worked up over nothing. If they really had solid evidence, wouldn't that lawyer of hers have at least hinted at what it could be? If the so-called evidence they have is legit, why all the secrecy?"

"I think she did," Geneva said, reminding them that Vivana's lawyer had suggested that some of the evidence may have been tampered with or even manufactured, and those kinds of things would point directly back to the authorities. "Maybe that's why she became so vague when the reporter asked her that question. Besides, I don't think a credible news station is going to air a story like that unless there are some legs to keep it running."

Everyone knew that Geneva was right, and that knowledge caused silence to fall over the room as they each processed the troubling turn of events. They were all exhausted from their long day, and they decided to end the night and retreat to their rooms to sort out their questions and fears.

A half hour later, Geneva lay in her bed watching her husband as he emerged from the shower. His muscular body was glistening from the beads of water still clinging to his smooth brown skin. She loved looking at Samuel, and she smiled as she remembered how different his body had been when they'd first met. Through her encouragement, in combination with healthy eating and regular workouts, Samuel had dropped over thirty pounds and had toned his muscles, reversing the hands of time. Geneva thought he looked good before his weight loss, and now he was even more handsome, but not just because his physical appearance had changed. He looked so good to her because of the goodness inside his heart. Samuel was kind, patient, and humble. Geneva thanked God every day for bringing him into her life.

"I'm glad to see you're smiling," Samuel said. "After the day you've had, to be able to smile is a blessing."

"I'm smiling because I know that regardless of what's going on, you have my back, and I have yours, and that's all that matters."

"It sure is, baby."

Samuel walked over to his dresser and pulled out a pair of boxer briefs. He stepped his right leg into them when Geneva said something that stopped him from making another move.

"Why put those on when I just plan to take them off?" She ran her tongue across her bottom lip and then smiled as she spoke. "Are you okay with that?"

Samuel nodded and closed the drawer. "I'm more than okay with that." Slowly, he walked over to Geneva's side of the bed, pulled back the jewel-tone damask comforter, and climbed in beside her.

Geneva felt safe and protected in Samuel's arms, and she needed that sense of security right now. She parted her lips as she welcomed Samuel's tongue into her mouth. She loved the way he kissed her because she could feel the passion and desire in each sensual movement of his lips and tongue. He started a slow, hungry dance, darting, retreating, and tasting her breath as he savored every inch of her mouth. All the while he caressed her back gently and rubbed his hands over her soft, chestnut brown-colored skin.

Geneva was glad that Samuel was the kind of man who liked to take his time making love, and she knew that tonight would be no exception. In fact, he would take extra care with her because he knew that's what she needed. He pressed his pelvis, along with his hard erection, against her thigh as he held her close to his body with his right arm. She moaned with pleasure from the feel of his strong hands caressing her skin with his free hand. The combination of his sensuous kisses, gentle touch, and slow pelvic grind all felt so good she nearly let out a small scream. She knew she had to be quiet because they had guests down the hall, and even though their house was expansive in size, sounds carried through the large space.

"I love you, baby." Samuel whispered into her ear.

"I don't want you to worry about anything. I'm going to protect you."

Geneva felt as though the heavy weight of the day had just been lifted off her shoulders. She'd always felt safe with Samuel, because from the very beginning of their relationship he'd been true to his word. If he told her he was going to do something, he followed his words up with actions that she could believe in. "I love you, too, baby," she panted, and then moaned. "Ohhhh, baby."

When she felt him slowly ease his way inside her, kissing her in between each thrust, her body sank into an ecstasy so sweet she had to turn her head to the side and moan into her pillow. Samuel continued to thrust, kiss, rub, and grind until Geneva's body trembled from the intense orgasm that overtook her, leaving her helpless to the aftershocks that made her limbs weak. She was still enjoying her orgasmic high when she felt him explode inside her, causing a second wave of ecstasy to surge through her body.

An hour later Geneva had been fast asleep when she awoke in a cold sweat. She could barely catch her breath as she fought for air. She looked over to her right, saw Samuel fast asleep, and tried to steady her breathing. She inhaled deeply, releasing shallow breaths as she tried to calm herself. She'd drifted off to sleep in pleasure, and now she'd awakened with terrifying thoughts. But this time it wasn't Vivana that had been on her mind and in her bad dream; it was her ex-husband, Johnny.

Geneva's nightmare had felt so real that she had to swallow hard and blink her eyes through the darkness in the room to make sure that what had happened wasn't real.

Her dream took her back to the night that Johnny had been murdered, and she'd seen it so vividly that it jolted her from her a satisfied sleep. She could see his dead body lying on the kitchen floor, where he'd been found by the police in the early hours of the morning. But what had made her gasp and had jolted her awake wasn't his stiff corpse. She'd been frightened because the person standing over him, the woman who'd murdered him in cold blood, wasn't Vivana.

Chapter 7

CHARLENE

Charlene bit down on her bottom lip and let out a long, hard sigh. She squinted and looked at the near-empty bottle of wine sitting next to her glass on the end table beside her. She was feeling the effects of the alcohol, and she liked it. "I might as well finish this off." With careful and slow movements, she steadied her hands as she reached for the bottle and poured what was left into her glass. Three long swallows later, she set her empty glass next to the empty bottle and shook her head. "What the hell is Leslie up to, and what does she know?"

Charlene reclined back into the couch, kicked her feet up on the tufted ottoman in front of her, and re-played her phone conversation with Leslie Sachs. The purpose of Leslie's call was crystal clear, because she'd mentioned the breaking news story right away, and she'd asked Charlene if she'd seen it. But the underlying intent behind Leslie's call was what had Charlene worried enough to drink an entire bottle of wine.

Even though many years had passed, Charlene still knew Leslie well, and there were a few things about the top-notch attorney that had remained consistent over time; she was damn good at her job, every move she made was calculated and well thought out; and she never had a contingency plan because her strategy was to always win. That was the very reason she never took a case unless she was sure she could exonerate her client, and that last part troubled Charlene the most.

"The only reason Leslie took Vivana's case is because she knows that, unstable as Vivana is, and as guilty as she appeared to be, she's really innocent," Charlene mumbled, still coherent enough to make reason of her thoughts. "I wonder if Vivana contacted Leslie or if Leslie contacted her?" Charlene was hoping that it was Vivana who had reached out to Leslie, because if it was the other way around, Charlene knew she was screwed.

She lifted her hand to her head and ran her fingers through her freshly trimmed bob, then thought about her stylist. Thanks to Geneva, her hair always shined with a healthy gloss and looked as though she could shoot a shampoo commercial. She was the best stylist Charlene had ever had, and she was also one of the kindest people she knew. Geneva had a genuinely warm spirit and was compassionate to a fault, always wanting to help others. Charlene guessed that was one of the reasons she'd never associated Geneva with Johnny; the two couldn't have been more different. That difference was also what had attracted Charlene to him, as well.

Two and a half years ago, Charlene's world had drastically changed. The hurt and humiliation she'd experienced in her marriage had driven her to a breaking point, and she knew she could either sink in her misery or swim her way back to happiness. She'd been living her life inside the lines of order and respectability since she was a young woman, and in her estimation it had landed her in places so lonely she wouldn't have wished it on an enemy. She'd known it was time for something different. She wanted and needed change.

Her ex-husband, Reginald, had cheated on her numerous times over the course of their marriage, and each time Charlene had forgiven him, hoping he'd grow out of his philandering ways. She'd loved him, they'd built a life together, and she'd fooled herself into believing his indiscretions would one day be a thing of the past. She'd grown up seeing how her mother had put up with her father's infidelity, some of which had resulted in blatant disrespect and humiliation. So she'd been thankful that Reginald had, at the very least, been discreet.

But when it was revealed that one of Reginald's affairs had resulted in a son whom their daughter had unknowingly dated, Charlene couldn't take another minute of Reginald's lies. She'd kicked him out of the house, and then promptly divorced him.

At the time, Charlene had been so hurt and devastated that she'd wanted to move out of the large, stately home she and Reginald had shared for nearly thirty years. She couldn't bear to spend another day in the house that held so many lies and empty promises. Plus, both of her children were grown, and the thought of living in a five-thousand-square-foot home all alone seemed ridiculous. She'd wanted something smaller and more practical. Little did she know that her desire to downsize would result in a colossal mess.

Charlene started looking for a Realtor, and a young couple she knew recommended Johnny. They'd hired him to help them find their dream home, and he'd delivered top-notch service. They'd raved so much about his professionalism and knowledge of the area's real estate market that Charlene decided to meet him for coffee to discuss how he could help her find a new home.

Charlene shook her head as she thought about her first encounter with Johnny. "I should've turned around in my tracks and walked away when that bastard said hello," she said, slurring her words as she began to succumb to the effects of the bottle of wine. "Better yet, I should've taken all the traffic and road detours I ran into that day as a big warning sign to stay away."

Charlene had been running twenty minutes late for her meeting with Johnny, but she'd been determined not to stand him up because she prided herself on being a woman of her word. When she finally walked into the coffee shop and met Johnny face-to-face, she hadn't expected him to be so handsome, charming, and downright sexy.

Johnny's wide smile, full lips, and handsome face had made quite an impression on Charlene. She'd liked that he was clean-cut, sporting a top-quality tailor-made suit, and that he was well groomed with freshly cut hair and shoes that were polished to a high shine. She thought he looked like a Wall Street investment banker rather than a Realtor. Although he was clearly at least twenty years her junior, Charlene could see that Johnny was attracted to her, and it made her feel desirable and wanted—something her husband hadn't made her feel in a very long time.

She and Johnny talked business for the first fifteen minutes of their meeting, but then it quickly turned into something else. Charlene had recognized the signs, and she was flattered that a man as young and handsome as Johnny had been genuinely interested in her. He'd had a seductive look in his eyes when he told her that he wanted to show her a property.

"I think you'll really like what I'm going to show you," Johnny had said with a devilish wink. "I guarantee it will meet all of your needs . . . and quite a few of your wants."

Right then Charlene knew what Johnny had in mind. But instead of using her good judgment, she went along with him, high on the excitement and flirtatious moves that he'd put on her. He hadn't been wearing a wedding band, and her divorce was imminent, so she convinced herself that there was no harm in having a little fun.

She'd followed Johnny to a small brick-and-stone apartment building that looked nothing like the type of stately, gated community–type of property she'd told him she was looking for. But then again, she'd known from the moment they left the coffee shop that the only thing Johnny wanted to show her was a good time. Before Charlene knew it she was in bed with him, having wild, hot sex in an empty rental unit. But just as quickly as she'd jumped into bed with Johnny and enjoyed their spontaneous tryst, it abruptly came to an end when Vivana showed up.

Vivana had been having an affair with Johnny, and

she'd become suspicious that he was cheating on her. Unbeknownst to him, she'd started following his every move. She'd tracked him to the apartment building, and that was when all hell broke loose. Vivana had walked up to them, knocked Charlene down to the ground, and then proceeded to punch Johnny square in the jaw.

At first Charlene had thought that Vivana must've been Johnny's wife, and in the split second that it all happened, Charlene realized that she'd become the other woman. She imagined that her low-down, cheating husband didn't wear his wedding band when he set out to seduce women, just as Johnny hadn't, and that her husband's mistresses were just as much a victim of broken self-esteem and lust as she was. But Charlene's thoughts quickly vanished, and she became outraged when Johnny and Vivana started yelling at each other, and the truth came out that Vivana *wasn't* his wife.

Charlene had been pissed to learn that not only was Johnny cheating on his wife, he was also cheating on his mistress, and in Charlene's eyes that sank him to a new low. She ran out of the building and never looked back.

She'd chucked the entire incident up to one colossal mistake, until several months later, when Johnny contacted her, asking for money. She'd thought he must have been out of his mind to think that she would give him a dime, but when he told her that he'd had a camera set up in the closet of the rental unit he'd taken her to, and that the video clip of the two of them would be e-mailed to practically everyone she knew, she changed her tune and started paying him hush money, in cash, every month like clockwork.

But Charlene eventually became fed up, and she decided it was time that Johnny paid the price for the damage he'd inflicted upon others. She'd hoped for months that he'd befall a bad accident, succumb to an illness, or that someone would outright kill him. But since none of those things happened, she knew she had to take matters into her own hands.

Charlene had been questioned during the murder investigation, and she'd remained cool under pressure. Being an attorney by trade, she knew how things worked, and she was certain that her meeting with Johnny at the coffee shop would eventually be revealed. She knew when the detectives went through his recent business dealings to find a motive, they'd discover the real estate contract she'd signed a few months prior to his death. Added to that, her hair stylist was Johnny's estranged widow. With that level of involvement, Charlene knew that once the murder investigations heated up, the detectives would eventually come knocking at her door. So she made a power move.

As soon as Johnny's death became public knowledge, Charlene immediately contacted the chief of police and the lead homicide detective on the case. She'd told them that she was shocked to see that the man she'd hired as her Realtor, but whose services she'd never used, had been murdered. She'd also told them that as a public official, sworn to serve and protect her constituents, that she wanted Johnny's killer caught as soon as possible so the citizens of Amber could feel safe. She'd polished it off by telling them that her office would provide any resources they needed for their investigation.

But despite Charlene's clever strategy, she knew that everything hinged upon Vivana being able to positively identify her as the woman she'd had an altercation with on that fateful day in the apartment building.

Charlene had nearly worried a patch of gray into the front of her head at the thought. But as it turned out, Vivana had been so distraught and angry that day that she couldn't remember the face of the woman whom she'd accosted. There had been no eyewitnesses, so it was as if it had never happened, and for that, Charlene had been grateful.

The prosecution had a field day picking apart Vivana's claim of the incident, and basically implied that she'd made the whole thing up. "How is it that you confronted and actually became engaged in a physical altercation with a woman who was seeing your boyfriend, yet you can't even remember what she looked like?" the prosecutor had asked. When Vivana responded by telling them that she'd been so angry she couldn't focus, it really made her seem like the kind of person who could easily go into a rage and commit murder.

Vivana's damaging testimony had sealed her fate, and from that point forward it was clear that she would be convicted. After she was locked away, life had begun to slowly return to normal for Charlene, that is, until a few months later when she received a cryptic text message. It had been very short and simple, but it had frightened her. Although she'd erased it right after she'd read it, she still remembered it word for word.

Unavailable: You're a murderer

CH: Who is this?

Unavailable: I'm the person who has proof that you murdered Johnny Mayfield

Charlene raised her arms, yawned, and then stretched out on the couch in her drunken haze. She was still dressed in her beige-colored silk blouse and her brown houndstooth skirt. She made no effort to remove her stylish gold necklace, matching earrings, or bracelet because at this point she couldn't maneuver the clasps or hooks, even if she tried. She was tired from the mental strain of the very real possibility that the crime she'd committed might soon be uncovered.

"What kind of evidence could they have?" Charlene said, slurring her words worse than before. She propped a pillow behind her head. "I was careful. I didn't make a single mistake. Maybe Leslie's bluffing." But deep down Charlene knew that wasn't true. A chill went through her when she thought about the fact that Leslie wanted to meet her for coffee at the Whole Bean Café, of all places.

As Charlene fell into an alcohol-induced sleep, she tossed and turned with the thought that she might not have gotten away with murder after all.

Chapter 8

DONETTA

Donetta had been in the produce section leafing through collard greens and talking to Geneva on her phone, when she saw the handsome man from the restaurant standing just a few feet away. She felt a jolt of excitement at the sight of him. But her sense of caution quickly kicked in. She knew from past experience that good-looking, sexy men like him couldn't be trusted any further than she could see them. And by the looks of this one, he was especially dangerous.

She'd caught him staring at her a few times while she'd been waiting for her food at Sebastian's, but she'd ignored him. Then Geneva had called, sounding worried and afraid, causing her to turn her complete attention to her dear friend, relegating the handsome man to an afterthought.

Now she was face-to-face with him again in, of all places, the grocery store. Her first thought was that he must be following her. She didn't want to become alarmed, but she also didn't want to discount the fact that she knew people were capable of just about anything.

Donetta tried not to look at him, but he was so tall—at six foot, four inches—and handsome—with the right combination of classic features and rugged sexiness—that she couldn't help herself. His faded Levi's were casual, with a well-worn vintage look, as if they'd been custom-made for him. She liked the way his broad chest and muscular arms outlined the black cashmere sweater that hung perfectly on his frame. She could spot style when she saw it, and he wore it as if he'd been born into it.

Donetta knew she needed to stop thinking about him and get back to doing what she'd come there to do. She was getting ready to place her bundle of collards into her shopping cart when she made the mistake of glancing his way. It was as if he'd been waiting for a cue because he smiled and waved a friendly hello.

"Damn it!" she whispered under her breath. She braced herself when she saw him walk toward her with a casual comfort, as if they were old friends. She steadied herself, put her hand on her hip, and stared him in the eyes. "Are you following me?"

The man looked startled and slightly offended as he lost his smile. "No, I'm not."

"Then why're you here?"

He chuckled. "I guess for the same reason you're here . . . to buy food."

"Oh, so you didn't get your order from Sebastian's?"

He gave her a puzzled look. "No, I mean, yes, I did. But it won't do anything for an empty refrigerator." He glanced down at the collard greens in her cart. "I guess you're in the same boat, too." He picked up a big bundle of greens and put them in his cart.

Donetta could see that he had no idea what he was doing, and she had the urge to tell him that the greens he'd chosen had too many spots and weren't as fresh as the ones in the back. He looked like he didn't know the difference between collards and cabbage.

"I see you like collards, too," he said with a smile. "Nothing like a good pot of well-seasoned greens for a holiday dinner."

There he goes again, trying to make conversation, she thought. Donetta ignored his last remark, rolled her eyes, and began to push her cart past him. But when she did, she got a whiff of his incredibly sexy scent and it made her stop in her tracks. *Damn, he smells good!* She loved colognes and perfumes, and she knew virtually every fragrance—male and female—upon first whiff. But she couldn't place what kind he was wearing. He smelled like a combination of Irish Spring soap, tangerines, and fresh pine needles. She knew she should have expected that a sophisticated man who looked as good as he did, would smell good, too. She had the urge to rest her nose against his neck and inhale deeply, but instead she quickly regained her composure and began to push her cart again.

"Hey, wait a minute," the man said playfully.

As much as Donetta knew she needed to keep walking, she found herself slowing her pace. His deep, velvety smooth voice sounded like pure seduction, and she wondered why she hadn't noticed it in the restaurant. She was intrigued, but she didn't want him to know that, so she stopped and turned around. "What?"

"Are you always this rude?"

She rolled her eyes again.

"Your attitude doesn't become a woman as beautiful as you. And rolling your eyes, which, by the way, are so hypnotic I could get lost in them, seems like such a waste when you do that. I think you're much, much better than the vibe you're giving off."

Donetta had been prepared to launch a sarcastic comeback to whatever the sexy stranger might say, but the words that fell from his mouth made her hold back. He'd managed to set her straight about her funky attitude while giving her what sounded like a sincere compliment. She looked into his eyes again and felt something stir inside her. She was a good judge of character, and she'd always followed her gut, which was now telling her that the man standing in front of her was a good one.

But just as quickly as she'd allowed herself to soften her hard stance, she turned cold again. A childhood full of hurt and an adulthood filled with pain had left her weary and cynical. And the last two years in particular had taught her just how cruel some people could be. It had taken Donetta a long time to climb out of the fog of dysfunctional and abusive relationships she'd experienced in her life, and only recently had she been able to lay old demons to rest. She'd made a promise to herself after her surgery a year ago that she would protect her heart at all costs, and she had no intention of breaking it.

Donetta cleared her throat as she pulled her long, silky hair behind her ear. "Since I'm so rude," she said with a slight smile, "I'll exercise what little home train-ing I have by saying thank you for that backhanded compliment. Now, if you'll excuse me, I've got some shopping to do."

The handsome man chuckled again and shook his head. "There was nothing backhanded about what I said. My compliment about your obvious beauty and lovely eyes was sincere, as was my comment about your attitude." He folded his arms. "I don't think you're as rude or as hard as you're trying to come off . . . so why don't you drop the barbed wire, which really doesn't suit you, and have a conversation with me."

Donetta looked down at her pink Uggs as the pit of her stomach fluttered. She knew she needed to resist the alluring sound of his voice and the welcoming smile that was spread across his face, which nearly made her smile back. She softened her tone. "You don't know a thing about me." She slowly pushed her cart past him. "Have a good evening."

She knew he was watching her walk away, and she fought the urge to turn around to make sure. The far-ther she walked, the more she could feel his eyes on her. When she rounded the corner at the end of the aisle, she glanced back, and sure enough, he was still staring at her with a smile on his face. Donetta quickly darted down the breakfast aisle, pushing her cart like she was on a mission.

With the holidays approaching, she planned to be out of the salon through the early part of next week, so she combed the aisles, placing items in her cart that she would need to tide her over. She strolled down the bak-ing aisle, and there he was again. The handsome man was looking at his phone and then at the shelves in front of him. Just as she'd thought before, he didn't have a clue about what he was doing. She figured his girlfriend, fiancée, or possibly his wife had probably texted him a list of things to pick up on his way home.

Donetta immediately became pissed. Here he was, out shopping for his woman, who was waiting for him at home, while he was hitting on a complete stranger, flirting and giving out compliments like a seasoned player. She took a deep breath and began placing more items into her cart, ignoring him as if he wasn't even there.

"Excuse me," the man said. "If you help me with this, I promise I won't bother you again."

She continued to ignore him.

"Miss, I know you hear me talking to you. I'm not asking for your number, I just need to ask you a question about an item on my list."

Donetta pushed her cart close to his. "What are you looking for?"

"Baking powder, self-rising yeast, and something called cream of tartar."

She looked at his cart and saw that he'd managed to find sugar and flour on his own. "Excuse me," she said as she reached in front of him, pulling the three items from the shelf.

"You must really know your way around the kitchen."

"And you obviously don't."

"You're a regular ray of sunshine, aren't you?"

She was about to roll her eyes again, but she caught herself.

"Actually, I'm pretty good in the kitchen," he said confidently. "But I don't bake at all, so I'm completely out of my element here."

Donetta walked back to her cart. "Your wife will

be very happy that you found the things she needs to do her baking."

He smiled and leaned against his cart. "I'm not married, I don't have a fiancée, and I'm not dating anyone."

Donetta shrugged her shoulders, trying to appear unaffected. "That's not my business, or my concern."

"No, but that's what you were thinking, otherwise you wouldn't have made the comment." He smiled. "I'm running errands for my mother. She's making a big Thanksgiving dinner, and I told her I'd get everything she needs to start cooking tomorrow. She works really hard and this will save her some time."

Donetta nodded her head and watched him as he looked down into her cart and then back into her eyes.

"Looks like you're cooking a big Thanksgiving feast, too."

"I thought you said after I helped you, you wouldn't bother me again."

"I won't . . . I'm not bothering you, I'm talking to you. There's a difference."

"Depends on who you ask."

The man had been smiling up until now, then he became very serious. "Miss, I don't know who or what has hurt you, but whatever it is, I hope you can move beyond it. Life is too short to be so hostile and angry all the time. It's ironic, too, because if you're this beautiful with a bad attitude, I can only imagine how stunning you'd be if you let down your guard and allowed yourself to be happy."

The handsome man's words stung because they were right, and for the first time in a long time, Donetta was speechless. The things he'd just said sounded eerily similar to many of the lectures Geneva had given her over the years, especially in the last few months. "You need to stop acting like the stereotypical angry black woman," Geneva had said. "If you act ugly, that's exactly what you're going to attract."

Donetta swallowed hard, struggling with what to say. "Um, listen, I apologize for my rudeness and my funky attitude. I had a very long day that didn't end too well."

His smile came back. "You're in luck because the day hasn't actually ended yet, so the way I see it there's a very good chance that you can turn things around."

"You think so?" She gave him a hint of a smile.

He nodded. "Absolutely. You have to have hope."

"I guess you're right."

"No, I'm Phillip," he said with a smile. "And you are?"

She giggled and cleared her throat again. "I don't usually give my name to strangers."

"I'm not some pervert who's gonna hunt you down or anything. I'm just a good brother who wants to know the name of the beautiful young woman who's gonna help me find the rest of the things on this list so I can get the hell out of this grocery store and head back home to eat my dinner from Sebastian's before it freezes out in my car."

"My chicken marsala is calling my name," Donetta said. Her stomach fluttered again, and she didn't know if it was because of hunger pangs, or the man standing in front of her.

"Wow, that's the same thing I ordered for my mom. It's her favorite dish from there."

Donetta raised her brow. "You got dinner for you and your mother, and now you're getting groceries for her. You're a good son."

"Thank you . . ." he paused and then held out his hand. "It sure would be helpful to know your name."

She looked into his eyes again, and she believed what he'd said about getting dinner and groceries for his mother, and she also believed he was a good man. For the first time tonight, she looked at him with a genuine smile and placed her hand in his for a warm shake. "I'm Donetta. Now, let's finish getting the things on your mama's list."

Chapter 9

PHILLIP

Phillip had always been told he had the Midas touch. Everything he set out to do resulted in success, whether it was being voted most valuable player on his high school basketball team, graduating at the top of his class from Stanford, or being the youngest associate ever to be considered for partner at his law firm, he always came out on top. So when he stood in the grocery store and spotted the beautiful woman from the restaurant standing in the same aisle, he couldn't deny his good fortune.

Phillip had hoped that fate would bring him face-to-face with the mysterious, beautiful woman again, but he had no idea that ten minutes later she'd be standing just a few feet away, carefully mulling over a bin of collard greens, inspecting each leaf as if she'd grown them herself. Although her body language made it pretty clear that she didn't want to be bothered, he had other plans in mind.

She seemed to have a power over him that drew him in and made him want to get to know her better. As a lawyer, he was trained by profession to ask questions and look for nonverbal clues that could explain one's motives and actions. He'd mastered the art of paying close attention to people's body language, because it spoke volumes, even if they refused to open their mouths. When he watched the beautiful woman, he saw that her body had been tense and that her eyes longed for something. The more he engaged her, the more he broke down her walls of defense, until she finally gave him a genuine smile that opened the door for more.

For the past thirty minutes, Donetta had been helping him find various items on the long grocery list his mother had texted him. After he'd broken through her hard shell, he found that not only was she much nicer than she'd acted, she was smart and had a wickedly biting sense of humor. Donetta was unlike any woman Phillip knew, and that alone put her in a special category. She cursed like a sailor—which was normally a turnoff for him—but coming from her delicately shaped lips, four letter words sounded almost melodic. And he could see that she had no filter because she said whatever came to her mind. In his experience, most women tried to be diplomatic in their approach, especially in the early stages of getting to know someone. But Donetta was just the opposite.

"My mouth is dry," she said, picking up a container of salt. "I'd love a dirty martini right about now."

Phillip laughed. "Experts say that water is the best thirst quencher."

"Fuck the experts. I'm an expert on me, and my throat is saying a dirty martini would set me straight."

As they pushed their carts from aisle to aisle, picking up boxes, cans, and containers of food, he learned that Donetta was quite the cook because she knew where everything was located in the store. He paid close attention to the little things about her, like the way she held her head to the side when she was questioning something he said, the way she put her hand on her hip when she was trying to make a point, and the way every move she made was graceful, like a ballet dancer's, and smooth like flowing water, and it turned him on. But most of all, he paid attention to her eyes. They were large and expressive, and looking into them he realized that the longing he'd seen earlier was actually sadness. He didn't know what had happened in her life to make her that way, but he hoped she would give him the opportunity to find out, and possibly to change it.

Phillip purposely tried to prolong their shopping adventure because he knew they were nearing the end of his list. He'd added a few items that his mother didn't need in order to spend more time with Donetta.

"We should get in separate lines so we can check out faster," Donetta said as she pushed her cart toward the checkout lanes.

Phillip nodded, reluctantly. "Okay, that makes sense."

He stood in line and glanced over at Donetta in the next aisle. She'd picked up a chocolate candy bar and then put it back down as she shook her head, no doubt talking herself out of the delicious indulgence in favor of watching her slim waistline. He smiled to himself and noted that she had a sweet tooth. He could see that her checkout line was moving much faster than his, and before he knew it she'd paid the cashier and was pushing her cart full of groceries toward the exit door.

She was walking slowly, and it made him think that maybe she was contemplating whether to stay or go. Slowly, she turned around, smiled, and waved good-bye before walking out of the store.

"Damn it!" Phillip said out loud, drawing a few stares from other customers. He'd hoped that he and Donetta would finish at the same time so he could get her number, and if he was lucky, continue their conversation later tonight over drinks. While they'd been browsing the aisles, he'd learned that she didn't have a boyfriend, which had been hard for him to believe, and that she hadn't been on a date in more than six months, which was nearly impossible to imagine. When he'd asked her why, her short response had been, "It's complicated." He'd wanted to know more, but now that she was gone, so was his chance.

Phillip's thoughts were interrupted when he heard a text alert come through on his phone. *It's probably Mom wondering how much longer it's gonna take me to bring home her chicken marsala,* he thought. He pulled his phone from his back pocket and frowned when he saw that the message was from Sabrina, an attractive anesthesiologist he'd been seeing on and off since last summer.

Dr. Sabrina Matthews was a cultured woman, and well-known among the who's who of DC's young urban professional sect. She had the right credentials, came from a prominent family, had a lucrative career, and was easy on the eyes. But for all her seemingly great attributes, she couldn't hold Phillip's attention for long, because everything about her screamed of a life he didn't want—proper, dull, and devoid of passion. He needed something more than simple window dressing.

He also didn't like the fact that Sabrina was overly concerned with outward appearances and social status, and that she was trying to pressure him into a deeper commitment. He'd told her from the very beginning that he wasn't interested in a serious relationship, but he could tell she had other plans. Last month she'd even hinted that she was ready to settle down and start a family, to which he'd told her he wasn't. Phillip knew that Sabrina was the type of woman who was willing to use anything at her disposal, including her body, to get what she wanted, so he had to be careful with her. He had to admit that sex with her was good, but not good enough to claim his heart, let alone warrant an engagement ring.

"I'll deal with her later," Phillip said as he slid the phone back into his pocket and looked out the exit door. He hoped that Donetta was still within sight, but she wasn't. He looked through the large glass window in front of him that provided a view of the parking lot, but he didn't see her out there, either. He figured she must have parked on the side of the building because if she'd been out front she'd still be loading her car with grocery bags right now. Phillip didn't want her to slip away for a second time. He looked at the cashier, who was moving as if he was stuck in quicksand. "Hey, man, can you speed it up? I'm trying to get out of here."

After the bag boy put the last item in Phillip's cart, he paid the cashier and quickly pushed his cart toward the exit. He walked out the door, and a smile returned to his face when he saw Donetta leaning against the side of the wall with her shopping cart in front of her. "You're still here," he said in a low, sexy voice, happy to see her.

She smiled back at him. "You didn't think I'd leave without saying a proper good-bye, did you? After all, I'm not a rude person . . . at least not anymore." She laughed and it made him laugh, too.

He moved his cart next to hers. "I'm glad you didn't leave."

"Five more minutes, and you would've missed me because it's freezing out here." She shivered, rubbing the sides of her arms to keep warm. "The temperature dropped while we were inside."

"Yeah, I think you're right. I wish I had a jacket to offer you."

She smiled and shook her head. "Thanks, but once I get to my car I'll be fine."

Phillip wanted to wrap his arms around her to warm her up, but he knew he couldn't do that . . . at least not yet. "I'll walk you to your car. Where are you parked?"

She hesitated, and then pointed her slender, perfectly manicured finger. "Over there. Follow me."

Now Phillip was certain that Donetta didn't want their time together to end, either, because instead of briskly walking to get out of the cold, she was taking her time, pushing her cart at a snail's pace. When they finally reached her car, he wasn't surprised to see that she drove a sleek BMW, similar to the one he owned that was parked in the garage of his town house. "I'll put your bags in your trunk while you sit inside and warm up," he offered.

Phillip quickly loaded her bags and then returned her cart to the stand in front of the store. As he walked back to her car, he could see that Donetta was staring at him, the same way he imagined he'd been staring at her in the restaurant. When she realized that he could see her watching him through her windshield, she averted her eyes. He knew that was a good sign. When he came up to her driver's side door, she had the window rolled down and the heat turned up high.

"You getting warm yet?" he asked.

"Yes, but I can't say much for my food. It's going straight into the oven when I get home."

"The oven? You don't microwave your food?"

Donetta tilted her head and flipped her long tresses to the side as she spoke. "Not with chicken marsala. The sauce they make it with is delicate and the chicken breast can dry out in the microwave. It's best reheated, on low, in a conventional oven. That way it retains its moistness and flavor."

Phillip loved that she was a woman who knew a lot about food. He was a firm believer that one of the best ways to a man's heart was through his stomach. "You sure do know a lot about cooking."

"It's my second passion. My customers at the salon rave about my cakes and pies."

"I bet they're delicious." Phillip paused, then licked his lips. "I'd love to taste them one day."

There was a short moment of silence that passed between them. He could see that Donetta wanted to say something, but instead she remained silent. He paid attention to her eyes, which darted around, trying to find a comfortable place to land. Even though he could tell she was unsure of what to do next, it was clear to him that Donetta was just as interested in him as he was in her. He was a decisive man of action, and he didn't want to stand in the cold hemming and hawing when he knew what he wanted, so he told her. "Donetta, I enjoyed meeting you tonight, and I'd like to get to know you better. I want to see you again. Do you think that's possible?"

Donetta looked down and then back up to him. "Anything's possible."

Phillip drove back to his mother's house feeling as though he'd just won a big case. He couldn't believe he'd been so persistent with Donetta. Normally, he didn't have to be aggressive in his pursuit of a woman because they flocked to him. But with Donetta, things were different. It wasn't just her striking beauty and unchecked boldness that made her stand out, it was the fact that she was one of the most genuinely authentic women he'd ever met. She didn't try to put on an act to impress him, which he found refreshing.

As he turned into his mother's driveway, Phillip's mind went back to the question he'd asked himself back at the restaurant, and was now begging to be answered. *What would his mother think of Donetta?*

In all the years that Phillip had been dating, and of all the women he'd been with, what his mother would think of them was a question he'd never really pondered because he'd never had a relationship that he thought was serious enough to consider. But he also recognized the strength and comfort of what it could mean to have the right person by your side.

After two trips back and forth from the car to the house, Phillip had unloaded all the bags and was now putting the food in the pantry and the refrigerator. He was surprised that his mother hadn't answered back when he announced that he was home, or that she hadn't come to help him put things away. He could see that the light was still on in the family room, which meant she was probably so involved in whatever movie or documentary she was watching that she didn't hear him. He reached into the cabinet and pulled out two dinner plates. "Mom, are you ready to eat?" he called out in a voice loud enough to be heard throughout the entire downstairs. She still didn't answer, so he walked into the family room, where he'd left her sitting earlier this evening.

Phillip was startled when he surveyed the scene before him. His mother was stretched out on the couch— still wearing her tailored skirt, silk blouse, pantyhose, and jewelry—fast asleep. His eyes roamed over to the empty bottle of wine sitting next to an empty glass. He couldn't believe she'd drank an entire bottle by herself, let alone that she'd fallen asleep, fully clothed.

"Mom," he said gently. "I'm home."

She didn't move a muscle, and he realized she was out cold. He knelt beside her and gently put his hand on her shoulder. "Mom, I'm going to take you down the hall to your bedroom, so I need you to stand up, okay?" He tried to gently nudge her to help her get up. But instead of rising from the couch, she simply repositioned herself to get more comfortable.

Phillip knew his mother needed the rest, so he decided to leave her where she was. He walked over to the decorative basket she kept in the corner and retrieved a soft, chenille blanket. He knelt beside her again and gently covered her with the warm throw. He leaned in and kissed her on her forehead, the same way she used to do to him when he was a little boy. "Good night, Mom."

He was about to walk away when his mother began to speak.

"I didn't mean to do it," she mumbled in a low, slurred voice. "But I had to . . . I had to stop him."

Phillip could see the tension covering his mother's face. He'd initially thought she was simply talking in her sleep, but as he continued to look at her he could see that it was much more than that. It appeared as though she was having a nightmare, and he wondered what was going on in her life that was bad enough to make her drink an entire bottle of wine and then fall into a bad dream.

"Mom, are you all right?" he whispered. A line of tension was streaked across her forehead that matched the pained look on her face.

Phillip didn't want to overreact, but he knew his mother well, and he was sure that something wasn't right. He watched and listened as her mumblings became incoherent. Then she turned onto her back, pulled the warm throw close to her face, and began to snore. "Whatever's going on with her, I'll have to find out in the morning," he whispered.

He knew she'd be out for a while, so he quietly left the room. He returned to the kitchen and placed his T-bone steak and baked potato in the microwave. A few minutes later he was sitting at the table barely touching his food as he continued to think about his mother. The first thing that came to mind was his father. "That's gotta be it," he said aloud. "Dad's the only person who can rattle Mom's nerves like that. Damn, I wonder what he's done now."

Phillip imagined that his father probably wanted to come around for the holidays, and heaven forbid if he'd been bold enough to ask if he could bring a "friend" with him. That would have surely set off his mother, and he didn't even want to think about what Lauren's reaction would be. But after giving the idea more thought, Phillip dismissed it. "Dad's not that stupid," he reasoned as he rubbed the light stubble on his chin. "I can't worry about what I don't know, so like I said, I'll just have to wait to talk to Mom in the morning to find out what's going on with her."

Phillip covered his half-eaten plate and put it in the refrigerator along with his mother's. He walked upstairs to his room and sat on the edge of his bed. He had to admit that although the home he'd grown up in was beautiful, and it had held precious memories of holidays and celebrations, his mother's new home, in a more trendy location, was now his favorite. It was large, but not grandiose. She'd created her own renovation design and had hired an independent contractor to help her bring the rooms to life, which resulted in a chef-grade kitchen, ample entertaining space, a beautiful main-level master suite, and a custom home office that was comfortable and chic. Each of the three bedrooms upstairs had its own private bathroom, complete with a rain showerhead. Phillip was still decorating his luxury town house, and he was looking forward to his mother coming up in two weeks to help him finish in time for a Christmas party he planned to have.

As he lay back on the bed and reflected on his day, his mind immediately went to thoughts of Donetta. Even though he'd just met her, he knew without a doubt that she was special, and she'd intrigued him enough to want to get to know more about her. He pulled his phone from his back pocket and pressed the contact button that he'd entered for her that read, BEAUTIFUL.

Donetta picked up on the second ring. "I wanted to give you time to eat and get settled in before I started blowin' up your phone," Phillip said.

"Thank you for that courtesy."

He could hear the smile in her voice, and that gave him encouragement. "You're welcome. And I'm glad you made it in safely."

"Thanks, you too. How was your dinner? What did you order, by the way?"

"Steak and a baked potato. How was your chicken marsala?"

"It was divine. Did your mother enjoy hers?"

Phillip thought about his mother still asleep on the couch downstairs. "When I came home she was knocked out. She had a really long day and was pretty exhausted."

"I know how that can be. I had a long day myself."

"Me too. But my night's been great."

"Really?" she giggled. "So . . . tell me, what's been so great about it?"

Phillip walked over to the window and looked out at the small flower garden and brick-paved patio below the deck in the backyard. "For starters, I met a beautiful woman. Actually, she was stunning."

Donetta giggled again. "Tell me more."

"Sure, I'll tell you all about her over drinks tonight, if you're up for it." Phillip heard her breathe into the phone, and he imagined she was debating whether or not she should meet up with him. "Listen, Donetta, I really enjoyed our conversation and I want to get to know you better. I was thinking since both of us had a long day, what better way to wind down than with a nice, relaxing drink at the Roosevelt?"

Donetta remained silent on the other end, and Phillip immediately realized his blunder, so he quickly corrected it. "I'm not trying to get you into a room."

"Uh-huh."

He laughed. "Seriously, I only suggested the hotel because their bar is open later than any of the restaurants in town, and I want to have plenty of time to tell you all about the amazing woman I mentioned."

This time Donetta didn't hesitate. "What time do you want to meet up?"

Phillip walked over to the closet, removed a black blazer from a black velveteen hanger, and laid it across the bed. "Can you meet me in thirty minutes?"

"The Roosevelt is a good twenty minutes from my house, and I need to change clothes. How about forty-five?"

He smiled. "Forty-five it is. I'll see you then."

Phillip hung up the phone feeling rejuvenated. He walked over to the bathroom on the other side of the room and removed his shaving cream from his black leather grooming kit. He wanted to look extra good for Donetta, and he was going to pull out all the stops to make an impression. He lathered his face with the citrus-smelling cream and realized that not only was he excited, he was actually a little nervous, which was something he rarely, if ever, experienced. He couldn't explain how he knew it, but he was certain that his date with Donetta was going to be the beginning of something special.

Chapter 10

GENEVA

Geneva filled her stainless steel teakettle with water, placed a chamomile and lavender–flavored tea bag in her cup, and sat on the bar stool at her large island while her water boiled. It was late, and she should've been lying beside Samuel, sound asleep after having made passionate love. But instead, she was sitting in her kitchen, feeling worried, shocked, and confused. A half hour ago she'd awakened after a terrible dream about Johnny that had seemed so real she'd almost screamed out loud. She was puzzled about what the dream had revealed, and she didn't know what to make of it.

Geneva shook her head as she replayed the dream in her mind. She'd been inside the home that she and Johnny used to share when they'd been married. It was early fall, and there was a crisp chill throughout the house because Johnny had always preferred cooler temperatures. Geneva was sitting on the opposite end of the couch from Johnny, staring at him as he turned a glass up to his lips. She was literally a fly on the wall, observing everything he was doing.

The house was a bit untidy, which was unusual because Johnny had been a neat freak. He loved a clean house with everything in its proper place. Geneva watched as Johnny took a slice of pepperoni pizza from the Pizza Hut box on the coffee table in front of him, and washed it down with a glass of what she knew was rum and Coke, which had been his longtime favorite drink. She knew this was one of several glasses he'd already consumed because he was drunk, and he reeked of alcohol so badly that she could smell him from where she was sitting.

She knew Johnny well, and he was a man who knew how to hold his liquor, so for him to be this drunk, she knew he'd probably been drinking all day.

She watched as Johnny took a small bite of his pizza slice, then put it back into the box without finishing it. He lifted his glass again and swallowed until it was empty. Geneva had no interest in watching her ex-husband drink all night, but what he did next made her sit up and pay attention. He put down his glass and picked up a small blue box. It struck her because the box was decorative, like the ones on display in arts and craft stores, used for keepsakes or supplies. Geneva had never seen the box while she'd been living with him, and she assumed that it must have belonged to some woman Johnny had been seeing after she'd moved out and asked him for a divorce. Geneva watched as he opened the lid of the box and started taking out what appeared to be photos. He shook his head as he looked at each one of them. Then he picked up a DVD sleeve that looked to have at least four or five discs inside. She tried to rise from her place on the couch to get a better look, but she was stuck, as if sitting in cement. She tried to move again, but she still couldn't budge from where she sat.

Geneva knew that whatever Johnny was looking at, it wasn't good. He shook his head again, looking visibly disturbed by what he saw as he held the photos and DVDs in his hands. He took a deep breath and lowered his head. "How could I have done something like this? What the hell was wrong with me?" He put the pictures and DVDs back in the box and then reached inside and picked up a small black phone. Geneva knew right away that it was a burner phone. She watched as he scrolled through the screen, and whatever he was looking at made him frown and shake his head even more before putting the phone back inside. He took another deep breath and then set the box on the floor. He leaned forward, picked up his glass, and drank the rest of its contents.

"I'm truly sorry, Geneva, and I hope one day you can forgive me," Johnny said, letting out a deep breath.

Geneva's heart beat fast when she heard him say her name. Now she really wanted to inspect the box, but she still couldn't move. She concentrated with all her might, but she couldn't even wiggle her toe, let alone move her legs to stand.

"I fucked up a good marriage to a good woman," Johnny continued, slurring his words as he spoke. "I have to give it to Bernard, he tried to warn me, but I wouldn't listen."

Geneva's heart sank when she thought about Bernard Seymore, who'd been Johnny's best friend. Bernard had been a playboy, just like Johnny, but once his wife of eleven years left him, his entire world changed. He'd plunged into depression mixed with heavy drinking, and it wasn't until he'd started therapy that he rose out of the darkness. He'd reformed his old ways, met a wonderful woman named Candace, whom he'd become engaged to, and had gotten a promotion on his job. But Johnny didn't liked the changes Bernard had made, because Bernard no longer hung out late or chased women with him like they used to. Plus, Johnny despised Candace and held her responsible for what he'd said had become Bernard's wimpy ways.

Bernard and Johnny's relationship continued to disintegrate, and ended in an all-out brawl that resulted in bruises and broken bones, but what had made their fight so bad was that it had taken place in Bernard's office at work. Bernard had been fired, and couldn't find another job. His truck was repossessed, his electricity was turned off, his house went into foreclosure, and his spirit was broken. He'd started drinking heavily again, and when Candace came over and caught him passed out naked beside another woman, she'd called off the engagement and left the ring he'd given her on his coffee table on her way out.

Bernard had been one of the prime suspects in Johnny's murder, especially because he didn't have much of an alibi, other than his word that he'd been at his house drinking the night Johnny had been murdered. Two months into the investigation, Bernard couldn't take the questions and scrutiny any longer, so he ended it all by putting a gun in his mouth to silence the world.

"Poor, poor Bernard," Geneva whispered. She was drawn from her thoughts when she heard Johnny's voice again.

"This is what it feels like to be shit on," he sighed and moved toward the edge of his seat on the couch. "I guess I'm getting my payback."

A bad feeling gathered in the pit of Geneva's stomach because she knew what was going to happen next. She didn't know how she knew it, but she was certain that Johnny was getting ready to be murdered. "Dear Lord, this is the night Johnny was killed," she said with a chill in her voice.

Geneva's eyes followed Johnny as he picked up the blue box and walked into the kitchen. She looked down at her feet, willing them to move, but she stayed planted where she was. She heard ice cubes clank against glass, and knew that Johnny was pouring himself another drink.

"Ahhh, that's what I needed," she heard him say.

Suddenly, there was a knock on the kitchen door. "Oh no!" Geneva said in horror. "She's coming to kill him."

Geneva was surprised that Vivana's knock wasn't more forceful because her nature was loud and rough. But Geneva realized that killers didn't want to bring attention to themselves. She thought if she could rush into the kitchen, she might be able to stop Vivana. But she still couldn't move. Then she tried to yell so she could warn Johnny, but when she opened her mouth, nothing came out. So she sat as still as she could and listened carefully.

"What're you doing here?" she heard Johnny ask.

Geneva's breathing became shallow and her heart raced fast. She continued to listen, but she didn't hear an answer. A minute went by before Geneva barely heard the faint sound that she'd known was coming. When the single gunshot rang out, she'd expected it to be louder, but then she remembered that the detectives had said that the killer had used a silencer to muffle the sound. She heard Johnny fall to the floor with a hard *thud*. His groans and gurgling coughs told her that he was in great pain.

Several minutes went by, which felt like hours, and Geneva became sick to her stomach with the thought of what had just happened. Then she heard Vivana talk so delicately that it didn't even sound like the crazy woman's voice. Geneva no longer wanted to move her legs because she didn't think she could bear the sight. But now, as if by command, her legs moved, and she rose from the couch involuntarily. She didn't want to see Johnny dying on the floor, or the deranged look Vivana probably had on her face at the pleasure of killing him.

Geneva closed her eyes so she wouldn't have to witness the gruesome scene, but just as she hadn't been able to will her legs to move on her own, she was unable to block out her sight, and she could still see what was happening through her closed lids. She drew in a deep breath as she looked down at the man she'd once been married to and had loved, sprawled out between the refrigerator and the cabinet, lying in his own blood. But as Geneva looked closer, she nearly lost her balance when she saw that Johnny's killer wasn't Vivana.

The killer was a female, for sure, but Geneva couldn't make out who she was. The woman was cloaked in shadow as she loomed over Johnny's body. She stood there for a moment, as if she was savoring his death. Then she kicked him in the side and walked out the door as casually as if she was taking a midafternoon stroll.

The whistling sound of the teakettle brought Geneva back to the waking present. She shivered at the thought of what she'd seen in her dream, and again, she couldn't shake the feeling that it seemed to be more than a dream; it seemed so real.

"I'd better turn off the kettle before it wakes everyone up." She hopped off the bar stool, went over to the stove, and poured her tea. She sipped slowly, listening to the peaceful silence in the house. While everyone was asleep, she was wide awake, filled with questions. She looked at the clock on the stove and realized that she'd never heard back from Donetta after they'd talked earlier that evening. Geneva reached for her phone and dialed her friend's number.

"Hey, girl," Donetta answered on the first ring.

"I thought you were going to call me when you got home." Geneva could hear noise in the background, and it sounded like Donetta was outside. "Where are you?"

"In my car, headed downtown."

Geneva stopped sipping her tea. "The last time I talked to you, some guy was stalking you in the grocery store, and now you're headed downtown . . . What's going on?"

"Sorry I didn't call you back. Everything's been happening so fast."

"Everything like what?"

"Well, for starters, that fine-ass man wasn't stalking me. He's a really nice guy, and—"

"Donetta, please tell me you're joking. I know you're not on your way downtown to see him."

Donetta let out a deep breath. "Just listen, okay?"

"Okay . . . I'm listening." Geneva shook her head and took a sip of tea to calm herself.

"We talked in the store for like, thirty minutes," Donetta said in an excited voice. "He was at Sebastian's picking up food for him and his mother, and then he went to the grocery store to get items from her shopping list. He looked like a deer in the headlights, because he didn't know where the hell anything was, so you know me . . ."

"You laughed at him?"

"Very funny . . . but no, I helped him find everything on his list."

"Wasn't that kind of you," Geneva said with a little sarcasm.

"Yes, it was," Donetta said as they both laughed. "Then I gave him my number. Girl, that brother didn't waste any time. He called me and asked if I'd meet him at the Roosevelt Hotel for drinks. So here I am, all dressed up, trying to find a parking space downtown."

"I'm in shock," Geneva said. Her conversation with Donetta felt like a dream, too, so she banged her foot against the bottom of the bar stool she was sitting on to make sure she was awake. "Ouch."

"What's wrong?" Donetta asked.

"After what you just said I had to kick something to make sure I wasn't dreaming."

Donetta laughed. "You're a regular comedian tonight. But I can't say that I blame you for thinking that because this is completely out of character for me. You know my ass is as cynical as they come. But girl, trust me when I say that this man is different."

Geneva knew that Donetta was jaded about most things, and she didn't trust anyone with a penis. She knew that her friend had been hurt in nearly every relationship she'd been involved in, and she'd become tough over the years to stave off disappointment. Geneva had thought that once Donetta completed her surgery last year, she'd feel more comfortable in her skin, and she'd have more success in her relationships, but it had been just the opposite. Donetta had dated more when she'd been transitioning than after she'd completed her transformation.

Geneva was happy to hear that Donetta was finally going on a date, but she was surprised at her friend's sudden change of heart. Earlier today Donetta had proclaimed that she refused to spend the holiday with her relatives, and now she was going out to meet a perfect stranger, late at night. "Who are you and what have you done with my best friend? Her name is Donetta Pierce, and if you see her please tell her to call me," Geneva teased. "Because I know the person I'm talking to on the other end of this phone isn't her."

Donetta laughed again. "I know, right? I can't believe it either. But remember earlier today when you asked me where my optimism was? If this doesn't show I'm trying to find it, nothing will."

"Wow! Okay, that's a major turnaround."

Donetta chuckled. "You should know by now that I don't take baby steps into anything. Once I decide on something, I'm all in."

Geneva had to agree. Donetta was an all-or-nothing kind of person, and for her to change her mind this quickly, Geneva knew the man she'd met must be special. "So, does this fine-ass man have a name?" Geneva asked.

"Yes, his name is Phillip! He's smart, and sexy, and taller than me, thank You, Jesus!"

"Donetta, I know you're excited, but please, please be careful. He may have seemed nice on first blush, but he could be crazy for all you know."

"No crazier than I am."

Geneva nodded her head, knowing her friend had just made a valid point. Donetta wasn't straitjacket crazy, but she could be a handful, and some of the situations she'd found herself in over the years were worthy of reality TV. "You know what I mean. Crazy, as in you could end up in his freezer."

"Stop it," Donetta said playfully. "You know I can handle myself. But wait a minute, what the hell are you doing up this late? Are you all right?"

Geneva finished the last sip of her tea. "I had a bad dream, so I'm sipping tea to calm my nerves."

"Oh, I'm so sorry, sweetie. You want to talk about it?"

This was one of the reasons why Geneva loved Donetta as if they were sisters. Donetta's offer to listen wasn't just a polite gesture; she really meant it. She was the type of friend who took her relationships seriously, and despite the fact that a handsome man was waiting to buy her drinks at the most exclusive hotel in downtown, she was ready to put him on pause if she felt Geneva needed her. "No, I'm okay. I'll tell you about it later. Go ahead and meet that handsome man and have a good time."

"Are you sure you're okay?"

"Yes, I'm certain. And listen, call me in the morning and let me know how things go. Don't forget, because if I don't hear from you by eight o'clock, I'm going to start blowin' up your phone."

"Okay, I'll call you. Now go to bed and get some rest."

Geneva hung up and prayed that Donetta would be all right. She washed out her cup, walked upstairs, and got back into bed. She snuggled next to Samuel and prayed for an answer to the mystery that she thought had been solved two years ago—who really killed Johnny?

Chapter 11

CHARLENE

It took Charlene a few minutes to figure out which room she was in when she opened her eyes. She slowly sat up on the couch before putting her feet to the floor in an effort to steady herself. Even though the room was dimly light from the elegant, flush-mount chandelier hanging above, she squinted as if she was sitting under a spotlight because her head felt like it weighed a hundred pounds. "What time is it?" She fumbled for her cell phone sitting on the ottoman in front of her and looked at the time. "I can't believe it's one o'clock in the morning." She blinked several times to focus her eyes, but all it did was make her head throb even more.

Charlene's stressful day, accompanied by a night of heavy drinking, had left her feeling listless. She strained her eyes when she saw a note lying beside the empty bottle of wine she'd drained. When she bent forward to pick it up, the room began to spin, so she leaned back into the soft pillows until she could gain her bearings. She looked to her left and saw a glass of water on the end table. She could tell it had been sitting there for a while because of the beads of condensation covering the glass and the half-melted ice cubes floating at the top. "Where did this water come from?" she mumbled. For the life of her, she didn't remember putting it there. Charlene licked her dry lips and swallowed the bad taste resting on her tongue. She was so parched at the moment that it didn't matter to her if the devil himself had put the glass there and had laced it with poison; she was thirsty, and she was going to drink it.

Slowly, Charlene reached for the water and held it tightly. When she brought the cool liquid to her lips, she gulped the entire glass down as if she hadn't had anything to drink in days. "Aaaaahh," she said. She set the empty glass back on the end table and looked at the note again. This time when she bent forward, she moved slower and stretched her arms. She picked up the piece of paper and saw that it was a handwritten note from Phillip.

> *Mom,*
> *You were asleep when I came home with the food. Drink all the water in the glass, that should help with the headache you're going to have. If you get hungry, your food is in the fridge, but don't microwave it because it's better warmed in the oven. I'm meeting up with a friend for drinks. Don't wait up.*
> *Love,*
> *Phillip*

The thought of Phillip finding her drunk and passed out on the couch made Charlene feel slightly embarrassed. But she knew, being the kind of person he was, he wouldn't judge her, or even be disappointed in her for having a very human moment. In fact, knowing her son the way she did, she knew he'd probably been worried about her, wondering what terrible thing had happened to cause her to get wasted.

"If he only knew," Charlene said to herself. But then again, she was glad he didn't know the details of what had caused her current state. She'd always tried to protect her children from hurt, and even though Phillip was now a strong, confident man, deep down he was a sensitive soul with a big heart. As a young boy he'd been polite, thoughtful, and kind, and again, she couldn't help but think about what a good husband he was going to make some woman one day—that is, if he could find it in his DNA to settle down. He was, after all, his father's child, and he loved the ladies.

Unfortunately, Charlene also knew that her ex-husband's philandering ways had had an impact on both of her children, and as a result they were on opposite ends of the spectrum in how they operated in relationships; Phillip had too many, and Lauren was in a perpetual dry spell.

Even though Phillip was honest with the women he fooled around with by telling them up front that he had no interest in having a committed relationship, he juggled more women than one man should. Charlene knew she couldn't control the actions of a grown man, but she wished her son would change that part of his life. She knew all too well how things could turn nasty if a woman felt scorned, whether she willingly knew what she was getting herself into or not—after all, that's how Johnny had ended up dead.

Thinking about the potential danger surrounding her son's love life made Charlene's head pound even harder. She wished she'd only drank two glasses of wine as she'd initially intended to do. But she'd gotten worked up over Vivana Jackson, Leslie Sachs, and the ghost of Johnny Mayfield, so she'd turned to alcohol in an attempt to chase her troubles away.

Charlene folded Phillip's neatly written note. "I've got to get up and go to bed," she said aloud. She adjusted her blouse and moved her skirt back into place as she slowly rose from the couch. She stumbled down the hall, and after walking what felt like the equivalent of a 5K, she finally reached her bedroom. She dragged herself over to her custom walk-in closet and removed her clothes. She reached into one of the built-in drawers and pulled out a long, silk nightgown and laid it across the small sitting bench near her shoe collection.

She wanted nothing more than to fall into bed and continue to sleep, but she knew she couldn't do that. She stripped off her clothes and stood under her rain showerhead as the warm water beat down on her skin. But instead of feeling peaceful relief, Charlene was bombarded by images that flashed through her mind of the night she'd murdered Johnny.

Charlene had come home after killing him and had immediately jumped into the shower. She'd scrubbed with a solution she'd purchased with cash from a pharmacy in the next county over, that would wipe away any traces of bacteria, blood, and gunpowder residue. She'd showered for thirty minutes, and had used the entire bottle in her efforts to wipe away the evidence of her crime.

Now, as Charlene lathered up her netted sponge, her mind shifted from the past back to the present, and in particular, to the phone call she'd received from Leslie Sachs. Charlene was certain that Leslie had evidence that would clear Vivana, otherwise she wouldn't have bothered holding a televised interview, or even taken her case pro bono. But Charlene wasn't sure whether Leslie had evidence that would implicate anyone else, and if she did, Charlene hoped the finger wouldn't point back in her direction.

After Charlene toweled off and slipped on her nightgown, she fell asleep as soon as her head hit the pillow. But as she rested under her 1,600-thread-count sheets, little did she know that the situations her two children would soon find themselves in would make murdering Johnny look like child's play.

Chapter 12

DONETTA

Donetta had just ended her phone call with Geneva, and now she was more worried about her friend than before. It was late, and instead of being sound asleep Geneva was up, traumatized and confused about a bad dream she'd had. "She thinks she needs to check on me, but I'm the one who needs to check on her," Donetta said to herself. "I'll call her in the morning."

She said a quick prayer for her friend as she maneuvered her car toward a space on her right. She preferred parking at a meter on the street whenever she ventured downtown, especially after business hours when parking was free. She didn't think the expensive parking decks and overpriced valet services were worth their touted convenience. But tonight as she drove down the mostly empty street with plenty of available spaces, she changed her mind. Keeping in line with her newfound attitude, along with the fact that it was cold outside and she didn't feel like walking several blocks wearing peep toe–style three-inch stilettos, she decided to splurge.

Donetta took a deep breath as she steered her car under the portico of the Roosevelt Hotel. She had to admit that she felt special pulling up to the luxury building. Despite being frugal in certain areas of her life, she loved high-end things, and she adored opulence. The Roosevelt was the epitome of style and refined taste, with its stately brick veneer, beautiful potted plants, and fragrant flowers flanking the front entrance to greet guests as they arrived. The lighting was so bright and perfectly staged that she felt as though she was stepping out at a Hollywood premier. There was even an actual red carpet leading from the front door to the lobby.

Donetta was about to open her door when a bellman, decked out in coat and tails, replete with a top hat, opened it for her. He extended his hand to help her out of her car. "Welcome to the Roosevelt, ma'am," the bellman said. "Will you be checking in, or are you here to meet a guest?"

Geneva cleared her throat. "I'm here to meet someone."

The bellman tipped his hat and spoke into his wireless earpiece to alert the front desk. *This is definitely my kind of place,* Donetta thought to herself as a valet came around to her door and handed her a yellow ticket stub. "We hope you enjoy your time here at the Roosevelt, ma'am."

"Thank you," Donetta said as she walked through the hotel entrance.

Although Donetta had been living in Amber for quite some time, she'd only been inside the Roosevelt on one other occasion, and that had been several years ago for a charity event. She'd fallen in love with the elegance and beauty of the grand hotel. Her taste had always gravitated toward high-end sophistication, which hadn't always matched her bank account. She let out a sigh when she looked around and thought about her beloved grandma Winnie. Her grandmother had been a plain woman who enjoyed the simple things in life, but she'd always encouraged Donetta to aspire beyond the boundaries of their life in rural South Carolina. "The only limits you won't be able to overcome in life is the ones you put on yo'self," her grandmother had told her.

"Grandma, you'd really like this place," Donetta whispered as she looked at the bright lights and blooming flowers surrounding the entrance. "And if I'm right, I think you'd like him, too." She smiled when she thought about Phillip, the reason she was there in the first place.

When Phillip had asked her to meet him for drinks, Donetta had hesitated and had almost told him no. All she'd wanted to do after a long day at the salon was relax with a hot bubble bath and a glass of wine after enjoying her dinner. But when he'd suggested the prestigious Roosevelt Hotel, she didn't hesitate. She knew that men who favored the Roosevelt for casual drinks didn't come along often, so she wasn't going to pass up the opportunity.

As she entered the lobby, she was greeted by a petite woman with a smile that seemed much too bubbly for so late at night.

"Welcome to the Roosevelt, ma'am," the woman said with a toothy grin. "How may I assist you tonight?"

Donetta smiled politely. "I'm here to meet some-one at your bar."

"Fantastic! Just walk through the lobby and veer to your left, and you'll see the Kylemore Room straight ahead."

"Thank you."

"My pleasure. And by the way, you look absolutely beautiful. Are you a model?"

Donetta smiled again and shook her head. "You're too kind. No, I'm not, but honey, I'll take that compli-ment any day."

Donetta walked through the lobby at a slow pace because she wanted to take in the grandeur of the room, letting the sights, sounds, and smells engulf her senses. She listened to the soft, instrumental jazz play-ing through the speaker system as she strolled, taking measured steps so she wouldn't miss a thing. She brushed her hand against one of the plush, leather high-back chairs and ran her fingers over the intricate nail-head trim. "Nice," she whispered. She glided across the floor as the heels of her stilettos sank into the rich Aubusson rug, and her eyes took in the bold tapestry of the heavy, silk jabot swags that adorned the floor-to-ceiling windows, accented by ornate crown molding. *I'm in my element,* she thought. She inhaled the sweet smell of fresh flowers and vanilla that filled the air, and made a note to herself that she needed to stop by Trader Joe's tomorrow to get some flowers.

For Donetta, the Roosevelt wasn't just a hotel, it was an experience, and she planned to enjoy every minute of it because she didn't know when she'd have the chance to do so again.

She saw the ladies' room just after exiting the lobby, and she ducked inside to take one last check of her makeup. When she walked inside she felt like she was in heaven. "Damn, this is nice!" She took in the long marble countertop that stretched the entire length of the room, boasting raised porcelain sinks and chrome fixtures that looked like they were straight out of a magazine. Two vases of fresh flowers added a special touch to the softly lit room, while the jasmine and lavender–scented reed diffusers made her feel as though she was smelling a fresh meadow. Donetta pulled her phone from her small purple clutch and started snapping pictures. "I'm gonna replicate this in my bathroom at home."

Donetta put her phone away and smiled as she looked at herself in the mirror, pleased with what she saw. At first she'd had no intention of getting dressed up because she didn't want Phillip to think she was trying too hard. She'd decided to go for the "I look good, but this is no big deal" look, so she'd pulled a pair of gray slacks and a cream-colored blouse from the hangers in her closet, and laid the outfit across her bed. But as she stood in the middle of her bedroom staring at the drab getup, she had to be honest with herself and admit that the very opposite was true. Her date with Phillip *was* a big deal, and not only did she want to look good for him, she wanted to impress him, and she knew she needed to put forth effort to show him.

She pulled together a knockout look in no time flat, and was out the door in record time, looking as though she'd spent hours preparing. The subtle golden highlights in her dark brown, razor-cut hair were flowing in sleek layers down her back. She'd applied smoky hues of gray and eggplant–colored eye shadows that made her look alluring, and she'd finished it off with a barely-there lipstick that brought out the pinkish tint of her full lips. Donetta nodded with satisfaction while she continued to look into the mirror.

She turned from side to side and smiled, knowing why the young woman in the lobby had mistaken her for a model. Her black skinny jeans showcased her long legs, and the subtle bling design on her back pockets accentuated the curve of her behind and her slender hips. She smoothed her manicured hand across the soft material of her white silk cami, and adjusted her zebra-print bolero-style jacket so the lapels brushed against her cleavage. Her bold, silver bangles and silver hoop earrings pulled the outfit together. She was stylish and chic with a hint of sass, compliments of her black suede and rhinestone-studded peep-toe stilettos. "Okay, Donetta, go out there with an open mind and just see where the hell this goes," she said, encouraging herself to be hopeful, and as she'd told Geneva, optimistic.

Donetta walked out of the restroom and veered to her left, as the bubbly woman in the lobby had instructed, and saw the Kylemore Room right in front of her. She suddenly became nervous with each step she took. This was a foreign feeling for Donetta, because there were very few things that could shake her. After all the battles she'd had to fight and hurdles she'd had to maneuver on her journey to find peace in her life, she rarely blinked an eye at difficult situations. And that was why she knew that drinks with Phillip was going to involve more than simply sipping alcohol with a handsome man. Her gut told her that he was very different, and her trembling hands reinforced that feeling.

She looked at the time on her phone and was glad

she'd arrived ten minutes early, because she needed those moments alone to calm her nerves, and maybe even order a drink to relax herself before Phillip arrived. If she had him pegged right, he was the type who would be there right on time.

Donetta's heart started racing when she walked into the large, dimly lit room and saw that Phillip was already there. *Damn it!*

She loved promptness, and she had a healthy respect for time, but in this case she wanted to adjust the hands on the clock. But that wasn't possible, so she knew she had to gather herself before she sat down in front of him. She took her mind off of being nervous by concentrating on each detail of the room as she walked in.

Although it was a large space, the mahogany furnishings and soft lighting made it feel intimate and warm. The chrome wall sconces and candles flickering inside tall, rectangular-shaped glass hurricanes gave it a daring edge. Donetta looked at Phillip, and it struck her how comfortable and relaxed he seemed to be, as if he owned the entire building. He was clearly self-assured and confident, which excited her. She loved a man who was secure and without pretense.

Donetta could see that he was staring at her, and the closer she got, the bigger his smile grew. He stood when she reached the table, and she couldn't help but smile back. She'd made an effort to look good for him, and she could see that he'd done the same in return. She knew she'd been right about Phillip having style when she saw how well he'd worn old Levi's and a sweater at the grocery store. Now he was sporting dark jeans, paired with a white shirt and a black blazer with a black-and-white polka-dot pocket square. His outfit was simple and classic, and the pocket square let her know he had a bit of flare.

"You beat me here," Donetta said.

Phillip reached for her, gathered her in his arms for a light embrace, and delivered a small, but sensual kiss to her cheek. She breathed in the scent that had stopped her in her tracks earlier tonight. "I'm always early," Phillip said. "And I'm glad you are, too. You look amazing, Donetta."

"Thank you, and you look very nice, too."

"I clean up okay."

Phillip pulled out the chair beside him and slid it closer to his, then extended his hand, motioning for Donetta to have a seat next to him. She appreciated that he was the type of man who pulled out chairs, opened doors, and showed up on time. As she watched him take his seat beside her, her cynicism tried to rear its head, and she began to think like she always did—the bigger the fish, the bigger the flaw.

Phillip seemed so perfect and much too good to be true. She wondered what kind of chink was buried deep in his armor. But as soon as the negative thought came to her mind, she heard Geneva's voice telling her to stop feeding in to negative energy. "If you look for bad things, think about bad things, and speak bad things, that's exactly what you'll get," her friend often told her. Donetta calmed herself, took a deep breath, and put her worries on hold . . . for now.

Chapter 13

PHILLIP

If there was one valuable lesson that Phillip could say his father had taught him, it was the importance of being on time. Phillip was always prompt in whatever he did, and tonight was no exception. He'd arrived at the Roosevelt Hotel nearly twenty minutes early with the anticipation of meeting Donetta. The hotel was one of his favorites, and in his opinion, it ranked above the prized Four Seasons in both quality and service. He wanted to show Donetta a good time, and he knew this was a great place to have what he considered to be their first date.

He'd thought Donetta was beautiful when he first saw her walk through the door at Sebastian's a few hours ago. But when she sashayed into the bar of the Roosevelt Hotel, he realized that she wasn't just beautiful; she was a work of art. He sat in his chair and took in every inch of her tall, elegant presence until she reached the table.

He appreciated a woman who knew how to wear a pair of jeans, and he thought Donetta could teach a class on how to pull off the look. Her curves were delicate, and nearly hypnotizing in their effect. He loved the way her body swayed from side to side when she walked, like a gentle breeze. When he stood to hug her, he'd wanted to give her a full-frontal embrace, but he was cognizant to remain respectful, so instead he lightly wrapped his right arm around her waist and gave her a quick kiss on the apple of her smooth cheek. He loved that she smelled good, not too sweet and not too bold, but a great combination of something in between.

They settled into their seats and ordered drinks and crab cakes. Phillip watched as Donetta sipped on the dirty martini that she'd said she'd been craving earlier that evening. He'd ordered a Scotch, and savored the taste of the Glenlivet 25, which went down smooth. He was glad that Donetta seemed more relaxed than she'd appeared to be when she'd first sat down. He didn't know if credit for that should go to the alcohol, to him, or both, but whatever the cause, he was appreciative.

The more he talked with Donetta, the more fascinated he became. One of the first things most women asked him within a few minutes of meeting him was, "What do you do?" DC was a power city, and in many circles, unless one could pinpoint your socioeconomic strata, they wouldn't entertain a conversation with you. He'd gotten so accustomed to being asked the question that he'd come to expect it right away. But after talking with Donetta in the grocery store about the holidays, their favorite foods, and what kind of music they each liked, the first question she'd actually asked him was, "You don't live with your mama, do you?" He'd laughed and told her that he lived in Washington, DC, and that he was in town visiting family for the holidays. He thought she'd follow up with the what-do-you-do question, but instead she'd simply pushed her cart and scanned the aisle for Ritz Crackers. And even now, she still hadn't asked him what he did for a living.

"I'm intrigued by you," Phillip said, taking a sip of his drink. "I know you're a hairstylist because you mentioned it when we were shopping, and it's written on the business card you gave me. But you have no idea what I do, yet you agreed to meet me here, why?"

Donetta tilted her head to the side and reached for a crab cake with her fork. "Um, correction. I'm a stylist, *and* I'm also the *D* in G&D Hair Design."

"You're a business owner." He smiled. "Congratulations. How long have you been in business?"

"I've been doing hair since college, but my best friend and I didn't open our salon until nearly two years ago."

"Very impressive, Donetta."

She smiled politely. "Thank you."

"Now, tell me, are you avoiding my question on purpose, or do you just not care?"

Donetta drank the last of her martini and moved the glass to the side. "No, I'm not avoiding your question, and yes, I do care what you do for a living. I'm not the kind of girl who'll date a brother who doesn't have his shit together. I have standards."

"I see." He chuckled.

"There's something you should know about me." She paused and looked him in the eyes. "I curse . . . a lot."

Phillip couldn't help but laugh. "Get outta here."

"I know, right? But I'm working on it."

"I like that you say what you think and feel. It's refreshing." Phillip gave her another smile. "Now back to my question."

"I didn't have to ask what you do for a living because I already knew five minutes into our conversation in the grocery store."

"Really? What is it that you think I do?"

"You break women's hearts."

Phillip was startled by her answer, which he hadn't expected.

"I'm sorry," Donetta said as she bit into her crab cake. "I meant to say you're *a lawyer* who breaks women's hearts."

Phillip shifted in his seat. "I don't think that's any better. But you did get the lawyer part right. How did you know?"

"Because you know how to ask invasive questions without coming off too pushy, and you pay attention to the small details of everything. You're well-spoken and very direct, and you leave very little room for rebuttal once you know what you want . . . like luring me out of my pj's in the middle of the night to have a drink with you at this bar."

Phillip leaned back in his seat and observed Donetta even closer than he had before. Beyond the lovely features of her face, she possessed something that he thought was a thousand times more beautiful, and that was her genuinely honest spirit. She wasn't pretentious like most of the attractive and accomplished women he knew. Donetta could easily be a model, and even be stuck on herself because of her beauty and entrepreneurial achievements. But instead, she was down-to-earth and sincere in the things she said and did. He was used to women saying things to impress him. But Donetta didn't do that, and she'd actually launched a few unintentional insults his way.

He had to admit that she was right about everything she'd said, including the part about breaking women's hearts. Although he was always up front about not wanting a serious commitment, a few of his relationships had ended in broken hearts and hard feelings. "Donetta, you're something else," Phillip said, giving her a wink.

"Tell me something I don't know."

When she blinked her long lashes and smiled back at him, Phillip wanted to kiss her, but he knew he needed to bide his time. He also knew he had to deal with the question he could sense was coming.

"So . . . how many hearts have you broken?" Donetta asked.

There it was. Phillip shifted in his seat. "I'm a very honest person, and I'm sensitive to others' emotions, that's why I'm always straight-up about my intentions, what I want and what I don't want. That minimizes broken hearts. But I can't control how others will react, I can only control how I handle things."

"You just said a lot of stuff, but I don't understand how that answers my question."

When the server came by to see if they wanted more drinks, they both ordered another round. Phillip knew he needed to keep his wits about him because Donetta was quick on her feet, and he wanted to be prepared to answer whatever she threw at him. The bartender was efficient because by the time the server walked back to the bar, another server was bringing out their drinks.

Donetta glided her finger across the rim of her glass. "What is it that you want and don't want in a relationship?" she asked.

"That depends on who the particular woman is. To be honest, I can't remember the last serious relationship I had. And when I say serious, I mean an exclusive commitment."

"Me either."

Phillip shook his head from side to side. "C'mon, Donetta. I know you said you haven't dated in a while, but do you really expect me to believe that you can't remember the last serious relationship you were in?"

"I believed you, so why is it so hard for you to believe me?"

"Because you're a beautiful woman, and men don't let beautiful women go unattached for long. Is it by choice?"

Donetta shook her head. "While I appreciate that compliment, in no way does being attractive mean a man will want to make a commitment to you. You're gonna make me start giving you the side-eye if you keep saying crazy shit like that."

Phillip laughed. "What I said isn't crazy, it's real."

She rolled her eyes.

"Okay, let's take the premise of a serious relationship off the table and talk simply about dating. Before tonight, how long has it been since you were on a date?"

"Six months."

Again, Phillip was in disbelief, and he found it hard to fathom that the amazing woman sitting across from him was dateless and alone. His degrees in psychology and law, combined with his natural ability to think logically, had all made him an excellent judge of character. Donetta had been right when she'd said he paid attention to everything, because he'd been sizing her up from the moment he'd laid eyes on her. He'd watched her every move and had listened carefully to the answers she gave and the comments she made, and so far, nothing she'd said or done had been contradictory. Being the rational-thinking person he was, he knew that her lackluster love life had to be self-imposed. "Having a date and making a commitment are two different things. I believe the only reason you haven't been on a date in so long is because you haven't wanted to."

"Partly yes, and partly no. I've kissed so many frogs in my life I may as well own a lily pad in a pond."

"Wow, that bad?"

"You have no idea," Donetta replied as they shared a laugh. "But I'm serious. I've been in some very unhealthy, dysfunctional relationships."

"I can identify with that. You women can be a trip."

"And you men can be ruthless."

The moment the words came out of her mouth, Phillip knew that was where the sadness that he'd seen in her eyes in the restaurant had come from. She'd experienced deep hurt at the hands of a man. He couldn't imagine how anyone lucky enough to be involved with Donetta could abuse that honor. But then again, he knew it didn't have as much to do with who she was, as it did with who they weren't. He thought about how his brave and beautiful mother had fallen victim to his father for so many years until she couldn't take it any longer. "I'm sorry you've been hurt," Phillip said. "Some men are straight-up fools, some just don't care, and some have never been shown love, so they really have no idea how to operate in that emotion."

Now it was Donetta's turn to lean back in her chair. "I completely disagree with that last part."

"What I'm trying to say is, how can you understand or appreciate something that you've never known or experienced? And that doesn't only apply to men, women can be the same way. If you've never been shown love, chances are you're not going to be good at showing it, or even recognizing it."

Donetta shook her head and re-crossed her long legs. "That's true about it not being gender-specific because anyone can be an uncaring asshole. But I still disagree with what you said about love."

"Tell me why." Phillip enjoyed seeing the spark of energy in her eyes and in her body, and he liked the fact that Donetta spoke her mind and challenged him. "I'm all ears."

"We all have a choice, that's what free will is all about. Everyone wants to be loved, period. Even the most hard-core badass wants a soft place to land, and to know that someone's in their corner. That's why God made Eve for Adam, so he would have companionship and that he wouldn't be alone. Love is a human desire we're wired with from the time we take our first breath."

"How about the person who's not wired for love and doesn't have a clue?"

"I don't buy that, because love is natural. People just express it differently."

Phillip stared at her. "You really believe that?"

"Yes, I do. My late grandma Winnie used to tell me all the time that the only person who could set limits on my life was me. I believed that then, and I believe it now. That's why even though I can't remember ever seeing an example of a truly healthy relationship growing up, and I've had some shitty ones of my own—and I'm talkin' commode-style—I know that ultimately it's up to me to create my own happiness, and that starts and ends with the choices I make. Like I said, free will."

"Your grandmother was a wise woman."

"Yes, she was. She taught me a lot, and I miss her dearly." Donetta's eyes flashed with sadness. She took a deep breath and smiled. "It's because of her that I know anything is possible. Just because someone has never seen an example of a loving relationship, it doesn't mean they don't know how to love or that they won't ever experience it. They'll simply have to work hard to get it. We all do, whether we've been damaged or not."

Phillip shook his head. "I appreciate and respect what you're saying, but some people don't have the capacity to . . ." Phillip stopped in midsentence because once again, he thought about his father. *Damn!* He realized he was about to argue the case to excuse his father's inability to be a good, loving husband and father. Then it occurred to Phillip that he was also trying to justify why he'd never wanted to commit to anyone. It wasn't that he didn't have the capacity, it was that he simply didn't have the desire. He cleared his throat. "On second thought, I stand corrected. I think you might be on to something."

Donetta raised her brow. "What caused your sudden change of mind?"

"Honestly . . . my father, and me too."

"What's your relationship like with your father?"

"We don't have one."

Donetta swirled her olive around in her glass. "Why not?"

"He's hurt everyone he supposedly loved. He knew he was doing wrong, but he chose to continue doing it anyway."

"Wow, I'm sorry to hear that." She paused and looked at him closely. "So what about you?"

Phillip took a deep breath. "How did we get on such serious topics? We're supposed to be having a lighthearted discussion over fantastic drinks in a relaxing atmosphere. We're getting kind of heavy, don't you think?"

"Phillip, my life weighed a ton from the moment I was born." Donetta paused again. "But over the last couple of years I adjusted my lifestyle and lost a lot of that weight. I'm finally getting healthy, the way I was meant to be, but in order for me to maintain it, I've got to constantly work at it. I refuse to be overweight ever again, so dealing with heavy stuff is how I make sure I stay in shape."

Now it was his turn to raise his brow. "You're not talking about your physical weight, are you?"

"I'm talking about life, boo."

Phillip couldn't help but smile when she called him boo. It was a pop culture term that he'd always thought was silly, but coming from her, it was endearing. There were so many things about Donetta that he found fascinating, and he could feel his emotions starting to take control in a way they never had before. With each new discovery, he became more and more drawn to her. Here they were on their first date, in a beautiful, romantic setting, sipping expensive drinks, eating pricey appetizers, and talking about the ugly, shitty side of relationships and life.

Before he knew it, Phillip found himself telling her about his childhood and the dysfunction between his parents that he'd witnessed since he was a teenager. He even told her about the time he'd stumbled upon one of his father's many affairs, and how his father had sworn him to secrecy, and then used Phillip as an alibi to do even more dirt. He'd never confessed that to anyone, and now that he'd told Donetta, he felt as if a burden had been lifted from him.

Phillip felt safe with her in a way he'd never experienced. Her eyes held enormous beauty, as well as miles of pain, and it allowed her to understand him instead of judge him. He was about to ask Donetta more details about her life and her upbringing, but two things suddenly happened that interrupted him. Their server came to their table to let them know that the bar was closing, and his cell phone chirped with a new text message. He didn't have to look at the screen to know who it was, because he'd assigned Rachel a specific ringtone.

Rachel Belmont had been the only woman he'd dated who'd been able to make Phillip remotely think about the possibility of a commitment. They'd gone to law school together at Howard University, and they had always been friendly, but at the time she'd already been in a serious relationship and he'd been a serious player. Several years had passed before Phillip spotted her two years ago at an alumni mixer during homecoming weekend. One thing led to another and before he knew it, she was spending the night and waking up the next morning in his bed. That by itself said a lot, because rarely did Phillip invite women over to his place, let alone let them spend the night.

Rachel was self-assured, and a bit of a control

freak. She was a defense attorney, and he represented plaintiffs, so by their very nature they were opposing sides. That was one of the reasons Phillip had never felt fully connected with her. She was great on paper, but there was something lacking where it counted. He felt an internal struggle when they were together. Lately she'd been pressing him for a commitment, and she had even asked if she could travel home with him for Thanksgiving. It had been hard, but he'd told her he thought it was time for them to move on because they wanted two different things. However, Rachel had other plans, and much like Sabrina, Phillip knew she was the kind of person who didn't stop until she got what she wanted. But he couldn't think about that now. He needed to concentrate on Donetta and deal with both Sabrina and Rachel at another time.

Phillip closed out their ticket, left a generous tip, and then escorted Donetta toward the lobby. It was the wee hours of the morning, everything was closed, but he didn't want his time with her to end. "Are you tired?" he asked.

"I should be, but no, I'm not."

Phillip nodded. "Neither am I." He led the way over to a love seat against a large window on the far side of the lobby. They sat close to each other and continued their conversation.

"So, who rang your phone for a booty call?" Donetta asked.

This was the first time that Phillip didn't want to be honest, but he knew he had to be. "A woman I've been involved with."

"Is it serious?"

"I told you earlier, I haven't been in a serious relationship in years."

Phillip noticed that Donetta's entire body language changed. She looked out the window into the darkness. "Donetta, are you okay?"

She let out a heavy sigh. "I want a serious relationship, Phillip." She said this without blinking, and it made Phillip's heart beat fast as she continued. "I want to get married. I want to raise children. I want to have a family. Talking to you tonight made me realize that I need to stop being afraid. If I want something, I need to make it happen." She gathered her small clutch, as if she was preparing to leave. "Phillip, you're a wonderful person, and I know that once you're ready to settle down you're gonna make some lucky woman a great husband. But I also know that's not going to happen anytime soon. You're in town for the holidays, and you're looking for a good time, which I think we've had tonight. But I know that's all it can be, because we want two different things, so let's not waste each other's time and just end this night on a high note."

Phillip felt as though he'd been punched in the gut. Donetta had just said the exact same words to him that he'd told Rachel. A part of him felt horrible, because for the first time, he fully understood how much he'd hurt some of the women he'd been involved with, whether it was intentional or not. Donetta's rejection was honest and straightforward, but it still stung, and he wasn't ready to accept it. "Wait, how do you know that we want two different things?"

"Because you said so. You said you don't want a commitment or a serious relationship, but I do. From where I stand, that's two different things."

Phillip rubbed his chin and thought about what she'd just said, and in that instant, he discovered something new about himself. "When you asked me what I want and don't want in a relationship, I first told you it depends upon the woman I'm seeing."

She nodded. "Yes, I remember."

"Donetta, you're unlike any woman I've ever met, so anything I may have thought or felt before is irrelevant." He looked deep into her eyes so he could make sure she understood what he was about to say. "I know this might sound crazy, but I believe you and I have something special going on between us. The thoughts that have been popping up in my head all night, ever since the moment I first saw you, are like nothing I've ever imagined, and the fact that we just met doesn't negate that it's real."

A long pause crawled by between them, filling the air. He could see that Donetta was processing what he'd just said, and he wanted to give her all the time she needed, but as much as he tried, he couldn't. He leaned in, wrapped his long arms around her slender waist, and brought her so close to him that their foreheads touched. He could feel the rise and fall of her chest and the tremble of her body against his. He looked into her eyes again, and without saying another word, he brought his lips to hers.

Chapter 14

GENEVA

Geneva rose from bed while Samuel and her in-laws were all still asleep. The only other person stirring in the early-morning hour was precious little Gabrielle. When Geneva went into her daughter's room, Gabrielle was already sitting up in her crib, and when she saw Geneva walk into the room she burst into a smile that was brighter than the sun. Geneva knew some things in life could get old, but watching the smile on her daughter's face wasn't one of them. "How's my beautiful girl this morning?" Geneva said in a cooing voice.

Geneva lifted Gabrielle from her crib and kissed her cheeks until her daughter squealed with delight. She couldn't believe how much her baby girl was growing every day. She'd been long and skinny when she was born, and now she was long and plump, like an adorable Gerber baby. Geneva walked over to the changing table and sang to Gabrielle as she wiped, powdered, and fastened a fresh diaper around her bottom.

Geneva felt blessed that Gabrielle was such a good and low-maintenance baby. She'd inherited that quality from both Geneva and Samuel. While Geneva had been pregnant, many of her customers had talked about the challenges and rigors of pregnancy, birth, and then the task of raising an infant. She'd expected sleepless nights, exhaustion, frustration, and at times, resentment for having to make such a drastic life change. But to Geneva's amazement, it was nothing like she'd thought it would be.

Her pregnancy had been smooth, and she'd worked at the salon up until a few hours before Gabrielle had been born. The first three weeks after Gabrielle had come home were a huge adjustment. Geneva had been tired and worried every second, wondering whether she was doing the right thing. But when the fourth week rolled around, it was as if a new chapter had been written. Gabrielle started sleeping through the night, she only cried when she needed to be fed or changed, and Geneva began to feel more confident each day that she knew how to be a parent. "My goddaughter has a better sleep pattern than I do," Donetta had joked. Not only did Gabrielle sleep through the night, she was a calm, happy baby, and it made Geneva and Samuel's life so much easier.

Geneva opened the mini-fridge in the corner of the nursery and pulled out a bottle. "Is Mommy's little princess ready to eat?" Geneva laughed when Gabrielle gave her a huge grin that erupted into happy giggles. Gabrielle knew the routine, and she was so ready to eat that she actually clapped her hands. This was Geneva's favorite part of her day. As she sat in the comfortable reclining chair and cradled Gabrielle while she fed her, she almost forgot about why she'd been so tired when she first got up; then she remembered, and it sent a chill through her.

After Geneva burped Gabrielle, she grabbed a handful of bibs and a few cloth diapers and headed downstairs. "I'm gonna sit you in here while Mommy makes breakfast," she said to Gabrielle. Once her daughter was secure in the portable playpen, Geneva knew that in another twenty minutes, Gabrielle would be fast asleep for another hour and a half. She walked over to the refrigerator and pulled out bacon, eggs, milk, cheese, and butter and set them on the counter.

As Geneva began to prepare food for the family, she tried not to think about the dream she'd had last night, but no matter how hard she willed herself not to, she couldn't get the image out of her mind of Johnny's dead body, and a woman cloaked in shadow standing over him. It had all seemed so real. Geneva had always heard that dreams were the thoughts and sensations that occurred in a person's mind during sleep. "Is it possible to actually see something from someone else's life?" she said out loud. She looked at the digital clock on the stove and saw that it was eight o'clock. She'd told Donetta that if she didn't hear from her by eight this morning she was going to call her, and as if like clockwork, Geneva's phone rang. It was Donetta.

"I was about to call you, but you beat me to it. I'm so glad you made it back alive."

"Of course I did," Donetta said in a groggy voice.

"Nowadays you can never be too sure when you meet someone new. I watch *Forensic Files*, and you'd be surprised at what people will do. There's a lot of nuts out there."

"I hear you, but there's no need to worry. The old me would've been caught up in some foolishness, but the new and improved Donetta don't mess around."

Geneva opened the pack of bacon and lined a large skillet, slice by slice. "So, how did it go?"

"Guuurrrlllll," Donetta said. "You just don't know."

"Wow, things went that well?"

"They're still going."

Geneva shook her head as she cracked eggs into a bowl. "Wait a minute, please tell me that you didn't sleep with him—and he's still there?"

"No, I didn't sleep with him, I had sex with him, and yes, he's in my bed right now and I'm in my kitchen about to make breakfast. Girl, I'm up early, cooking for a man. Hell has officially frozen over."

"Girl, stop! I can't believe this . . . I mean . . . damn, I don't know what to say."

"I know!" Donetta squealed with delight as she whispered into the phone.

Geneva turned off the skillet of sizzling bacon and moved the bowl of eggs to the side. She took a seat on a bar stool at the end of the island because she needed to fully concentrate on everything Donetta was going to say. "Give me all the details, and don't leave anything out."

"You know I love to kiss and tell."

"Well, tell me while I still have a few minutes of peace before everyone wakes up."

Donetta giggled. "Okay, so we had a great conversation in the bar, which is actually more like a sophisticated lounge. He's got daddy issues like most folks I know, but he's handling it. Anyway, we had such a good time that we closed down the place and had to end up going to the lobby to finish talking. We talked about relationships and what we wanted."

"Wow, y'all got down to the nitty-gritty right away."

"At this age, and after all I've gone through, I'm not interested in wasting my time."

"I hear you."

"Anyway, we talked enough for me to know that he's smart, funny, honest, successful, and an all-around good guy, but . . ."

"There's always a but."

"You got that right. He's had a lot of women, and he's never made a serious commitment, as in an exclusive relationship."

"Ever?"

"Not that I could tell, and that's why I promptly told him that even though I haven't been in a serious relationship in a long time, or even dated for that matter, I still want to. I told him that I want to get married and I want to raise a family of my own, then I picked up my purse and got ready to leave."

"Good for you. But obviously that didn't happen, so tell me how he ended up in your bed."

"He told me that he hadn't wanted a commitment in the past, but every situation is different, which I agree with. Then he leaned in and kissed me, and before I knew it we were back at my house taking off each other's clothes."

Geneva knew that Donetta had only had sex once since having her reassignment surgery, and that had been six months ago. Donetta had told her that it had been a huge disaster. She'd been so disappointed that Geneva believed it was the reason Donetta hadn't had any interest in going on a date since that night. As Geneva's mind briefly flashed back to that time, she now realized the true significance of what last night must have meant for Donetta, and also, that the man she was with was truly someone special. "He obviously knew what he was doing," Geneva said.

"Not only did he know what to do, he knew when to do it." Donetta's whisper carried a softness in tone that Geneva had never heard before. "He was so gentle. He took his time, he talked to me, he kissed me, he told me I was beautiful. Girl . . ." Donetta paused and her voice trembled. "It was magical."

"I'm so, so very happy for you, Donetta. You've waited a long time to feel this way, and I can't think of anyone who deserves it more than you."

"Thanks, honey. I don't know where this is going to lead, but I'm going to enjoy it while I can. I've learned that I can't worry about what might happen tomorrow, because the next day isn't promised. If someone had told me when I woke up yesterday morning that today I'd be waking up beside a handsome, caring man who rocked my world, I wouldn't have believed them. But it happened."

"You're right."

"So I'm just gonna live in the moment, and let this moment take me to the next one."

Geneva thought about what Donetta was saying, and she knew that she needed to do the same thing with her life and the worries she'd been having since yesterday, especially after her bad dream last night. "Donetta, I agree with you, and again, I'm so happy for you, girl."

"Enough about me, how're you feeling this morning?"

"I'm good."

"Geneva, it's me you're talking to. I know you're happy for me, but I can hear something in your voice that's not quite right. It's the same thing I heard last night, so don't tell me you're good, because I know you're not."

"It's nothing, really." Geneva didn't want to bring Donetta off her high by telling her about a crazy dream she'd had, but at the same time, she couldn't shake the feeling that her dream meant something. "I don't want to worry you."

"I'm already worried, and I'm gonna be upset in a minute if you don't tell me what's going on."

Geneva took a deep breath. "This is going to sound crazy, so just keep an open mind about what I'm getting ready to tell you."

"Okay, my mind and ears are open."

Geneva told Donetta from beginning to end about her dream, not leaving out a single detail. "I was literally there, watching Johnny in the moments before his murder. I just wish that I'd been able to move my legs so I could've gotten a good view of whoever it was that killed him."

Donetta was silent.

"I know you think I'm crazy. Say something."

Donetta let out a deep breath. "No, I don't think you're crazy, I'm just processing everything. You obviously had that dream because you saw Vivana on TV yesterday, and that brought the trauma of what happened two years ago back to the surface."

"Yes, that's true, and at first I thought the same thing. But Donetta, it was more than just a dream. I'm telling you, it was real. Vivana didn't kill Johnny."

"You know, it's funny," Donetta said with a sigh.

"I'm one of the very few people in this entire town who never thought that bitch was guilty. Is she nuts? Absolutely! Is she capable of murder? You bet. But did she kill Johnny? I don't think so."

"Up until last night I really believed she did, and you couldn't have convinced me otherwise. But after my dream, I know in my heart that she didn't."

"Tell me again, what was the last thing you remember seeing the killer do in the dream before she walked out the door?"

"Well, like I said, the person was definitely a woman. The shadow around her filled the entire space like a shade tree. She stood over him, and even though I couldn't see her face, I know she was smiling. She said something to him that I couldn't understand, and then right after that she waited for a minute or two, like she was waiting to make sure he was dead, then when he took his last breath she turned around, kicked him in his side, and walked away."

"Damn! She was one cold killer."

"It sent chills down my spine."

"I bet."

Geneva tried to remember as many other details as she could, and then something else came to her. "I think the killer took the blue box that I told you about. As a matter of fact, I know she did. When Johnny left the living room he had it in his hand, then once he was in the kitchen I could hear him fixing another drink, so he had to have set it on the counter in order to do that. But when I went in there after he was murdered, the blue box was nowhere to be found."

"That makes a lot of sense. Remember, during the trial when the detectives said that Johnny had been blackmailing all those women with videos and pictures he'd taken, but they couldn't find any physical proof, not even cell phone records because he'd used a burner phone. All that physical proof, along with the burner phone, was in that blue box, and after the killer murdered him, she took the evidence with her."

"Exactly!" Geneva hopped off her bar stool and started pacing the floor. She glanced over at Gabrielle, who was fast asleep, and then walked over to the other side of the kitchen. "In my dream, I distinctly saw Johnny pull out some pictures, DVDs, and a burner phone. I guarantee you all the women he blackmailed were in that box."

During the murder investigation, the only way the detectives had discovered that Johnny was blackmailing women was that he'd gotten sloppy, and had forgotten to erase a few e-mails he'd sent from the hard drive of his computer. Two of his victims had also sent him threatening texts on his regular cell phone. But because the authorities had figured out that Johnny must have primarily used a burner phone for his dirty deeds, they'd suspected that there had probably been more victims out there than they'd ever really know. Now Geneva believed it without a doubt, and one of those faceless victims had gotten away with murder.

"So what are you gonna do?" Donetta asked.

"I'm not sure. On the one hand, I don't want to go to the police because they'll never believe me. And besides, if Vivana is really innocent, that means she'll be released from prison. She vowed to kill me once, and if she gets out she might try to finish what she started."

"Like I said, she's capable, for sure. But I don't think she'll do anything because she knows the authorities will be keeping a very close eye on her."

"I guess you're right, but there's only so much the police can do."

"True. But if what you're saying has merit, which I believe it does, you need to talk to someone you can trust who's in a position to represent you if you need legal counsel and protection for coming forward with new evidence."

Geneva thought for a moment. "You're right, and I know just the person. Councilwoman Harris. She's a licensed attorney, she's well-respected in the police department, and I can trust her completely."

"I hadn't even thought about her, but you're right."

Geneva and Donetta talked for a few more minutes before hanging up the phone. Geneva felt a small sense of relief knowing that she could go to Charlene Harris for advice. Not only was she qualified to help, she was a friend. Geneva decided that she'd wait until after Thanksgiving to give Charlene a call.

Chapter 15
CHARLENE

Charlene woke up in a fog. If she thought her head had been hurting when she'd gone to bed in the wee hours of the morning, it was even worse now. Her temples throbbed so badly that she had to squint just to open her eyes. She was also nauseated, and her mouth was so dry that her lips were cracked. "I've got to pull myself together," she said as she looked at the alarm clock beside her bed and realized it was after ten in the morning. "Oh no, I'm going to be late picking up Lauren."

Lauren's flight was scheduled to arrive at ten thirty, and Charlene had told her daughter that she'd be standing at the baggage claim waiting to get her. Slowly, she sat up in bed and rubbed her eyes. She was tired, but she knew she needed to get up. Charlene knew that by the time she got dressed and on the road, she'd be an hour late. As it was, Lauren's flight would be arriving in the next fifteen minutes. "I need to ask Phillip to pick his sister up because he can get going quicker than I can."

When Charlene put her feet on the floor and stood, she felt as though she'd just stepped onto a carousel. She remained in place for a few moments until she could gather her bearings, and then she reached for her silk robe and tied it tightly around her waist. She walked down the hallway that led toward the front of the house where the staircase was, and called out for Phillip. That was a bad idea because it made her head ring like a bell.

Charlene went back into her bedroom and picked up her phone from her bedside table and found a text message from Phillip that he'd sent a half hour ago.

Phillip: Mom, I hope you slept well. I'm going to pick up Lauren from the airport. We will see you soon.

Charlene smiled and remembered that Phillip had told her he would pick up his sister. "I can always count on that boy." As she walked out to the kitchen, a thought came to her. She wondered whether Phillip had come home at all last night. When she'd gone to bed shortly after one o'clock this morning, he hadn't been home. She'd also awakened a few hours later at four, with an intense need to release the wine she'd drunk. Her throat had also been parched, so after a trip to the bathroom, she went to the kitchen to get a glass of water. She'd looked out the window and seen that Phillip's rental car wasn't there.

Now Charlene was almost certain that whomever Phillip had been out with last night, he'd likely stayed with them and had never returned home. Charlene shook her head. "Lord, please slow him down because he's moving too fast with all these women," she said aloud. She knew Phillip was a grown man with a life of his own, and that he could do as he pleased. But he was also still her child, and she knew it was her job to protect him until she took her last breath.

Ever since Phillip had been a little boy, she'd guided him and had given him sound advice, and she had no intention of stopping now. He needed help before his casual love 'em and leave 'em lifestyle landed him in more trouble than he could handle. Johnny Mayfield was a prime example of what could happen if a man continued to pursue the wrong women, and although Phillip was far from the conniving scoundrel that Johnny had been, Charlene knew that one bad move with the wrong woman could land her son six feet under. As she thought about Phillip, her mind took her to her own set of troubles that had started yesterday.

Charlene walked to the kitchen, pushed the Power button on her Keurig, and pulled her favorite coffee mug from the cabinet. She reached for the TV remote so she could watch the last of the morning news on the small flat-screen television mounted under the cabinet. She turned the channel to MSNBC and was busy gathering cream and sugar when she heard an announcement that froze her in her tracks. "Up next, an exclusive interview with Leslie Sachs, the woman who wants to set a convicted killer free," the serious-looking commentator said.

Charlene's mouth fell open and her hands began to shake. She'd known yesterday that Leslie and Vivana's claim of new evidence was going to garner a lot of interest, but she hadn't anticipated it would make national news so quickly. But then again, Johnny's murder had made national news two years ago. The fallout over his blackmail scheme involving several women, combined with the fact that there were a half-dozen prime suspects, had made the big murder in the small town worthy of national attention. That was also how Shartell Brown had been elevated from a busybody town gossip into a respected columnist for one of the nation's top entertainment news websites. She'd provided weekly updates and inside information to curious minds who had wanted to be in the know. Shartell had delivered and was still doing so to this day.

Charlene could barely sip her coffee as her heart raced with each commercial. Finally, the reporter was back on screen, announcing her live interview. This time Leslie was alone, sitting at her desk. Charlene could tell that the interview was being conducted in Leslie's home because there were beautiful drapes in vibrant colors hanging against the wall, just under the ceiling's crown molding, and she could see houses on the street through the window behind the chair where Leslie was sitting. Charlene also noticed that Leslie had clearly paid a visit to her salon and the makeup counter at the local department store since yesterday because her blond hair was perfectly coiffed, cascading to her slim shoulders, and her face glowed flawlessly under the bright camera lights. Charlene turned the volume up high so she could hear every word that was being said.

"Ms. Sachs," the reporter began. "You're representing Vivana Jackson, who was convicted two years ago for the murder of Jonathan Mayfield, pro bono, and you announced yesterday that you have new evidence that proves Ms. Jackson's innocence. Can you tell us how you became involved with this case?"

Leslie looked into the camera with her steely ice-blue eyes. "First, I'd like to address what you said leading into this interview. I'm not trying to set a convicted killer free, I'm working to exonerate an innocent woman who was wrongly accused of a vicious crime that she didn't commit."

Charlene had to admire Leslie's grit and tactics, and she had to admit that if she was ever wrongly accused of anything, Leslie would be the first person she'd contact—and that was the very reason why Charlene was worried out of her mind. She listened as Leslie continued.

"Now, to answer your question. As a criminal defense attorney for over thirty years, I receive requests every day from individuals who claim they've been wrongly convicted of a crime. But when I read Vivana Jackson's letter, two things stood out for me. One was that it was a case I'd followed closely because it happened here in Amber, Alabama, where I live. And the other reason was that her impassioned plea led me to pay her a face-to-face visit, and when I did, I discovered a detail during our conversation that had been overlooked during the trial."

Charlene's heart was thumping so hard she could barely breathe.

"As you know, Ms. Sachs, the Mayfield case received national attention, and the overwhelming majority of citizens as well as legal professionals who followed the trial were convinced by the evidence and the testimony that the prosecution proved beyond a shadow of a doubt the right person was convicted. What specific evidence do you have to dispute that?"

Leslie paused for a brief moment, leaned forward, and gave a hint of a smile. Just when she was about to open her mouth, she paused again and looked to her right, as if she was distracted by something. But Charlene knew that Leslie wasn't distracted; what she'd just done was intentional. Leslie was building up suspense to whatever she was going to say next, knowing that the real killer could possibly be in front of a television watching her right now, hanging on her every word in a complete state of fear and panic, just as Charlene was doing at this very moment. "Damn her!" Charlene said.

Finally, Leslie spoke. "After my conversation with Ms. Jackson, I went back over the sworn statements, testimony, and interviews of every person associated with the case. Then I went over all the evidence found at the crime scene, and matched it up to something that Ms. Jackson had told me. That's when I discovered a small, but crucial missing link that proves Ms. Jackson's innocence."

"What's the missing link?"

"I'm not at liberty to give the full details at this time, but I'll be submitting it to a judge in the coming week."

"Is your proof indisputable?"

"Anything can be challenged, whether it warrants merit or not. But I believe what I've uncovered is definitive proof that my client did not murder Johnny Mayfield."

"So you're certain that the evidence you found will clear your client of this crime?"

"I don't take cases unless I'm completely confident of my client's innocence, and that I can prove it. So yes, I'm certain that after I do my job, Vivana Jackson will once again be a free woman. At which time I'll make sure the real killer is convicted, as they should've been from the beginning."

"There you have it," the reporter said, looking into the camera. "I guess we'll all have to wait and see what develops. Be sure to stay tuned to MSNBC for follow-up developments on this breaking story."

Charlene turned off the TV and sat in silence. Her head was no longer pounding, her mouth was no longer dry, and her stomach felt settled. But what had replaced her hangover symptoms was a dull numbness that ran through her entire body. Even though her heart was still beating fast, she could barely move because her mind had her stuck on the last words Leslie had said. After she made sure Vivana was exonerated, she was going to make sure the real killer was convicted. Charlene knew that if Leslie said she was going to do something, you could consider it a done deal.

Charlene's heart sank when she thought about what would happen if the truth came out. Phillip and Lauren would be devastated, her good name would be ruined, and she would surely spend the remainder of her days in prison. She'd known during the time that she'd been planning Johnny's murder that one day she'd have to pay for her sins, which she thought would be the Day of Judgment, at which time she'd answer only to God. She'd planned Johnny's murder so well that she didn't think there was any possibility of her getting caught. Then her mind immediately went back to the cryptic message she'd received a few months after Johnny's murder. There was someone out there who knew that Charlene was the real killer. Whoever that person was, combined with Leslie "the Pit Bull" Sachs, was going to make sure Charlene paid for what she'd done.

After Charlene had received the text, she'd spent months worrying about it. She'd tried to think of any possible slips she could have made the night she'd killed Johnny, but she couldn't think of one. She'd planned everything to the tiniest detail, even figuring into the equation what she would do if by chance someone came forward who could identify her as the woman whom Vivana had alleged she'd had an altercation with at the apartment building. But Charlene quickly dismissed that possibility for a number of reasons. For one, not a single resident living in the building who'd been questioned had been able to corroborate Vivana's story. Luckily for Charlene, she'd been with Johnny during a time of day when most people had been at work.

Another thing that had been in Charlene's favor was that the small building had been located in a quiet area that was spread out and not easily accessible. During the week that she'd planned Johnny's murder, Charlene had covered her tracks by returning to the apartment building late one night to search for security cameras at the building, and in the nearby area, that could place her at the scene that day. To her relief, there hadn't been any. Then Charlene thought about how she'd spent painstaking time and effort into framing Vivana with the murder weapon.

She'd reached back to her days of practicing law and had come up with a list of people and places where she could get her hands on a gun that couldn't be traced. She'd driven to a town two hours away that was known for criminal activity, and used a burner phone to call her contact. She'd met with him late at night and had parked her car a mile away from the area where they'd agreed to meet. With cash in one pocket and a Taser in another, Charlene set out on foot to purchase the weapon to kill Johnny. She'd even worn a wig that was a dead ringer for Vivana's weave, and had padded herself under her ex-husband's large trench coat, to give her body the girth Vivana was known for. Even though, in theory, the steps Charlene had taken to buy the gun had been dangerous, it had turned out to be quite easy in practice. She'd known that the real trick would be making sure Vivana stayed put in her house the night of the murder so she wouldn't have an alibi.

It had been mid-fall, and daylight hours had been short, which served to help Charlene put her plan into motion. She'd parked her car a good distance from Vivana's neighborhood, and had walked in the dark behind each house on the neatly lined block until she'd reached Vivana's. Charlene quickly ran up to Vivana's doorstep and placed a small, colorful bag stuffed with tissue paper there before ringing the bell and making a mad dash to the bushes on the side of the house. She'd crouched her body to the ground and prayed with all her might that Vivana was at home; otherwise, she'd have to wait for another time to kill Johnny.

It had taken Vivana a few minutes to open the door, and when she did, she spotted the colorful bag and immediately looked around to see who'd left it. Charlene watched in the darkness as Vivana stood on her porch, under the light, and cautiously peered inside the bag. She pulled out the note, read it, and smiled wide with delight. Charlene had wanted to jump for joy, and when Vivana then pulled out the cupcake inside and took a big bite out of it, Charlene had actually pumped her fist up and down.

Once Vivana went back into her house, still chomping on the dessert, Charlene sprinted back to her car, focused and already thinking about what she had to do next. Earlier that day, she'd made a bowl of cupcake batter, but had only poured it into one cupcake holder in her muffin pan. She dumped the rest down her sink and waited for the single cupcake to bake. She then typed a note on her computer, printed it off, and read it twice to make sure it sounded right.

> *Dear Vivana,*
> *I was wrong and I hope you can forgive me. Here's a little treat for my sweet. I will be home later tonight, please call me.*
> *Always,*
> *Johnny*

Satisfied that the note would serve its purpose, Charlene folded it twice and put it inside the decorative bag along with the cupcake. She waited until seven o'clock that evening to drive over to Vivana's house. Dressed in black from head to toe, she prayed that no one would see her cutting through their backyard, and if they did, she was in good enough shape to make a run for it.

Once Charlene returned home safely, she poured herself a glass of wine and then waited until she knew that Vivana would be fast asleep before she headed over to Johnny's house. Charlene had researched what kind of drug she should use in the cupcake. She needed something that would knock Vivana out for up to twelve hours, and would leave her system quickly without a trace of it having ever been ingested. There were dozens of odorless, tasteless pills floating around on the black market that Charlene knew would do the trick, and instead of wasting time trying to obtain something exotic, she decided to go with Rohypnol, commonly known as the date rape drug.

During the trial when the prosecutor questioned

Vivana about the phone records they'd obtained that showed she'd called Johnny just a few hours before he was murdered, Vivana had said that Johnny had asked her to call him, and that he'd left a note and a cupcake on her doorstep. She'd kept the note as proof, but it was as useless as a counterfeit bill because, as the prosecutor had pointed out, anyone could've typed that note, even Vivana herself. It hadn't been difficult for the jury to believe that she'd made up the entire story, especially after she'd spent four months pretending to be someone else, all in an effort to get close to Geneva.

Charlene had been extra-careful in her planning, right down to the way she'd killed Johnny. She'd been meticulous about every detail. However, if there was one thing she could've changed, it would have been that she'd lingered inside the house a little too long. If she could do it all over again, she would have killed Johnny the minute she'd walked through his back door. But she'd enjoyed seeing the doomed look in his eye when she pulled the gun on him, and she'd savored it for a few minutes longer than she should have.

Charlene had felt triumphant because she'd avenged dozens of women whom Johnny had wronged, and she'd also given him payback for the life of an unborn child he'd taken as a result of his selfish ways. But as the investigation had heated up, she'd realized that Johnny's murder had actually caused further hurt to the women he'd blackmailed, because now their dirty little secrets were exposed for their friends, families, and fellow church members to see. The saying, "What's done in the dark will be brought to the light," had never been more true, which brought Charlene back to the present—and the fact that her own sins had come back to haunt her.

Charlene closed her eyes and exhaled deeply. She'd been sitting at the breakfast table for more than thirty minutes, and she knew she had to pull herself together before her children came home. She thought about them, and the repercussions that would surely follow. "I can't let that happen," Charlene said aloud. "I need to find out who sent that text to my phone, and then I need to make sure I handle them so I can deal with whatever Leslie has up her sleeve."

Chapter 16

DONETTA

Even though Donetta had been tired when she'd called Geneva twenty minutes ago, she'd also been filled with joy because she'd awoken with her head resting in the crook of Phillip's arm, secure in his embrace. But by the time her conversation with her friend had ended, Donetta's lower pelvic area had begun to ache and she had a bad feeling she couldn't shake.

From that fateful morning when the police had come by the salon and questioned Geneva's coworkers about Johnny, to yesterday, when Vivana and her attorney had announced there was evidence proving Vivana's innocence, Donetta had always felt there had been something very sinister at hand surrounding Johnny's death, and now she felt it more than ever. It might have been a dream, but what Geneva had told her was convincing, and Donetta hoped that Council-woman Harris could help her friend finally get to the bottom of the ugly mess.

"I know it's too late to make wishes, but I wish to God in heaven that Geneva had never married that arrogant, no-good son of a bitch, 'cause right now this would be someone else's shit to deal with," Donetta mumbled as she shook her head. "Geneva's upset and scared, and my stomach is in knots because of a man who's still raising hell from the grave. I've got to refocus my mind before I make myself sick with all this worrying."

Donetta looked at the turkey sausage and eggs she'd set on the counter, and thought about how nice it was going to be to eat breakfast in bed with Phillip. But when she walked over to her spice rack to retrieve some seasonings, another sharp pain punched her lower abdomen, followed by a sudden and intense throbbing between her legs. She wasn't wearing panties under her nightie, and when she looked down at the floor, she saw small specks of blood at her feet. "What the hell?"

Donetta held her legs together and quickly walked to the powder room down the hall. She drew in a startled gasp when she wiped herself and saw bright red blood on the tissue. "Shit!" she hissed. She knew she needed to be quiet because she didn't want to wake Phillip, but at the same time she wanted to scream at the top of her lungs because she was in pain, and she was scared about what the bleeding meant.

She wiped herself again, gently placed a wad of tissue between her legs, and gritted her teeth to temper her scream. "What the hell is happening to me?" Donetta whispered as she washed her hands and stared into the mirror. To have woken up and not done anything in the way of beautification, she still looked like a million bucks. Her eyes were bright and her bed-tousled hair had a wild, sexy look. But her outward appearance belied what was inside, because she was beginning to feel worse by the minute. Then it came to her. "Oh no. Please don't let this be happening because I had sex."

Donetta hadn't bled six months ago when she'd had sex for the first time after her surgery. But then again, the guy she'd been with, who she'd later found out had been married, had only penetrated her halfway before he'd ejaculated, at which time he'd put on his pants and had left her lying in bed in the hotel room they'd checked into only fifteen minutes before. But she and Phillip had made love for an hour, and it had been the most satisfying, wonderful experience she'd ever had.

She'd been nervous at first, praying that her encounter with Phillip wouldn't be as disappointing and uncomfortable as it had been with the married jerk.

He'd touched her gently, caressed her with care, and kissed her passionately—all over her body.

"I'm going to go slow and take my time," Phillip had said.

Donetta moaned with pleasure as his fingers moved between her legs while he kissed her softly. She'd been glad that her surgeon had been right when he'd told her that the clitoris he'd sculpted from the sensitive skin around what had once been her penile head would produce erogenous sensations when properly stimulated, and lead to fulfilling orgasm. Phillip not only knew how to properly stimulate her, he'd made her climax twice.

But now all Donetta could feel was severe discomfort. "Urrrghh," she moaned as she held one hand over her vagina and the other over her lower abdomen to help stifle the pain. Slowly, she tiptoed back to the kitchen and wet several paper towels in the sink. She whimpered and gritted her teeth as she bent down and cleaned up the small specks of blood she'd hemorrhaged onto the floor. "I can't believe this is happening," she moaned. She was starting to feel dizzy, and sadly, she had a feeling it was about to get worse. She grabbed her phone off the counter and headed to the bedroom. With slow and measured steps, she eased past the bed and was relieved to see that Phillip was still sound asleep, snoring on his back. Another sharp pain hit her as she limped into the bathroom and quietly closed the door behind her. She knew exactly what she needed to do, so she opened the closet where she kept her medications.

She pushed the bottle of Percocet to the side in search of the high-octane painkiller she'd hoped she'd never have to take again. "There it is," she whispered, grabbing the bottle of Dilaudid.

Donetta put one of the powerful pills in her mouth and limped over to the sink. She cupped her hands under the running water and gulped until the painkiller slid down her throat. "Lord, please let this work fast." She felt as if she'd run a marathon, and now when she looked at herself in the mirror she could no longer see the sexy, bright-eyed woman who'd stared back at her just moments ago. Large beads of sweat dotted her forehead, her eyes looked red and tired, and her skin looked flushed. She practically staggered over to her marble soaker tub and plopped down on the edge. The pain was so great she began to feel hot and nauseated. "Lord, please let everything be all right with me. Please." Donetta dialed the number to the clinic where she'd been going for the past several years, and waited for someone to answer.

When she was finally patched through to one of the nurses on duty, Donetta could barely speak, but she gathered the strength to explain in detail what had happened to her. "I was fine during sex last night," she whispered.

"Was it moderate or rigorous?"

"Rigorous . . . and good."

The nurse cleared her throat. "Okay."

"I felt fine when I woke up this morning. I even talked on the phone with my best friend for a while. I was about to make breakfast when all of a sudden my lower pelvic area started hurting, and then my vagina felt like it was on fire. I looked down and saw blood. I'm still bleeding now. I'm hot, nauseated, and I feel terrible. What's wrong with me?"

The nurse explained that even though it had been a full year since her surgery, bleeding could still occur if this was the first time she'd had rigorous intercourse. The nurse instructed her to take her temperature while they were on the phone. When Donetta removed the digital thermometer from under her tongue, she was grateful to see that it was normal.

"You're sore and you're in pain," the nurse continued, "and that can cause the headache, nausea, and fatigue that you're experiencing. You need to drink plenty of fluids and monitor your temperature. If it rises, that means you have an infection and you'll need to get in here right away."

"How long will this last?" Donetta asked.

"It's hard to say. You could feel better in just a few hours, or it might take a few days, depending upon how quickly your body heals. Most likely you'll have some residual discomfort due to the intercourse you described, but that will get better over time. The most important thing for you to do is to stay calm and listen to your body."

"Okay, I'm just so scared."

"Anxiety will only worsen your symptoms and elevate your blood pressure. The Dilaudid you took should start working pretty soon, and that will immediately help to ease your pain and calm your body. In the meantime, get plenty of rest and monitor your temperature throughout the day because as I mentioned, that will be a direct indicator of infection. Also, make sure you douche this morning and dilate later tonight."

Donetta hung up the phone and wanted to cry. The thought of putting anything inside her right now made her feel weaker than she already was, and took her mind back to the hell she'd suffered after her surgery.

She'd experienced a range of emotions the morning of her surgery, vacillating between whether to go through with it or not. She'd always been sure that it was what she'd wanted to do, because she'd felt it was the final step in making her outside match up with who she was on the inside. But when she'd been lying in the prep room, waiting to be wheeled into the OR, her fears about the pain she would experience dominated her mind. She'd done years of research and had thoroughly discussed the procedure with her surgeon. She'd talked to as many trans women as she could who'd had the surgery, she'd watched hundreds of YouTube videos and read equally as many blogs of women who'd chronicled their experiences before and after surgery. Some had recovered without a single problem, while others had been plagued with one catastrophe after another, sometimes resulting in the need for additional surgical procedures. But no matter their individual experiences, one thing rang true with every testimonial that Donetta had heard, seen, or read, and that was the fact that there would be no getting around some amount of pain.

Donetta had been beyond thankful to have Geneva there by her side, holding her hand each step of the way. She knew if it hadn't been for her best friend, and her beloved grandma Winnie's spirit praying over her from above, she couldn't have made it through. When she'd awoken in her hospital bed after surgery, Geneva's determined and caring face had been the first thing she'd seen, and it had made Donetta smile, but that was the last time she would smile for several weeks.

The pain that Donetta had experienced had been so excruciating that she hadn't wished it on her worst enemy—not even Johnny, from the grave—and that had been saying a lot because she'd despised him. She'd lain on her back in pain for five days before her surgeon removed the packing inside her new body part. She'd tried to think positive about what was about to happen, and she had focused her mind on the women who'd described the feeling as liberating, once they'd been unpacked. Unfortunately for Donetta, it had been so painful and uncomfortable that she'd had to ask for another dose of Dilaudid just to get through the procedure. It had taken several minutes to remove what had felt like miles of gauze from the new space between her legs. And if she'd thought the unpacking had been bad, the dilating had been downright torture. Just as she'd done research about the surgery, she'd educated herself as much as she could about dilating, especially because it was something she'd have to do for the rest of her life.

Donetta still remembered the sharp pain she'd felt when her surgeon had inserted the long, hard plastic dildo inside her immediately after removing the packing. In retrospect she'd realized later that he'd actually been as gentle as a lamb, but at the time she'd been so swollen and sore that it had felt as though he'd jammed hot coals inside her.

"Dilation is a lifelong commitment, and something you must continue from this moment forward," Donetta's surgeon had told her in a calm, steady voice as he pushed the dildo farther and farther inside her. "If you do not dilate on schedule, it will result in a shortening of your vaginal depth, and once you lose depth you can never get it back." One of the trans women in Donetta's support group had explained it in more basic terms. "It's like getting your ears pierced. If you don't wear your earrings, your hole will close up."

For the first eight weeks after surgery, Donetta had had to dilate five times a day for twenty minutes each time. From week eight to week twenty-four, she'd gone down to three times per day. From week twenty-five to fifty-two, it had dropped to once a day. And now, she only had to dilate once a week. In the beginning, Donetta had felt as though her entire life centered around the exhaustive exercise and the extreme amount of time it took to lube up, dilate, and then clean herself, as well as the dilator, after each session. She'd gotten to a point that she'd planned her days around her dilation. Fortunately, it got better over time, and now dilating was as normal and easy for her as brushing her teeth. But not this morning.

Donetta grimaced when a hot burst of pain shot through her lower body as she leaned against the back of the commode, inserted the douche nozzle, and squeezed. She closed her eyes and saw bright lights and stars. "Sweet mother of Jesus," she called out in pain. At this point she didn't care whether Phillip woke up or not, and as a matter of fact, if he did she would ask him to douse her lower body with a bucket of ice.

Slowly, Donetta rose to her feet and ran cool water over a washcloth. She gently pressed it between her legs and held it there, praying for the Dilaudid to kick in. She wiped away more blood and then reached into her cabinet and pulled out a box of Always with wings. Suddenly, she felt light-headed, and she knew her prayer had been answered—the medicine was taking effect. "Thank You, Lord."

From past experience, Donetta knew she only had a few minutes before the powerful drug would begin to make her feel loopy, because once it kicked in, it took her down for the count. Back in the bedroom Donetta walked gingerly to her dresser and removed a pair of cotton panties. She was about to walk back to into her bathroom to insert her pad while she was still coherent enough to do it, but when she turned around she saw Phillip sitting up on his elbows, staring at her.

Donetta was holding her panties in one hand and her pad in the other. She didn't have the energy to explain anything to Phillip, so she stood where she was without saying a word. She watched him as he tossed his long, muscular legs over the side of the bed and reached down to pull on his boxer briefs. Even in her dizzy state, Donetta could still see that his body was a thing of beauty. He walked over to her, gently embraced her, and kissed the top of her forehead.

"Good morning," he said.

She did her best to smile. "Good morning."

Phillip looked down at her hands. "Come on." He

led her to the edge of the bed and helped her sit down. He took the panties from her hand, lifted her feet, and pulled the underwear up her legs. He placed the pad in the center of her panties. "I'm not sure how this works, but if you guide me, I can help."

Donetta burst into a flood of tears. She didn't know if it was because of the throbbing pain between her legs, the ringing she felt in her head, or the gentle way Phillip had just treated her, but what she did know was that she felt completely safe and loved. "I'm sorry, Phillip," Donetta sobbed.

"Shhhh." He put his finger to her lips. "You don't have anything to be sorry about. It's okay, I'm here for you."

Donetta pulled herself together long enough to secure her pad in place, then Phillip helped her get back in bed. He tucked the comforter around her body and kissed her forehead again. "Do you need to take anything?"

Donetta shook her head. "I already took some medicine . . . and it's starting to make me feel drowsy."

"Close your eyes and rest. I'm going to get dressed and head out because I have to pick my sister up from the airport this morning."

The last thing Donetta remembered was Phillip telling her to rest. She closed her eyes and was sound asleep within seconds.

Chapter 17

PHILLIP

At first Phillip didn't know what to think when he saw Donetta standing in front of her dresser looking as if she'd just finished a long day at work. He'd been sleeping soundly until he'd heard her crying out in the bathroom. It had taken him a minute to gather himself, and by the time he'd propped himself up on his elbows, Donetta was walking out of the bathroom. Right away he'd known something was wrong. The gate of her stride was different, her straight shoulders were hunched, and her back was bent. He watched in silence as she reached into her dresser drawer and pulled out a pair of panties. But when he looked at her other hand and saw what he knew was a sanitary pad, he realized that she'd come on her period.

Growing up in a house with two women whom he

was very close to, and having countless women in and out of his life, Phillip was well-acquainted with the discomfort, and in some cases, agony, that accompanied a women's menstrual cycle. It was one of the reasons he was glad he was a man, because he didn't think he could go through what he saw as torture every month.

He could see the pain on Donetta's face, and all he'd wanted to do was take care of her. He'd helped her get situated as best he could before tucking her in bed. The next thing he knew she was fast asleep. He looked at the clock on Donetta's nightstand and noted that he still had an hour before he needed to leave to pick Lauren up from the airport. He walked over to the other side of the bed and found his pants, shirt, and blazer lying on the floor where he'd left them. He smiled as he dressed, thinking about last night, or actually, early this morning.

After he'd kissed Donetta in the lobby at the hotel, he'd known right then that he was finally ready for what his mother had talked to him about earlier that day. He was ready for a real, committed, grown-up relationship, and he wanted it with Donetta. He wanted to build something with her and watch it grow. Her lips had felt soft and perfect, and when he'd held her in his arms he'd known that was where she belonged, with him.

Twenty-five minutes later he'd found himself parking his rental car behind hers in her driveway and then he'd followed her into her house. The only light inside had come from a pendant in her kitchen, but even in the darkness he could tell that Donetta's home was tastefully decorated. An aromatic smell filled the air and tickled his nose.

"Listen," she'd said. "I know when you suggested

that we get a room at the hotel I said we should come here, but don't get it twisted."

He smiled. "What is it that you don't want me to twist?"

"Phillip, I'm serious. I don't want you to think that I bring strange men over to my house when I first meet them."

"I know that you don't."

"Good, because it's the honest truth."

"I know that the reason I'm here is because I'm different. I'm special."

She shook her head and folded her arms. "And what makes you so sure?"

"Because you're different, and special. What you and I are experiencing with each other is rare, and I'm glad we're both open and honest enough to put our fears aside so we can deal with it."

Donetta was silent.

"This is the first time I've ever talked to anyone the way I'm talking to you. Donetta, we have a real connection going on between us, and I'm ready to see where whatever is happening between us can go. That's not a come-on, or a mack move, it's the simple truth. And I promise you that as long as we're together, I'll always be honest with you."

"Are you saying you want to have a relationship with me?"

Phillip didn't hesitate. "Yes."

"We just met."

"Yet I'm here, standing inside your home in the wee hours of the morning, prepared to take a chance on wherever this goes."

"This is happening so . . . so fast."

"Yes, it is, and that's why I know this is right for me. I've been cautious, taking my time with relationships my whole life. But I don't have any reservations about pursuing one with you. Are you having reservations about pursuing a relationship with me?"

Donetta inhaled deeply. "Phillip, I've made so many terrible mistakes in my life."

"I understand, and so have I. But for me, it's not about what I've done or what has happened in my past, it's about what I see right here, right now. I'm not some twenty-something dude who's trying to live it up. I'm a man who wants more than I've ever had, and I'm willing to take a chance to get it." Phillip had been amazed that he'd made himself so vulnerable to a woman he barely knew. In his experience it had usually been the other way around, but here he was, exposing his most intimate feelings, and it felt right.

He moved in close, pressing his hard body against her soft one. He wrapped his arms around her waist, pulled her in even closer, and kissed her as he'd done at the hotel. Their passionate kisses turned into soft caresses. Their soft caresses gave way to gentle moans. And their gentle moans led them to Donetta's bedroom. Her blinds were still open, allowing the moon to fill the room with soft light. Phillip admired the sexy silhouette of her slender frame, and he counted himself lucky to be standing where he was, about to embark on what he knew was going to be an experience like no other.

"I'm a little nervous," Donetta said.

"Please don't be. I know you've been hurt deeply, and I know how much it means that I'm standing here. Donetta, I promise you, I won't take that for granted and I won't abuse the honor. Your home is where you feel safe, and I want you to know that you're safe with me, too."

She looked into his eyes and placed her arms around his neck, massaging his skin with her delicate fingers. Phillip loved the way it felt when she touched him, further proof to him that he was where he was supposed to be, doing exactly what he was doing. He tilted his head and kissed her slowly, rubbing his hands up and down her body. They took their time taking off each other's clothes. He admired her long, lean frame and the soft curves that made her look like a centerfold model. When he cupped her perfectly shaped breasts, she'd fidgeted. "I um . . . I had them done a year and a half ago," she said.

Phillip had been able to tell as soon as he'd unhooked her bra that she either had implants or some type of augmentation surgery because he'd been with a few women who'd had both. And while cosmetically altered breasts didn't hold the same buoyancy and sensual jiggle that only Mother Nature could provide, they still served the same purpose as far as he was concerned, and he was looking forward to taking great pleasure in Donetta's. He gently placed his hands over each of her breasts, slowly massaging them. "You're beautiful in every way," he told her.

He kissed her again and slowly, they made their way over to her bed. He removed her peach colored lace panties and she slid off his black boxer briefs. They kissed, caressed, sucked, nibbled, and fondled, until Phillip couldn't take it anymore. He reached over to his pants on the floor and pulled a condom from his wallet. When he returned to the bed, he saw that Donetta was searching for something inside her nightstand. She pulled out a tube, which he could see was lubricant, but what had startled him were the other objects that caught his eye inside the drawer. Even with the hazy, indirect light, he'd been able to see that she had four or five vibrators lying inside.

She caught him looking at them. "I have them for a reason."

"Most women do. But you won't need them tonight."

Making love to Donetta had been tender, hot, exciting, and sexy. But more than anything, it had been a game changer for him, because it had been the first time Phillip had made love to someone whom he wanted to be in a relationship with.

Now, as Phillip stood beside Donetta's bed, watching her sleep peacefully, all he could think about was how right it felt to be with her. It had felt natural for him to help her the way he had moments ago. He looked at her again, studying the peaceful expression on her face as she slept. He felt bad that she'd been in so much pain, but he was glad she was getting some rest. He hoped she'd be feeling better by this afternoon so he could come over and spend time with her.

Phillip stood in place for a few moments, enjoying the silence. He looked up at the ceiling and smiled. "Wow," he whispered. It had been dark when they'd come in during the wee hours of the morning, but now that it was daytime, he had the opportunity to take in his surroundings, and the first thing that stood out was the crystal-and-chrome chandelier hanging above. It was bold and glamorous, and he thought it fit Donetta's style perfectly. As he looked around, it was clear to see that she had given attention to detail in the way she'd decorated her home. The color scheme in her bedroom was a mixture of varying shades of grays, purples, and creams, all mixed in with metallic accents. Her large upholstered headboard was outlined with bold stitching and rich fabric, and her bedding was equally as elegant. When Phillip had drifted off to sleep after they'd made love, he remembered thinking that her bedsheets were the softest he'd ever lain under.

He was drawn from his thoughts when Donetta turned on her side and pulled the comforter up to her neck. He decided it was time to leave, and because it was still so early he had time to go back to his mother's house and freshen up before driving to the airport. He walked into the living room and stood for a moment, admiring the tasteful and stylish décor, just as he'd done in Donetta's bedroom. Even though her design and color palette was made up of bold colors that grabbed his attention, her home still felt cozy. Phillip walked around her living room, which was an open concept design, and saw that she had left food on her kitchen counter. He was about to store the turkey sausage and eggs in her refrigerator when an idea came to him.

Twenty minutes later, Phillip sat at Donetta's kitchen table eating breakfast. Instead of putting the food away, he'd sautéed the turkey sausage with seasonings from her pantry and made cheese omelets and toast. He quickly finished his meal and then washed and dried the dishes before putting them away. He sent Donetta a text letting her know that her breakfast was waiting on her in the microwave when she got up, and to call him later. Then he texted his mother, who he knew was more than likely still asleep with her hangover, and told her that he would pick up Lauren from the airport.

Phillip walked back to Donetta's bedroom and found her still resting comfortably, which put his mind a little more at ease because he was worried about her. He sat on the side of her bed and watched her sleep. He wondered if she had problems like this every month. He knew some women had difficulty with their periods, while others didn't. Her pain must have been bad because it had caused her to cry out while she'd been in the bathroom. He didn't think he was the cause of her bleeding—or at least he hoped he wasn't. Nothing like this had ever happened in the past after he'd made love to a woman.

He ran his hand gently over her hair, enjoying the softness of each strand that slipped through his fingers. It was amazing to him to think that of all the places to find love and of all the times, it had snuck up on him in his hometown, out of the blue. He stroked Donetta's hair again and smiled, but then she let out a painful-sounding groan. He waited a few minutes to see if she would do it again, but thankfully, she continued to sleep as soundly as she had before. He made a mental note to ask her about her health when he saw her later that afternoon. Then he gave her a soft kiss on her forehead and headed to the airport.

Chapter 18

GENEVA

After eating a large breakfast of bacon, scrambled eggs, cheese grits, home fries, freshly brewed coffee, and biscuits with strawberry jam, Geneva, Samuel, and her in-laws were all satisfied and full.

"Geneva, you outdid yourself," Herbert said. "This breakfast was better than anything I could've ordered in a restaurant."

"It was absolutely delicious," Sarah complimented. "And you must give me your recipe for those biscuits. They melt in your mouth!"

Geneva smiled. "Thank you both."

Samuel walked behind Geneva as she stood at the kitchen sink and he hugged her. "My baby can throw down." He kissed her on her cheek. "Mom and Dad are right, everything was delicious. Thanks, baby."

Geneva loved cooking, and it made her feel good to feed people a meal made with love, especially if it was her family members. But although she appreciated their gratitude and kind words, right now her mind was focused on something far more complex than bacon and eggs. She wanted to be alone with Samuel so she could tell him about the dream she'd had last night.

Even though her in-laws knew intimate details about Geneva's past with Johnny, having received information directly from her and Samuel, as well as from online articles during the time of the trial, Geneva didn't want to involve them in her worries about the dream she'd had and what it might possibly mean. She needed to think of a way to get them out of the room so she could talk privately with her husband.

When Gabrielle woke up, it gave Geneva the opportunity she'd been looking for.

"Look at my precious little granddaughter," Sarah said. She walked over to Gabrielle and lifted her out of the playpen, kissed her on her chubby cheek, and cooed. "Did you get enough rest, my little sweetie pie?"

Gabrielle giggled and laughed as though she'd been given a new toy.

"She's probably ready for a changing after her morning nap," Geneva said.

Sarah smiled. "Grandma's got that covered."

"Maria usually takes her for a morning walk after her nap," Geneva said, referring to their sitter who came to the house three days a week and took care of Gabrielle during the day while Geneva worked at the salon. "It's a beautiful fall morning, why don't you and Dad take her for a stroll?" Geneva suggested.

Herbert perked up. "We'd love to. Sarah and I go for a walk every morning, and now we'll be able to keep up our exercise routine while we enjoy our grand-daughter."

"Yes, this is perfect," Sarah chimed in. "We'll take turns watching her while we shower and get dressed, and then we'll head out for a nice long walk around the neighborhood. But before we head upstairs, do you need help cleaning up the kitchen?"

Herbert nodded. "Two hands are better than one, and you've got four right here, willing to help."

Geneva smiled. "No, Mom and Dad, don't worry about the kitchen. Enjoy this time with Gabrielle because I know it'll be a treat for you two as well as for her."

Geneva watched as Samuel's parents walked upstairs with Gabrielle. Now she had to find a way to get Joe out of the room. Luckily, she didn't have to try to persuade him with anything because he had plans of his own.

Joe stretched his arms and yawned. "This is my vacation, so I'm gonna relax. I think I'll go back upstairs and take a nap so I can sleep off some of this food." He rubbed his plump stomach and shuffled down the hall toward the stairs.

"Honey, can you help me with the dishes?" Geneva asked her husband. "I want to talk to you while we get this kitchen back in order."

Samuel grabbed a kitchen towel and shook his head. Frustration was etched across his face.

"What's wrong?" Geneva asked.

"He saw all these dirty dishes in this kitchen, but unlike my parents, not once did he offer to help wash a single plate. And beyond that, he was the only one who didn't thank you for getting up early to cook us a delicious breakfast, yet he ate double what everyone else did."

"You know how Joe is."

"Yeah, I do, and it pisses me off. Whenever Joe does something rude or inconsiderate, or acts like a complete ass, like he did last night, everyone always says, 'You know how Joe is.' I'm sick of it."

Geneva knew that Joe got on Samuel's last nerve, as his brother did with most people, and they'd been adversaries since their days in the sandbox. But normally Samuel didn't let Joe get to him. Other than Geneva's late mother, Samuel was one of the most calm, easygoing people she'd ever known. But this morning he'd seemed irritated from the moment he'd come downstairs. Geneva knew her husband well, and she knew something was wrong. "Honey, are you okay?"

"It was a bad idea for Joe to come here. I tried to be okay with it, but I don't want him in our house."

"I know you two have your issues, and you've never quite seen eye to eye. But it's the holidays and he's family, so try to tolerate him for the next two days. After that he'll be on a flight back to Maryland."

"If I'd known he was planning to come, I would've told him to stay home, and I think he knows it. That's why he didn't tell me ahead of time."

"He said he wanted to surprise you."

"He fed our parents that same story, and asked them not to say anything, but I know he's lying through his teeth."

"How can you be so sure?"

"Because I know my brother. He's a selfish bastard."

Geneva nearly dropped the plate she was loading

into the dishwasher. "Samuel! What's gotten into you?" She'd initially been focused on telling him about her dream, but now her concern had shifted to why her husband was so upset with his brother. Samuel rarely used harsh words, and the only time she could ever remember him cursing was during the time right before Johnny's murder, when Samuel had wanted to kill Johnny for causing the accident that had led to Geneva's miscarriage.

"Geneva, I want him out of this house. There are plenty of hotels in town with vacancies."

"Honey, it's the holidays."

Samuel looked at her as if to say, *So?*

"Joe has always gotten on your nerves, but this is something different. Tell me what's going on."

Samuel looked away from her. "I just want him out of here."

"Samuel, please tell me what's wrong. What's the real reason you're so upset with Joe?"

After a pause filled with silence, Samuel let out a deep breath. "Let's sit down so we can talk," he said as he led Geneva into the family room.

Geneva sat on the couch in the exact spot where she'd been sitting yesterday afternoon when she'd been speechless while listening to Vivana's interview, and now, she was speechless again as she listened to Samuel tell her the real reason he was so upset with his brother.

Chapter 19

CHARLENE

Charlene had been sitting at her breakfast table all morning, unable to move as her mind continued to race. She'd been concentrating so hard that a worry line had formed across her forehead. "Who could've sent that text?" she questioned, trying to figure out who had sent the cryptic message to her phone. She desperately needed that answer because she knew it was going to be the key to preventing her undoing.

She wished she'd dealt with the troubling situation when she'd first received the message. But at the time she'd been stressed beyond her limits. She'd justified killing Johnny by likening herself to a moral Robin Hood, exacting justice for the innocent. It had been the only way she'd been able to live with the sobering fact that she'd allowed her hurt and anger to turn her into a cold-blooded killer.

But at the time what had concerned Charlene even more than the fact that she'd killed someone were the disturbing changes she'd begun to see in her daughter. After Lauren and the rest of the family had discovered that Lauren's boyfriend was actually her half brother, it had changed her daughter from the inside out. Her mannerisms and her outward appearance began to morph into those of a person whom Charlene didn't recognize. Charlene had also been so drained from the multitude of her life crises that a few times she'd actually considered turning herself in so at least she'd finally have peace of mind about something. That was one reason that, although the text had frightened her, she'd never acted upon it.

Charlene had fully expected to receive another cryptic message right behind the initial one, this time asking for hush money, the way Johnny had done. She'd been prepared to tell the mysterious blackmailer no, and let the deck of cards simply collapse around her, because she had no intention of entering into the same type of blackmail scheme that had led her to become a murderer in the first place. But a few days went by without so much as a peep. Eventually, days turned into weeks, and those weeks morphed into months. "I can't worry about the things I can't change," Charlene had told herself. "I have to move forward with my life, regardless of what happens."

Charlene shook her head. "I should've put fear aside and gotten to the bottom of it a long time ago," she said. "I should've addressed that text the same way I addressed all the other problems going on in my life. But instead I put it off, and now it's coming back to bite me." Charlene let out a deep breath of frustration. But again, she knew she couldn't beat herself up over something she couldn't change. She couldn't undo Johnny's murder, or the fact that there was someone out there who knew she'd done it. Suddenly an idea occurred to her. "The person who texted me has got to be Leslie's source of evidence." But the more she thought about it, the more confused she became.

The mysterious texter had said they had proof that Charlene was the murderer, and during Leslie's solo interview this morning, she'd hinted that the new evidence she'd uncovered had come from something Vivana had said in a conversation that she and Leslie had had. This meant there were actually two separate sources that could point the finger back to Charlene. She knew she had to think strategically about what her next move should be. "I'll handle each problem one step at a time," she told herself. She'd deal with Leslie next Monday morning when they were scheduled to meet for coffee. But right now, Charlene's main focus was to uncover the identity of the person who'd sent her the text.

"I need to think about everyone who has my number." Charlene used two cell phones; one for business and one for personal calls, and she rarely allowed her contacts lists for the two to merge. The text had been sent during business hours while she'd been in her office at City Hall, but it had come through on her personal phone. By the process of elimination, she knew the texter had to be someone within the tight-knit group of people who had access to her private cell. She immediately eliminated her children and other close family members as suspects, then she thought about her friends and acquaintances. Charlene had always been very private and selective about her home life and who she allowed into her world, so the list was small.

"The texter probably knew Johnny, as well," Charlene mused aloud. "Who could that be?" She thought about the other women whom Johnny had blackmailed. But she dismissed that theory, because each one of them had said that although they didn't kill him, they'd wanted to shake the killer's hand and thank them for a job well done. Then Charlene thought about Mark and Marjorie Thomas, the couple who'd referred her to Johnny. But then she dismissed them, as well, because the two had been far too busy at the time with a toddler and a newborn to involve themselves with murder. "It has to be someone who wants something from me," Charlene said aloud. "But then again, they haven't asked for any money." The only other person she could think of who had her private number, and who'd been associated with Johnny, was her stylist, Geneva.

She'd become close to Geneva in the nearly two and a half years that Geneva had been her stylist. Charlene admired Geneva's professional skills, and she respected the fact that she always stayed above the fray of petty salon gossip. Geneva was one of the few people Charlene truly trusted. After Johnny's death, ironically, Geneva had come to Charlene privately for legal advice. The two lead detectives assigned to Johnny's murder had begun to hound Geneva and Samuel, and although both of them were innocent, their motives were the strongest of nearly all the other suspects. Charlene had been more than happy to help Geneva, though, as it kept Charlene close to the investigation with inside information.

But as Charlene thought more and more about Geneva possibly being the texter, she had to dismiss her, as well. She'd gotten to know Geneva during the dozens of times she'd counseled her, and there wasn't anything about her character to make Charlene believe she'd do something so conniving.

"It has to be someone who's devious, deceptive, and cunning," Charlene whispered to herself. The person didn't want money, so she knew there had to be something non-tangible they stood to gain. She also knew the person had to be someone who enjoyed playing games, because they'd dangled the threat over Charlene's head, probably taking pleasure in knowing Charlene would live in fear of it each day of her life. "The person wants power and control." Then, as if a light switch had been turned on, Charlene knew exactly who it could be. "Why didn't I think of her before now?!"

Just then Charlene heard a loud *thump* that jarred her from her thoughts.

"Hey, Mom!" Lauren screamed with excitement as she burst into the room. She rushed over to Charlene's chair and wrapped her heavy arms around Charlene's chest. She squeezed so tightly Charlene could barely breathe. "I'm home!"

Charlene was so startled she nearly fell out of her chair. She'd been in such deep thought about her circumstances that she didn't hear Phillip's rental car pull up, nor did she hear him roll Lauren's enormous suitcase against the hardwood floors.

"Mom, are you okay?" Lauren asked.

Charlene wanted to tell her that no, she wasn't okay. But as she scanned Lauren from head to toe, she wanted to ask her daughter the same thing.

Each time Charlene had seen Lauren during holidays and school breaks over the last two years, her appearance had changed, and not for the better. Lauren used to be a well-dressed, meticulous, attractive young woman who took care of herself and had pride in her appearance. Her hair had always been neatly styled, her clothes had always fit well and were appropriate for her shape, and she'd always paid close attention to her diet, exercising regularly so she could maintain a healthy weight for her medium-size frame. Lauren had also been very focused and highly driven in her approach to everything from school to her social life. Charlene had often told her to loosen up and not be so serious about things. But now, Lauren had gone in the opposite direction, and Charlene was more than a little worried.

Charlene had begun to notice the change almost immediately. Lauren went from wearing a combination of trendy shirts, classic blouses, and flirty dresses, to sporting sweatpants and T-shirts. She'd gone from a neatly tapered pixie cut that had suited her angular face, to a dried-out, misshapen Afro that did nothing for her appearance. And her once-fit body that had comfortably carried a size eight, had ballooned to a size twenty. There was once a time when if Charlene had called Lauren to check on her, she'd have been deep in a book at the library, or studying in her off-campus apartment. But these days, no matter when Charlene called her, Lauren was hanging out with friends, or she wouldn't pick up at all, giving Charlene no other choice than to leave a voice message and hope that she called her back within a week.

Charlene had become so worried about the changes she'd observed that she'd asked Lauren what was wrong several times. "Baby, I know the things that have happened in our family have had an impact on you," Charlene had told her, "but I want you to know that you can talk to me about anything. Please tell me, what's going on with you?"

Despite Charlene's constant probing, Lauren would simply smile and tell her not to worry because everything was fine. That was another reason Charlene knew without a doubt that something was very wrong—Lauren rarely smiled or acquiesced if she felt she was being challenged about something. She was the type of young woman who stood resolute in her beliefs and serious in her demeanor.

Now Charlene longed for those days, because Lauren had become a serious party girl, and if Charlene's guess was right, her daughter hadn't seen the inside of Johns Hopkins' library in weeks.

"You startled me," Charlene said as she gave Lauren a kiss on her cheek. "I'm so glad you're home, baby. Let me stand up and give you a proper hug." Charlene's embrace used to envelop Lauren, but now her arms barely covered less than half the surface of her daughter's back. Lauren didn't even smell the same. There was a time when she'd always emanated a sweet scent of some new lotion or perfume she'd be trying out. But, as Charlene inhaled, her nose was filled with the smell of onions.

"What did you eat this morning?" Charlene asked.

"I got a burger from Steak 'n Shake on our way from the airport. Why?"

"Because you smell like onions. Why are you eating hamburgers this early in the morning?"

"Restaurants start serving lunch at ten thirty, Mom. Besides I haven't had a good burger in forever."

"Okay, well, you could've gotten a salad. The last time we talked, you said you were going to start eating more healthy."

Lauren let out a deep, frustrated breath and rolled her eyes. "It's good to see you, too, Mom."

"Don't get sarcastic with me, and don't roll your eyes, young lady."

Lauren walked over to where her suitcase was propped against the wall and started rolling it toward the hall. "I wasn't being sarcastic."

"Stop right there," Charlene said in shock. She couldn't believe how blatantly disrespectful Lauren was behaving. She walked over to her daughter and looked her in the eye. "Don't walk away from me when I'm talking to you. What's gotten into you?"

"I'm fine, but it seems that you have a problem with me for some reason, because instead of being happy to see me, all you can do is find fault about what I eat."

"I told you I was glad you're home when I hugged you. You're only upset because I called you out about the way you've been eating. Lauren, you're in medical school, so you've got to know that eating the way you've been doing this past year isn't healthy."

Lauren put her hand on her wide hip. "Oh, I get it. You're embarrassed because you have a fat daughter now."

Charlene was appalled. It was as if she was standing in front of a total stranger, trying to make sense of the irrational, defensive things coming out of the mouth that used to belong to her once logical and responsible daughter. "I'm not embarrassed, I'm concerned."

"Not everyone can be a size six," Lauren said, looking at Charlene's slim frame.

"I didn't say a word about your weight, because your health is more important than your size. And I'm telling you right now, you need to tone down your attitude. Like I said, I don't know what's gotten into you, but you need to change it—quickly."

Just then Charlene looked down the hall past Lauren to see Phillip coming in the front door pulling two large suitcases. Two travel bags also hung from each of his shoulders, and Charlene could tell they were heavy because her strapping son looked weighed down.

"Hey, Mom," Phillip called from down the hall. He left the luggage at the foot of the stairs and walked back to where Charlene and Lauren were standing. "How're you feeling, Mom?"

Charlene remembered that the last time Phillip had seen her was last night, when she'd been passed out drunk on the couch and he'd left her a note and a glass of water. She saw that he was dressed nicely, as usual, but she also suspected his outfit was what he'd worn when he'd left the house last night. She wanted to talk to him about it, but this wasn't the time to have that conversation. "I'm a whole lot better today," she said, then she looked at Lauren, "I think."

The expression on Phillip's face told Charlene that he knew exactly what she was talking about, and that perhaps Lauren had been a little salty with him as well. Charlene looked at the pile of luggage down the hall. "Lauren, why did you bring all that luggage home for a such a short trip?"

When Phillip folded his arms and looked at his sister with raised brows, Charlene knew the answer wasn't going to be good. Lauren hesitated, so Charlene asked her again. "Lauren, why did you pack so many bags?"

"Go ahead and tell her," Phillip urged.

Lauren lowered her voice. "I was hoping I could stay here for a while."

Phillip's phone rang and temporarily distracted everyone. Charlene watched as he looked at the number, frowned, and then returned the phone to his back pocket. Charlene refocused, turning her attention back to Lauren. "What do you mean, stay here for a while?"

Lauren glanced at Phillip with a look that let Charlene know she wanted her big brother to help her explain something that was so bad it had left her unable to speak up for herself. But Phillip shook his head as if to say she was on her own. Finally, Lauren cleared her throat and spoke. "I'm not going back to med school, so I was hoping I could stay here for a little while until I figure out what I want to do next."

"Wait a minute." Charlene blinked rapidly. "When did you suddenly make this grand decision? It had to have been this morning when you packed all this luggage and boarded your flight, because as of yesterday afternoon when I talked to you, you didn't say anything about dropping out of school."

"Mom, I'm not dropping out. I withdrew, and—"

"Withdrew!" Charlene said, raising her voice. "When did you withdraw from your classes?"

Lauren lowered her voice to a whisper. "A few weeks ago."

"Lauren, what's going on with you? And don't you dare give me a sarcastic answer."

Lauren let out a loud sigh. "No one ever listens to me."

"I'm listening to you right now, but you're not making any sense."

"No, Mom. I'm making perfect sense, just not to you. And that's the problem. You and Phillip keep asking me what's wrong with me, over and over again, but neither one of you have taken the time to listen to what I've been saying. I'm fine and there's nothing wrong with me. I've decided to make some changes in my life, and just because you guys don't approve of them, or understand me, it doesn't mean that anything is wrong with me."

"You can't possibly believe what you're saying," Phillip said.

Charlene stepped toward Lauren, folded her arms, and looked into her daughter's eyes with a serious stare. "Are you doing drugs?"

Lauren laughed and shook her head. "Unbelievable. Now that I'm finally taking control of my life and making decisions that are best for me, you think I'm on drugs."

"Baby, you graduated valedictorian from Tuskegee and you have a full . . . let me say it again . . . a *full* scholarship at one of the most prestigious medical schools in the country, to pursue a career you've dreamed about since you were a child. And now you want to throw that all away? Yeah, that's why I asked if you're on drugs, because you clearly don't know what you're doing." Charlene shook her head with worry. "Lauren, I'm going to ask you again, what's going on with you?"

Lauren let out a deep, frustrated breath of air. "There you go again. You're still not listening to me. Mom, I'm not on drugs and I'm not depressed, or whatever else you've made up in your mind that you think is wrong with me."

"Phillip," Charlene said as she turned to her son, "did you know about this?"

He shook his head. "She told me after I loaded her bags in the car at the airport."

"I know you two don't respect my decision," Lauren said defiantly, "but I know what's best for me. Why can't you guys just be supportive?"

Phillip's phone rang again. He quickly pulled it out and frowned for a second time when he saw the number. He hit the Ignore button to silence it before placing it back into his pocket. "Sorry about that," he said. "Listen, sis, Mom and I love you, and we're not gonna stand around and let you mess up your life when we can both see that something's wrong with you."

"I should've known you two wouldn't understand," Lauren huffed. "Hakeem was right, I should've just stayed with him in our apartment in Maryland instead of coming back here."

"Who the hell is Hakeem?" Phillip asked.

"He's my boyfriend, and right now he's the only person who respects the fact that I'm capable of making my own decisions." Lauren looked directly into Charlene's eyes. "I didn't graduate number one in my class or win a full scholarship by making bad decisions."

Charlene balked. "That was the old Lauren. I don't know who I'm dealing with now."

"You're dealing with a grown woman who knows what's best for her. Just because my decision doesn't please you, it doesn't mean I'm wrong. I know what I'm doing and I don't understand why you two find that so hard to believe!"

"Because it's coming out of the mouth of someone who has mustard stains smeared across the front of her sweatshirt, breath that smells like onions, and hair that looks like a bird decided to build a nest in it, that's why," Charlene said in a matter-of-fact tone. "You've got to be on drugs."

Phillip's phone rang again, and this time when he looked at the number he smiled.

Charlene shook her head. "Please cut that phone off, or tell those women who keep calling that you're busy with a family emergency." She watched as Phillip answered the phone.

"Hey," Phillip said in a soft tone, dripping with sweetness. "Hold on a minute." He looked at Charlene and then at Lauren. "I'll be back in a sec."

Charlene watched as her son rushed off to the family room.

"I have to use the bathroom," Lauren said, then turned and practically ran down the hall and up the stairs.

Charlene stood where she was, frozen in disbelief and despair. She looked up toward the ceiling above, listening to her daughter stomp her way down the hall upstairs, oblivious to the fact that she was making the biggest mistake of her life. Then she turned her eyes and ears toward the family room, where she could hear her son speaking softly, probably to the woman he'd been with last night, no doubt trying to juggle her into his rotation. "Lord, please, please help me." She was worried about her children, and she felt helpless to what she could see were big problems brewing for both of them.

Then Charlene's mind turned to her own worries, and the terrible mistake she'd made that was now looming over her head. And once again, she knew she had to focus only on what she had the power to change. For now, that meant dealing with the person who'd sent her the cryptic text. So instead of spending happy family time with her children while she prepared the food they would eat for tomorrow's Thanksgiving dinner, Charlene walked down the hall to her study and sat behind her desk. She turned on her computer, typed in a name search, and wrote down the information she found. She opened another browser window and sent an e-mail to Shartell Brown, the person whom she now knew had sent the infamous text message.

Chapter 20

DONETTA

Donetta slowly opened her eyes and blinked. She was thankful that her throbbing headache was gone, along with the terrible pain that had gripped her entire pelvic area. She was still experiencing pain, but compared to how she'd felt earlier this morning, she was thankful it wasn't worse. "What time is it?" she mumbled in a groggy voice. She rubbed her eyes and looked at her digital alarm clock, only to see that she'd slept straight through the morning. "Damn, that Dilaudid knocked me out for the count." She looked around for Phillip and realized he wasn't there.

"Close your eyes and rest." Those were the last words Donetta remembered hearing Phillip say before she'd drifted off. She picked up her phone to dial his number and saw that he'd sent her a text while she slept.

Phillip: I hope by the time you read this message you're feeling better. Your breakfast is in the microwave when you're ready to eat. Call me when you wake up. See you soon.

Donetta couldn't help but smile at the thought of him. She actually felt giddy, which until now she'd thought was an emotion reserved only for teenage girls. But that was how Phillip made her feel: like a young girl full of hope. She shook her head, still trying to wrap her brain around how suddenly her love life had changed, as well as her frame of mind. When she'd awoken yesterday morning she'd been lonely and filled with pessimism about the holidays. Now, a little more than twenty-four hours later, she was in the beginnings of a new relationship and she was excited about the possibilities that were to come.

Donetta thought about Phillip and remembered how gentle he'd been with her that morning when she'd been in excruciating pain. They'd shared passionate moments last night when they made love, but that physical nirvana paled in comparison to the emotional intimacy and connection they'd formed this morning when he'd slid her panties up her legs, and then tucked her into bed. He'd turned an awkward moment into an endearing memory that she'd never forget. She dialed his number and he picked up on the first ring.

"Hey," he said in a sweet but hushed voice. "Hold on a minute."

Donetta could hear female voices in the background. She turned the volume button up and held the phone close to her ear so she could listen to what was being said. But the more she strained her ears to make out their words, the farther away the voices sounded. Even though she didn't know what they were talking about, she could tell by the women's pitch and tone that they were arguing.

"Sorry about that," Phillip said, still talking in a low, hushed voice. "I'm back. How're you feeling?"

"I'm better. Is everything okay?" She didn't want to rush to any conclusions, so she held her breath and waited for him to explain the commotion going on around him.

"Good, I've been worried about you. I'm glad you're better."

"Thanks." *And by the way, where are you and who the hell are those women that I hear arguing in the background?* She wanted to ask.

"Did you eat your breakfast?"

"Uh, no . . . not yet, but thanks for making it for me. I just woke up, read your message, and called you."

"Oh, okay. Well, I hope you'll enjoy it."

He sounded preoccupied, and it made Donetta wonder even more what was going on. The noise in the background had escalated, and then suddenly subsided. She refused to remain in the dark any longer. "Phillip, I hear women arguing. Where are you?"

"I'm in the middle of a family situation. It's, um, it's not good. I picked my sister up from the airport after I left your place, and now she and my mom are going at it."

Donetta started breathing regularly again. "Oh, I'm sorry to hear that."

"It's a really bad situation here . . . you have no idea."

"As much drama as I've experienced in my life, I completely understand. Do you need to go?"

"Yeah, I think I do, before things get too out of hand between them. Do you have plans for today?"

"None."

"Can I come over later this afternoon?"

She smiled. "You better."

"In that case, I'll see you in a little while."

Donetta hung up the phone feeling happy. Slowly, she rose from her bed and felt a twinge of pain. But that small discomfort couldn't take away her joy. She walked over to her cream-colored vanity on the other side of the room and lit a lavender-scented candle. As she watched the flame grow, she thought about last night and this morning and how incredible it was that life could change in the blink of an eye. But then doubt set in.

Every time Donetta thought she might be on the verge of something good, it had always turned bad, and that's why she'd learned to accept hurt and expect disappointment. She'd come to believe that if something seemed too good to be true, it usually was. What was happening with Phillip was almost magical, and she wanted desperately to hold on to it. She wanted to believe in it and trust it. But she also knew it had the real possibility of ending, especially once she told him that she was trans.

Donetta had been living life as a woman for many years well before her reassignment surgery, and she'd always been up front about who she was with the men she'd dated. She knew that first and foremost it was a matter of honesty, and she didn't want anyone to feel as if they'd been deceived. Most of the men she'd dated had known from the beginning that she was trans, as she'd been introduced to them by friends, or she'd met them online through LBGT forums. But there were instances when she'd met men who didn't know her background, and that had always been tricky.

In those cases, Donetta wanted the man to get to know her for who she was before she told them her full story. But she never let the truth linger beyond the first date. Even though none of her relationships had ultimately lasted, most of the men she'd met had continued to see her once she'd told them she was a trans woman. They'd accepted her for who she was, inside and out, and some had even been intrigued. There had only been a few who'd taken it badly, but those few situations had been disastrous. That was how Donetta learned the valuable lesson about how to break the news—never in person. The risk of danger in doing so was much too great.

Donetta had learned from talking with other trans women, and from her own personal experiences, that it could not only be dangerous, but sometimes it could be fatal, to tell a man you'd just met—face-to-face—that you were trans.

The incidence of hate crimes against trans people, especially trans women of color, was higher than that in any other minority group, and with the number of black trans women being killed skyrocketing over the last few years, Donetta was extra-cautious. She'd been the victim of violence several times in her life, and on a few of the occasions she'd gotten the better of the men who'd mistaken her slender frame for weakness. But ever since she'd begun her steady regimen of estrogen and anti-androgen drugs a few years ago, her bravado had softened, her physical strength had decreased, and she knew that put her more at risk if she ever found herself in a compromising situation again.

Last night, when she'd been getting dressed to go out with Phillip, she'd decided that if things went well she would tell him the next day. But in her wildest dreams she'd never thought she'd wake up lying beside him the next morning. Now she was in a quandary about what to do. Donetta looked at her reflection in the vanity mirror. "I already like him so much . . . How am I going to tell him?" Suddenly, her bright, airy mood turned dark and sullen. She rose from her fur-lined vanity stool, walked over to the window, and looked out her blinds. The dark clouds hinted that rain was on its way. "Just my luck."

She was about to go into the kitchen to heat her breakfast in the microwave when her phone rang. When she looked at the screen, she was surprised to see Shartell's number appear. She'd just done the nosy, worrisome woman's hair yesterday, and she wondered what Shartell wanted now. "What do you want, Shartell?" she asked.

"Well, good afternoon to you, too, Donetta."

"Uh-huh. Why're you calling me?"

"Damn, must you always be so rude? I thought after your hot date last night, you'd be on top of the world this morning."

Donetta froze where she was standing in front of the window. "What the hell are you talking about?"

"Awww, don't play coy with me. You should want to spread this good news all over town. There's nothing wrong with gettin' a little lovin' for the holidays."

"I don't know what you're talking about. And furthermore, why're you calling me, trying to get in my business?"

"Girl, I'm happy for you, I just wanted to call and congratulate you, that's all."

Donetta knew she needed to proceed with caution. She'd always had a love-hate relationship with Shartell, going back to the days when Shartell used to work at Heavenly Hair Salon with her and Geneva. Even though Donetta detested that Shartell was always into everyone's business, she respected the fact that the woman's information was always accurate and 100 percent true, which made it gossip rather than rumor. If Shartell opened her mouth to spread some news, you could bank on it being the truth. But what Donetta found troubling, and why she took issue with Shartell, was the way Shartell went about getting her information. Donetta was sure that whatever methods Shartell used, they had to be underhanded, because no one would willingly divulge the type of dirt that she had been able to uncover.

"I'm not playing your little game," Donetta said. "I've known you long enough to know that you're tryin' to get in my business for a reason. So before we fall out, you need to tell me what the hell's going on. And I promise you, if you lie to me, not only will I never do your hair, ever again, I'll personally come to your house—'cause I know where you live—and beat your ass!"

Shartell huffed. "Oh, stop it with the threats. You're always tryin' to break bad."

"Because I have to protect myself. Now, tell me why you're in my business."

"Okay, okay." Shartell let out a sigh. "You know

that article I was telling y'all about yesterday at the salon . . . about finding love during the holidays? Well, I thought it would be really cool to feature some diverse stories about love. I know for a fact that you haven't dated in a while, but now that you're back in the game, I thought . . ."

"Who says I'm back in the game? Where's all this coming from?" Donetta's heart started beating fast. What if Phillip wasn't the sweet, caring, upstanding man she'd thought he was? What if he was really a low-life gigolo who went around romancing women and somehow Shartell knew him? All these thoughts sprinted through Donetta's mind and made her head hurt again. "Tell me the truth, Shartell. I've always been straight-up with you, and now I need you to be straight-up with me. What makes you think I'm seeing anyone?".

"Because you were with him at the Roosevelt Hotel last night."

Damn! Donetta shook her head and bit down on her bottom lip. She didn't remember seeing Shartell at the Roosevelt last night. As a matter of fact, she was almost positive that Shartell couldn't have been there. Donetta had paid special attention, taking in every square inch of the beautiful scenery around her, and although Shartell might be a major sleuth, she was a hefty-sized woman who always dressed in blindingly bright colors, so there would've been no way she could have gone unseen. Plus, Donetta knew Shartell's MO, and she could tell by the way Shartell was talking that she was fishing for information. Otherwise she would have led off by mentioning how handsome Phillip was. Again, Donetta proceeded with caution. "Were you in the hotel last night?"

Shartell hesitated, and Donetta knew she'd been right. Shartell hadn't been there. "I asked you a question," Donetta said, "and I expect you to answer it."

"Well, not exactly." There was a long pause. Donetta refused to say another word, so Shartell spoke up. "I was downtown late last night because I had to pick my aunt up from the train station, and on my way I saw you walking into the hotel all dressed up. It was a great outfit, by the way. Loved the zebra-print jacket."

"I could've been going there for any number of reasons. What makes you think I was there with anyone?"

"I can't reveal my sources."

Right then Donetta knew it had to have been a member of the hotel staff. Entertainment reporters were known for having inside contacts at hotels, restaurants, and retail stores, who fed them information about customers for a price, and Donetta was sure that was the case with Shartell. "You're really low, you know that?"

"Donetta, I've done nothing wrong. As a matter of fact, I'm doing you a big favor because I'm coming to the source first, rather than just going ahead and printing the information in my article."

"You're not doing me any favors, and you know it."

"How can you say that? I'm on the phone trying to talk to you about it, aren't I?"

"Only because your hotel contact obviously couldn't give you the accurate information you need. I know how you operate, Shartell. You probably called them, described me, and then asked them who I was with, and when they couldn't give you a name, that's when you decided to call me."

Donetta was thankful that Phillip had pulled out two crisp hundred dollar bills to pay for their appetizer and drinks, rather than use his credit card; otherwise his name would end up in Shartell's online column. Donetta knew that the way gossip spread so fast, Phillip might find out things about her before she had a chance to tell him.

"Whether you believe me or not," Shartell said, "I'm trying to do the right thing by you."

"The right thing would be to forget about including me in anything that has to do with that article."

"Think about how much inspiration your story would give to trans people who're trying to find love. Did you know that the word *transgender* has been trending in the top ten on Twitter for a month? The exposure will be phenomenal . . . I mean, for helping people . . . you know?"

Donetta thought her head would pop off. She was through-the-roof mad, and she had to take a deep breath to calm herself. "Shartell, I want you to listen very carefully to what I'm getting ready to say."

"Um, okay . . ."

"I've spent my entire life living in the shadow of happiness. You have no idea how hard just doing simple things like going on a date has been for me. You don't know what it's like to live with the fear that someone might beat you up, rape you, or even kill you because of who you are. I've been beaten and I've been raped, but I'll be damned if I'm gonna allow you to put my life in jeopardy."

"Donetta, I would never do anything to put you or anyone else's safety at risk."

"That's not true. You have no idea what kind of consequences your actions have caused to the people you've hurt over the years by spreading gossip. What might seem like nothing to you could mean the difference between life and death for someone else."

"You know me, and you know I would never do anything to harm anyone."

"The old Shartell wouldn't have. Back in the day, when you were just the town busybody with a bad perm, at least you had a conscience. But the new Shartell, who writes sensationalized articles and has a six-figure book deal, doesn't give a damn about anyone but herself. I've seen the change in you." Donetta took another deep breath and swallowed hard. "If you have a shred of decency left in your body, you'll finish that article today, and when I go online to read it tomorrow, my name won't be anywhere in it."

Donetta hit the End button on her phone, looked out the window, and watched fluffy snowflakes begin to fall as tears rolled down her cheeks.

Chapter 21

GENEVA

If anyone had told Geneva at the beginning of the week that her Thanksgiving Eve would be spent doing anything other than enjoying her family and cooking food in preparation for their big holiday feast, she wouldn't have believed it. But as she rubbed her temples, feeling the beginnings of a colossal headache about to roar, a festive celebration was the last thing on her mind. It had been four hours since she and Samuel had put Joe out of their house, turning what should have been a time of family love and celebration into a flood of flared tempers and heated emotions. The family was just beginning to settle down from the chaos that had taken place, but the atmosphere was still tense.

Sarah was upstairs in bed, sleeping off the Valium

she'd had to take to help calm her nerves. Herbert had gone to the driving range down the street from Geneva and Samuel's subdivision so he could hit some balls and blow off steam. Samuel had just taken two Tylenol that Geneva had given him and reapplied a bag of frozen peas to his knuckles to help with the swelling from where he'd punched his brother in the jaw. And Geneva was outside, reclined on a lounge chair on their scenic back patio, wrapped up in two thick blankets, as she watched the flames dance inside the Tuscan-style brick firepit in front of her. The only person in the Owens household who was as happy as could be was little Gabrielle, who was oblivious to the adult commotion around her. She'd devoured her lunch and then fallen asleep with a satisfied tummy and a smile on her face.

Ever since yesterday it seemed to Geneva that nothing had gone right. First the interview with Vivana, then her bad dream about Johnny's killer, and now the revelation that her brother-in-law had been the major cause of the pain and scrutiny she'd suffered after Johnny's death. Geneva shook her head in disgust as she thought about the story Samuel had told her. "Now I know why Samuel didn't want that deceitful lowlife in our house or our lives," she said to herself.

Throughout the investigation of Johnny's murder, up to the point when Vivana had been indicted for the crime, the authorities had hounded Geneva and Samuel. The two had topped the list of prime suspects, and their every move had become a matter of interest to the authorities. The level of scrutiny around them had gotten so intense that Geneva and Samuel had suspected they were under surveillance. The police had known their schedules like clockwork, even when Geneva and Samuel would change up their routine. Neither of them could go anywhere without seeing squad cars or plainclothes detectives parked in dark sedans nearby. One of the detectives working the case had even shown up at restaurants on two separate occasions when Samuel had taken Geneva out to dinner.

As it turned out, Geneva and Samuel had been right; they had indeed been under surveillance. Their personal struggles, daily schedules, events they planned to attend, and intimate conversations had all been leaked by Joe, who sold the privileged information to none other than Shartell Brown, who then passed the details along to the police.

Shartell had met Joe in passing when he'd come down to visit Samuel a few days after Johnny's murder. Joe had been in Starbucks waiting for his coffee when Shartell walked in. At the time, Shartell hadn't risen to the notoriety she now enjoyed. Back then she'd simply been known as the town gossip, and she'd made it her business to buddy up to as many people as she could so she'd always be in the know. When she saw Joe's unfamiliar face, she'd immediately known he was new in town, so she struck up a casual conversation with him. She asked him where he was from, noting that he didn't have a Southern accent. Joe told her that he'd been in Birmingham a few days before for a business convention, and that he'd decided to drive to Amber to visit his brother.

Once Shartell found out that the stranger's brother was none other than Samuel Owens, a light had sparked in her eyes. Shartell was the type of person who could smell a conniving schemer a mile away, and Joe had been oozing with the scent. She knew she could use Joe's greed to advance her own ambition.

Shartell told Joe that she was a local reporter, which

was almost true, seeing that she was always asking questions, gathering information, and telling stories. She'd said she was working with authorities on the Mayfield murder investigation by providing them with inside information. She told Joe that if he gave her information about Samuel and Geneva, she would make it financially worth his while and his name would never be mentioned. The only catch was that he could never mention her name either. That had been fine with Joe, because he didn't want any dirt to be traced back to him.

Shartell had been so eager to enlist Joe's help that she'd reached into the large leather attaché draped over her shoulder and pulled out a confidentiality agreement right there on the spot. "Anonymity and confidentiality are crucial in my line of work," she'd told him, "and I'm always prepared in case I run into a juicy story." They walked next door to the UPS Store and had a notary public witness, stamp, and sign the agreement, sealing their deal.

Joe had made a pretty penny feeding Shartell the details of his weekly phone conversations with his brother. Time rolled on, and everything was good— until the day after Vivana was indicted. Samuel and Geneva were no longer news, and Samuel's usefulness had come to an end, along with the brotherly phone calls from Joe.

Samuel didn't find out what Joe had been up to until a month after Gabrielle had been born. He and Geneva had planned a big party to celebrate the birth of their daughter. They'd invited their close friends and family members, and at the urging of Samuel's parents—who'd purchased Joe's airline ticket—Joe had come to town for the festivities.

Geneva shook her head when she thought about that weekend. She remembered watching Joe and Shartell exchange glances during the party. She'd even caught them huddled in deep conversation at the edge of her flower garden beyond the patio. She'd thought they might be trying to hook up, but then Shartell abruptly stormed off, leaving Joe standing outside alone. Geneva had simply thought that it was a case of Joe being Joe, and that his abrasive personality had turned Shartell off. Little did she know at the time that her assumption was only half-right.

"I thought they were trying to hook up, too," Samuel had told Geneva a few hours ago when he'd broken the news to her. "I'd heard voices coming from the family room, which I'd thought was odd because everyone had been in the kitchen and living room. Anyway, I went to see who was in there and it was Shartell and Joe. They didn't see or hear me when I cracked the door, and that's when I heard them arguing in whispered tones. Joe told her that she still owed him money and he threatened to sue her. He told her that without the information he'd given her about you and me during Johnny's murder investigation, she wouldn't have been able to assist the police, which helped her become well-known and land her the job with Entertainment Scoop. He wanted a piece of the action. That's when Shartell reminded him about the agreement they'd signed, and she told him that if he opened his mouth about anything she'd make sure he ended up in jail for defamation and breach of contract."

After Samuel finished telling Geneva all the details of his brother's betrayal, Geneva had sat on the couch stunned.

"Why didn't you tell me this when you found out?" Geneva asked.

Samuel let out a long sigh. "Because we'd gone through so much and you'd finally gotten to a point where you were happy. I felt that telling you would only cause more pain, so I decided your happiness and peace of mind was much more important than my brother's scheming ways."

But Geneva's hurt soon turned to anger, and anger turned to rage. Samuel had barely finished his sentence before Geneva jumped to her feet and ran up the stairs—taking them two at a time—to the guest room where Joe had been napping. Samuel had tried to stop her, but she'd moved too quickly. She'd stormed into the room and shouted at Joe to pack his bags and leave.

"Are you crazy?" Joe had said. "What the hell is wrong with you?"

"You're a no-good, low-down, devious coward," Geneva yelled. "I want you out of our house right now!"

When Joe made the mistake of telling Geneva to go to hell, he'd found himself lying flat on the floor after Samuel punched him in his jaw. Sarah had stayed in their guest room with Gabrielle, while Herbert rushed in and broke up the one-sided fight. Fifteen minutes later a cab pulled up to the front door and took Joe to the Hilton Garden Inn.

Geneva pulled the soft lambs-wool blankets up to her neck and let out a long sigh as she thought about her money-hungry brother-in-law. Then her thoughts turned to her nosy friend, Shartell. Geneva had always known that Shartell was a bigmouthed gossiper; after all, she'd been nicknamed Ms. CIA because she had intel on everyone in town. But Geneva had also known Shartell to have a sense of honor, or at least she'd thought so. Geneva shook her head when she thought about what Shartell had said at the salon yesterday when Donetta had made a joke, and said that Shartell's family better be careful, lest they end up in Shartell's new book. Geneva had been appalled when Shartell had said it was actually a good idea.

"If she'll sell out her family, she'll certainly throw me under the bus in order to get what she wants," Geneva huffed. She closed her eyes and rubbed her throbbing temples. When she looked up, she was startled to find Samuel standing beside her lounge chair. "I didn't hear you come out."

"You looked like you were in deep thought and I didn't want to startle you." Samuel handed her a glass of wine. "Here, baby. I know it's the middle of the day, but I figured you could use this."

Geneva nodded her head and took a sip. "Thanks, honey. This is exactly what I need. How's your hand feeling? Is the Tylenol helping?"

"No, but the wine is. I already finished one glass and I'm about to have another."

"I might need a refill, too."

Samuel looked up at the dark clouds looming above. "The weatherman said this'll be the first time in over fifty years that this town has seen snow on Thanksgiving."

"Snow?" Geneva looked up at the sky. "You've gotta be kidding me. I didn't know they were calling for snow."

"They weren't, but apparently in the wee hours of this morning an unexpected clipper, mixed with a polar vortex, came from out of nowhere, and it's sweeping through the South. I didn't know anything about it, either, until I turned on the news right before I poured your drink."

"Wow, this is sudden."

"Yeah, this winter storm is fast-moving, and it's caught everyone off guard. They're saying it's an emergency situation. I'm glad we've got plenty of food, because it looks like we're gonna get over a half foot by nightfall."

Geneva took a sip of her wine and closed her eyes. "Can things get any worse?"

"Why don't you come back inside, baby? It's way too cold to be out here, and it's supposed to start snowing any minute."

Under normal circumstances, Geneva wouldn't have willingly gone outside in this type of cold for any reason. But what she'd just experienced wasn't a normal circumstance. She needed the solitude and the bone-freezing chill to clear her mind. "I'll come in after I finish my glass, which won't take long," she told her husband. "Between the fire, these blankets, and the wine, I'll be warm."

"Okay, but if you're not inside in the next ten minutes, I'm coming back out to get you."

Geneva took another sip of her wine and watched Samuel close the patio door. She'd wanted to tell him about her dream, but now it seemed silly in comparison to what she'd just discovered. She thought about how much Samuel had been hurt by his brother's betrayal, and how he'd kept it inside because he hadn't wanted to upset her. They'd suffered the loss of one child the year before, and he didn't want to ruin the celebration of their new baby girl by confronting his brother, which would have surely caused a scene.

Before Geneva knew it, she was swallowing her last sip of wine. She set the glass on the patio side table and looked up at the heavy clouds. "What's gonna be next? A plague of locusts?" She wished she could make a wish and return her life to normal. But when she thought about it, many of the things she'd thought were normal had really been lies. Her entire marriage to Johnny had been a lie. Joe's bond with Samuel had been a lie. Vivana's conviction for a crime she didn't commit had been a sham. And Shartell's claims of integrity had been a huge farce.

Geneva was hurt by her brother-in-law's betrayal, frightened by what her dream might mean, and angry that Shartell had used her and Samuel's pain to advance her own gain. Geneva was the type of person who always tried to look for the bright side of any given situation, but when she thought about the current set of circumstances, it was hard for her to see any good. She'd tried to keep a positive outlook, but right now all she could feel was the numbness that came with finding out someone had betrayed you.

"I guess I'd better go in before I catch pneumonia out here." Just as Geneva rose from her lounge chair and gathered her blankets, she felt a snowflake land on her cheek. She looked up into the sky and saw big, fluffy flakes starting to fall all around her. "What a beautiful sight." She stood perfectly still, enjoying the quiet beauty of nature, and for a brief moment she felt completely at peace. But her solitude was interrupted when she heard Samuel call out to her.

"Donetta's on the phone," he said.

"Okay, tell her I'm coming." Geneva folded her blankets and reached for her wineglass. She was looking forward to talking with her best friend, who was probably calling to give her another update about the wonderful new man she'd just met. Geneva couldn't wait to talk to Donetta, because she needed to hear some good news right now.

Chapter 22

DONETTA

"Geneva, what in the world were you doing outside? It's freezing," Donetta said when Geneva came on the line. "Samuel said you were out back on the patio wrapped up in some damn blankets."

"I had the fire going. It was nice."

"Geneva, you're talking crazy. It's thirty degrees outside, and it's snowing on top of that."

"It just started, and it's beautiful."

Donetta shook her head. "What's wrong with you? I know something's going on because Samuel answered the phone sounding like he just lost his best friend and you're about to turn into a Popsicle. Somethin' ain't right."

"You sound congested, are you catching a cold?"

Donetta had just finished blowing her nose to end

the long cry she'd had after hanging up on Shartell. She'd called Geneva to tell her about Shartell's scheming ways, but first she wanted to know what had made her friend so upset that she had to sit outside in the cold. "I hate it when you avoid my questions. What's wrong?" Donetta asked again.

Geneva let out a sigh. "I don't want to rain on your happiness with my drama."

"Ha, too late for that. But I'll fill you in on it later. Right now I want to know what's going on with you and Samuel. Is this about your dream? Did you talk to Councilwoman Harris about it?"

"No, I haven't had a chance to call her. As a matter of fact, I haven't even told Samuel because so much has gone on in this house. This definitely isn't the type of family holiday I'd envisioned. The last few hours have been so stressful I don't even know where to begin."

Donetta had a feeling she knew what was wrong. "Did that asshole brother-in-law of yours do something to piss everybody off?"

"How did you know?"

"Because with the exception of the trouble that Vivana's interview stirred up yesterday, everything with you was fine. You and Samuel get along great, Gabrielle is an angel, and your mother-in-law and father-in-law are super-sweet people, so by process of elimination, the only person left is Samuel's brother. I've met him, and he's a real piece of work, so I can only imagine what kind of stunt he's pulled."

Donetta had only met Joe once, and that had been when he'd come down for a visit shortly after Gabrielle had been born. Donetta hadn't liked him on sight, but because he was Samuel's brother, she'd tried

to be cordial. It had only taken her five minutes of conversation to assess that Joe was a complete ass, and
he'd turned her off by his rude manner and off-color
sense of humor. "Did he say something insulting to either of you?"

"Girl, if you only knew the half of it," Geneva
said.

"Oh my . . . I'm listening."

"We had to put Joe out of the house."

"What?! Why?" Donetta was still in her nightgown, so she walked back over to her bed and crawled
under her cozy comforter as she watched the snow fall
outside. "I just got back in my bed so I can lie down,
because I have a feeling I shouldn't stand up while listening to this."

"Joe and Samuel exchanged blows. Well, actually,
Samuel knocked Joe out, and after that we told him
that he couldn't stay under our roof, and that he had to
leave immediately."

"Shut the front door! You're shittin' me."

"No, I'm serious. It was awful. I'm just glad my
mother-in-law had Gabrielle in the guest room down
the hall, away from all the drama."

"Lord have mercy, Geneva. It's hard for me to picture Samuel raising his voice, let alone fighting."

"Tell me about it. He hit Joe so hard that his
knuckles are swollen. By the time the cab picked Joe
up, his jaw was already the size of a small baseball.
The sad thing is that I don't even care. As a matter of
fact, I hope his jaw swells even bigger. Maybe it'll
teach him a lesson."

"Damn. What in the world did he do?"

Donetta had been lying down when Geneva began

her story, but by the time she'd ended it, Donetta was sitting up in bed with her mouth hanging open.

"I always knew that Shartell had deceptive ways about her," Geneva said. "Otherwise she wouldn't gossip and spread people's personal business around the way she does. But I had no idea she could be this heartless and downright cold-blooded. I get mad every time I think about all the times during the investigation when she was working right beside me in the salon, talking and laughing with me as if she'd never done a thing. What kind of person can do something like that?"

"The kind who doesn't give a damn about anyone other than themselves. She's always been a greedy opportunist, she just hid it well. That's what deceitful people do, and that's how they're able to continue to shit on people."

"I guess you're right."

"Well, don't feel bad. You're not the only one Shartell has tried to screw. I got a phone call from her this morning."

Donetta went on to tell Geneva about how Shartell wanted to feature Donetta in an article that was set to run tomorrow, and that she'd been fishing for information on the man Donetta had been out with last night to include in the story. "That heffa actually had the nerve to tell me that she was doing me a favor by calling me before she runs the article."

"She's gone way too far this time. Do you really think she's going to go through with it?"

"I hope not, but I'm not sure. With someone like her, it's hard to say. What I do know, though, is that Shartell likes to name names and use direct sources to make her articles appear juicier and more controversial. She doesn't have Phillip's name, and without it there's no shock value. She doesn't like to leave anything up for speculation, because that undermines her credibility."

Geneva was quiet, and Donetta knew that couldn't be good. After a brief moment, Geneva cleared her throat. "I've had to learn the hard way that Shartell is ruthless. I wouldn't be the least bit surprised if she ran the story anyway."

"But she never spreads gossip unless she has a definitive source to back it up. Do you really think she'd pull the trigger without a smoking gun?"

"I sure do. Think about it. She could run the tagline, 'Trans Woman Finds Love During the Holidays with Mystery Man', and she'll say she doesn't want to reveal his name in order to protect his privacy."

Donetta's heart sank when she envisioned the caption. "After all the years that I've known her, if Shartell is heartless enough to do something like that to me, the Amber Police Department won't have to worry about spending taxpayers' money on an expensive investigation like they did Johnny's, because after I kill that bitch, I'll gladly go and turn myself in. Knowing Shartell's reputation, I'm sure a few people in uniform might actually thank me."

"Donetta, don't say things like that. Joking about killing someone isn't funny."

"I'm not joking."

Donetta hated that she was caught in this predicament. She knew that because Shartell's book was scheduled for release in the coming spring, she needed something salacious to boost views of her column on Entertainment Scoop, which would increase book sales and ensure that she made several bestseller lists. For this reason alone, Donetta knew Geneva was right. Shartell was ruthless, and she'd made it clear that her own welfare was her main concern. "This isn't good at all," Donetta said. "Damn!"

"Have you told Phillip yet?"

Donetta knew that Geneva was intimately familiar with her dating rules, and why she'd set them. Geneva had been there to nurse Donetta back to health after two attacks several years ago. One man had punched her in the stomach and fractured one of her ribs, requiring an overnight stay in the hospital. The other had waited until she'd left work one night and jumped her in the parking lot, beating her until she was bruised from head to toe.

Donetta knew that those incidents had left Geneva frightened for her, and she always worried that something like that might happen again. She knew that had been the reason why Geneva had been so concerned last night when she'd thought Phillip had been stalking Donetta in the grocery store.

"I had planned to tell him after our date," Donetta said. "I figured once I got home safely, I'd call him and explain things. But as you know, he ended up spending the night, which I totally hadn't planned on. And you know I wasn't about to tell him while he was here in my house."

"No, you did the right thing because you never know how someone will react."

"Right. Plus, I got really sick right after I got off the phone with you this morning. One minute I was fine, and then before I knew it I was practically doubled over in pain. I even had to take some Dilaudid."

"Oh no! What was wrong? Are you okay now?"

"I'm still in a little pain, but overall I'm much better than I was." Donetta told Geneva about the bleeding, the pain, and about how Phillip had taken care of her.

"Wow, Donetta. I don't know very many men who're in long-term, committed relationships who'll help to that level. He sounds like a really good person, and he obviously has a kind heart," Geneva said. "But even good, kindhearted people can lose it. Judging from what he's shown you, how do you think he's going to react when you tell him that you're trans?"

"I really don't know. He seems open-minded, but I can also tell he's very traditional. He has issues with his father, and from the little things he's told me, I think his papa was a rolling stone. His dad had a lot of women, and I know Phillip has, too."

"Hmmm . . . interesting."

"I know he'll be shocked, and he might even be angry. Even if he's both, I hope he'll be able to see me for who I am. That's been the hardest part of my entire life, every day I open my eyes." Donetta's voice trembled as she spoke. "All I've ever wanted is to live as the person I really am, and be accepted for what's inside of me. From as early as I can remember, I've never, ever felt like I was anything other than female. I remember how I used to dread trips to the barbershop when my mom would take me to get my hair cut. I didn't want a tapered fade, I wanted my hair to grow so I could have ponytails like the rest of the girls. Sometimes I feel so hollow, Geneva. Even now, when I finally look like who I really am, it's still not enough. I'm tired of having to prove, justify, and explain who I am. It's exhausting, and I'm worn out. I just want to be happy."

"Sweetie, I'm so, so sorry." Geneva's voice was

full of compassion. "I won't sit here and tell you that I
know how you feel, because I don't. But like that fa-
mous worldwide project says, it gets better."

Donetta nodded her head as she thought about the
It Gets Better Project that was started in 2010 as a way
to encourage, inspire, and give hope to young people
facing harassment. Everyone from well-known Hollywood celebrities to little-known community activists
were featured in video messages giving their account
of how they overcame the adversities and struggles
that came along with being gay, lesbian, bisexual, or
transgender.

"You know, I think about that all the time," Donetta
said, sadness coating her voice, "and I don't only want it
to get better, I want it to be great. You don't know how
blessed you are to have been born with your outside
matching up with your inside. You have a good husband who loves, values, and cherishes you, and a beautiful baby daughter who holds her arms out for you and
lights up every time she sees you. I'd give anything to
have that." This was the first time Donetta had ever admitted that she envied her best friend's life.

"My life hasn't been perfect," Geneva said. "I might
not have gone through the same kinds of struggles that
you have, but I've had my fair share of challenges. Yes, I
was born looking and feeling like a woman. But the difference between you and me, Donetta, is that I looked
like a woman and never really felt pretty. Regardless of
what you looked like on the outside, you always, from
day one, felt like you were the most gorgeous thing on
two legs. That's powerful, because it's what's inside
you that makes you so beautiful. I've always admired
your confidence and how self-assured you are. It took
me a long time to achieve what you've always had, so

don't sell yourself short. And don't discount finding a husband and child who love you. If you want it, go after it."

Donetta smiled. "You always know the right thing to say."

"Not only is it right, it's true."

"I pray that Phillip will think that way, too."

"He sounds like a caring person, but you won't know until you tell him. If he can't handle who you are, then he's not the one for you."

"Damn, life sure can throw you for a loop."

"It can change in the blink of an eye. Look how much has happened to both of us in the last twenty-four hours. Yesterday, if anyone had told me that Vivana was innocent of Johnny's murder, I wouldn't have believed it, but today I know it's true. And if anyone had told me that my husband's brother would sell us out"—Geneva paused—"on second thought, that's a bad example. But you get my point."

"I do, and I agree. Phillip came into my life and changed things, literally overnight. I've never been one of those sappy romantic types, but girl, I'm all in. That's why I'm so nervous about telling him."

"He just might be your happily-ever-after. I've never heard you sound this way, and in all the years I've known you, I can't ever remember you bringing a man over to your house, let alone letting them spend the night."

"Girl, I know. I'm so into him it scares me."

"You've got to tell him right away. Like now."

Donetta knew Geneva was right. "I'm going to call him after we hang up."

"Okay, call me back and let me know how the conversation goes."

Donetta hung up the phone and took a deep breath. She'd made a lot of mistakes in her life, and she'd also done some things that had been right. In just one day, Phillip had felt righter than anything she'd ever experienced, and she prayed that he would listen, keep an open mind, and continue to walk down the path they'd started on. "Okay, here goes." She dialed his number, heard it ring, and waited for him to pick up.

Chapter 23

PHILLIP

Phillip rubbed his chin and shook his head as he sat alone on the sofa in the family room. He'd just gotten off the phone with Donetta, and while their conversation had been brief, it had put a smile on his face to know that she was feeling better. He'd been worried about her when he'd left her house a few hours ago because she'd been in so much pain from the menstrual cramps she'd been experiencing. It was the first time he'd ever taken care of a woman the way he'd cared for her, and it had felt as natural to him as breathing.

Being with Donetta had been exhilarating, but that good feeling had ended as soon as he'd spotted his sister walking toward him in the baggage claim. Initially, he hadn't recognized her, and when he'd seen the hefty-sized young woman grab her bag and give him a quizzical look, he'd thought to himself that she looked an awful lot like Lauren.

"Um, excuse me, but a hello would be nice," the woman said.

Phillip blinked twice. "Lauren?"

He couldn't get over the drastic change in his sister's appearance. He hadn't seen her since back in the spring, when she'd taken the train from Baltimore into DC to spend her school break with him. He'd been surprised to see that she'd put on what looked to be at least forty pounds, and that she didn't look as put together as she usually did. Her once neatly combed hair had been matted atop her head, the bright eyes he'd been used to seeing had shown telltale signs of lack of sleep, and her normally smooth, caramel-colored skin had been blotchy with a breakout.

He'd had a heart-to-heart talk with Lauren about not only her appearance, but also her seeming overall lack of care about life. He'd asked her outright if her decline had anything to do with the anger and resentment she'd been carrying for her father since the incident involving their half brother. She'd been adamant that she didn't even think about their father or their half brother anymore, and that she'd simply decided to start living her life in a much freer way. That had been seven months ago, and as he now looked at his sister, whom he barely recognized, he knew there was something very wrong going on with her. She'd put on an additional fifty pounds since spring, which was a dead giveaway that something was definitely wrong. Her leggings and sweatshirt looked cheap, tight, and ill-fitting, and he could tell she hadn't combed her hair because her makeshift Afro looked as though she'd been wearing a hairnet, even though she wasn't.

After he'd gotten over the shock of her physical appearance, she'd given him another stunner when he'd loaded her last suitcase into the trunk of his car and asked her why she'd packed so many bags. When she'd told him that she'd withdrawn from medical school, he couldn't believe his ears. He'd spent the next thirty minutes standing in the cold parking deck trying to talk some sense into her. Finally, he'd given up. He didn't put up resistance when she'd asked him to stop at a local fast food restaurant and had ordered a triple bacon and cheese steak burger, large fries, and a large milk shake.

Phillip had known that as soon as his mother laid eyes on Lauren, it wasn't going to be good. She would hit the roof, and rightfully so, but he hadn't expected Lauren to act so disrespectfully to her, and he'd begun to wonder if his sister *was* using drugs. Right in the middle of their heated family confrontation, his phone had rung. Sabrina had called and he'd hit Ignore, choosing to deal with her later. A few minutes after that, Rachel called, and he ignored her call, as well. Then Donetta called almost immediately after, and he'd rushed out of the room to talk to her.

Now, as Phillip continued to sit alone in the silence of the family room, he was glad his mother and sister had finally stopped arguing. This certainly wasn't shaping up into the family-friendly holiday he'd thought it was going to be when he'd arrived in town yesterday. He'd had a rough week at work, and he'd been looking forward to relaxing in his mother's comfortable home, eating her delicious food, catching up with her and his sister, and then flying back out late Sunday morning. But it didn't look like any of that was going to happen now.

He thought about how close his family used to be, and how fractured they were now. He hadn't seen his father in two years, and even then their interaction had been tepid at best. His mother had always been the strong pillar of the family, but now she was drinking herself to sleep at night. And poor Lauren seemed to be drifting out to sea without a clue as to how to make it back to shore.

Phillip sat in silence for a few more minutes before he got up in search of his mother and sister, hoping they'd each calmed down and were in better moods. He walked down the hall toward his mother's study and found her there. She was sitting behind her desk, concentrating as she typed on her computer.

"You busy?" he asked, slightly startling his mother. He leaned against the doorway. "I can come back later."

"I'm never too busy for my children. Come on in."

Phillip walked into her spacious office and took a seat in front of her desk. The blinds were closed, and because it was already cloudy outside when he'd been out earlier, it felt like it was early evening instead of lunchtime. "Mom, I'm sorry about the way this holiday is shaping up."

"It's not your fault." She removed her reading glasses and rubbed her tired eyes. "This is what they call life, and as you know, life changes and so do people."

"I tried talking to Lauren on our way back from the airport, but it's like trying to get through a brick wall."

"Please keep talking to her. She's always looked up to you, and she respects your opinion."

Phillip shook his head. "I think she's more concerned with what that clown Hakeem has to say than anything I can tell her."

"How long has she been dating him?"

"I don't know. The first time I heard his name was when she mentioned him this afternoon, but apparently they're living together."

"Dear Lord."

Phillip watched as his mother slumped her shoulders and shook her head. Her eyes looked tired, and she was still wearing her nightgown and robe from this morning. It seemed that her hangover was gone and had been replaced by defeat. "Mom, are you gonna be okay?"

His mother gave him a small smile. "I'll be fine. Don't worry about me, I'm a tough bird."

"But even tough birds need to give their wings a rest every now and then."

"True." She leaned forward in her chair and looked into his eyes. "Tell me how you're doing."

Phillip smiled. "I'm good."

"Who is she?"

He smiled even wider. "Mom, c'mon."

"You didn't come back home last night, and as cold as it is, I know you didn't sleep in your car."

"No, I didn't. I spent the night at a friend's house." He felt slightly uncomfortable talking to his mother about his love life. She usually allowed him to go about his business with impunity. But he understood that because she was worried about her children, she would naturally ask questions. When he thought about Donetta, he knew his mother would like her.

"I don't understand, Phillip. Is this someone you just met? Because I've never known you to go out with anyone when you come home to visit."

"Yes, I just met her. But I feel like we've known

each other for a while. I can't explain it, but . . . All I can say is that she's an amazing woman, and I think you'd like her."

"Do you realize that you're smiling while you're talking about her?"

"No, I didn't." Phillip chuckled. "Enough with the interrogation, for now. I'll keep you updated as things develop."

His mother folded her arms, and Phillip noticed a weary look cloud her face. "I worry about you and your sister. I know the things you witnessed your father do while you were growing up didn't set a good example, but please, please don't follow in his footsteps."

"Wait, you knew Dad was creeping back in the day?"

"I didn't have definitive proof, but I suspected things. Then I noticed when you were in high school that the relationship between you two became very strained. When you were in college, I heard you two arguing one night and it finally made sense to me."

"Wow, I never knew you'd heard us."

"I did, and I put up with a lot of things that I shouldn't have for far too long. And now I feel like all those poor decisions have come back to bite me. You and Lauren don't even know how to have healthy relationships. And to be honest, I still don't."

Phillip shook his head. "Mom, you can't blame yourself for the decisions that anyone else makes. We all have free will." Phillip had to smile when he repeated what Donetta had said to him last night. "You're a great mother and a great example of how to do things the right way. I'll be fine, and so will Lauren. We'll get through this."

She raised her brow. "When did you become so wise?"

"I'm learning every day." Just then his phone rang. He glanced at it and saw that it was Rachel trying to reach him. He'd texted her last night and told her he'd call her when he returned to DC. But she was persistent. His battery was low, and he didn't want to waste precious juice responding to her, so he slid the phone back into his pocket.

"That's why I worry about you," his mother said. "Your phone's been ringing off the hook this afternoon with different women calling you. You're playing a dangerous game, son. You're juggling too many women, and pretty soon it's going to come to a head."

"Mom, it's not like you think, and I'm not doggin' out anyone."

"Like I've told you, you might not think so, but you don't know how these women feel. All it takes is the one bad move with the wrong woman, and . . ."

Phillip loved his mother, but he was starting to tire of her constant warnings. "You act like I'm Johnny Mayfield or somebody."

"What did you say?"

"Johnny Mayfield, you know, that dude who was murdered a couple of years ago and no one knew who did it because he'd been messing with so many women, even blackmailing some of them. Then they found out that a crazy chick he'd been messing around with did it. You remember, Mom. It made national news. It's sad that's how Amber got its name on the map."

She nodded, and he noticed that she looked even more worried than before. Then he realized that had been a terrible example to use. "I'm nothing like that guy, and nothing's going to happen to me. I'm careful.

And as a matter of fact, right now there's only one woman I want to spend my time with, so all these calls are about to cease."

His mother nodded and rubbed her forehead. "I'm exhausted, I need to take a nap."

Phillip and his mother left her office. She walked in one direction to her bedroom, and he walked in the other as he headed upstairs. He decided to have a talk with Lauren, but when he walked by her room she was sound asleep and snoring. He was beginning to feel tired, too. And after the late night and early morning he'd had with Donetta, and the drama with his mother and sister this afternoon, he knew he needed to get some rest. As soon as his head hit the pillow, he was out.

Three hours later Phillip awoke when he heard a knock on his door.

"It's snowing like crazy!" Lauren yelled with excitement.

"What?" Phillip rubbed his eyes and tried to focus.

Lauren rushed into his room, walked over to his window, and opened the blinds. "Look, there's at least four or five inches out there."

Phillip jumped up from the bed and rushed to the window. "Damn, I didn't know it was going to snow." He hadn't watched the news today, and this morning when he'd been scrolling through his phone while he ate the breakfast he'd cooked at Donetta's, he hadn't seen any weather alerts. "This is crazy," he said as he watched the big flakes fall. The top of his rental car was already covered.

Lauren nodded. "Tell me about it. I woke up about ten minutes ago, turned on the TV, and it was all over the news. This winter storm came from out of nowhere, without any warning, and now it's like an emergency."

The first thing Phillip thought about was Donetta. He rushed over to his phone, but when he tried to turn it on, it remained black. His battery was dead. He rushed over to his suitcase and searched for his charger.

"What are you looking for?" Lauren asked.

"My cell phone charger. I can't find it. Damn it! Hey, let me use yours."

Lauren looked at his phone. "My charger won't do you any good unless you turn that Apple into an Android."

"Damn, and Mom has an Android, too."

"If you know the number, you can still use my phone."

Phillip couldn't remember Donetta's cell number and the number on her business card was for her salon. He had no way of contacting her. He looked back out the window at the big flakes that kept falling in a steady stream. "How much snow are they calling for?"

"At least a half foot before nightfall. Some areas are gonna get up to ten inches," Lauren said with delight. "The forecasters are saying we'll have about nine inches by morning."

"I've gotta get going before I get stuck here."

Lauren craned her neck. "Where're you going in this weather?"

"To see a friend." Phillip walked over to the corner, grabbed his dead phone, and put it in his bag. He went into the bathroom and tossed his toiletries back into his leather case, added them to his bag, and headed downstairs with Lauren following him.

"Mom's gonna flip. She's not letting you out of this house in the middle of a snowstorm," Lauren balked.

"Let me out the house? Are you forgetting that I'm a grown man?"

His sister pursed her lips. "Not if you ask Charlene Harris. We're both babies in her eyes."

Phillip walked down the hall and peeked into the study, but his mother wasn't there. Then he went to the family room, and she wasn't there, either. When he walked past the kitchen, he was surprised that he didn't smell food cooking, so he knew there was only one other place she could still be. He walked to her bedroom and there she was, sound asleep. He knew this was very unlike his mother. She was the type of person who was always full of energy and on the go. But ever since he'd come home yesterday, all she'd done was sleep, and he hoped she hadn't had anything else to drink today. He thought about waking her up, but then he changed his mind because he didn't have time to debate with her whether it was a good idea for him to be on the road in the middle of a snowstorm.

Phillip walked back down the hall to where he'd left Lauren standing near his bag. "When Mom wakes up, tell her I'll call her later."

"Okay." She smirked and shook her head. "I hope she's worth it."

"What?"

"Whoever the woman is that you're about to risk your life to go see. I hope she's worth it. She must be a bad chick to make a man go through a snowstorm for her."

Phillip smiled. "Yeah, she is."

Chapter 24

CHARLENE

Charlene stretched her arms and yawned as she slowly opened her eyes. She felt tired, from the top of her head to the bottom of her feet, and even though she'd slept the better part of the day away, she still didn't feel rested.

Charlene shook her head as she thought about the events that had shaped her day to this point. She'd started her morning by listening to Leslie Sachs's live interview, which had left her with even more questions about what Leslie and Vivana were really up to. Then she'd followed that headache by having a big blowout with her daughter this afternoon over Lauren's decision to drop out of medical school. And if that hadn't been enough, she'd topped things off with a nerve-bending conversation with her son, who'd brought Johnny Mayfield's name into the mix.

Charlene had felt so defeated that all she'd wanted to do was sleep and forget about the troubles facing her. She'd gone to her bedroom, reached into her nightstand drawer, and pulled out a bottle of Lunesta that her doctor had prescribed for her several months ago when she'd been battling insomnia. The sleep aid was fast-acting and powerful, so she'd known that she had to be careful. She'd used a pill splitter to cut it before taking only half of a dose. The medicine had done its job, giving her the rest she'd needed to calm her anxiety, if only for a few stolen hours.

Charlene stood up, stretched again, and tied her bathrobe around her waist. She rubbed her stomach, realizing she hadn't eaten since lunchtime yesterday. "I'm starving. I need to eat something before I get sick."

She slipped her feet into her bright red velveteen bedroom shoes and shuffled down the hall. But she came to an abrupt stop at the sight she saw when she reached the edge of her kitchen. Although it was beginning to get dark outside, she could see that snow was falling. She moved faster as she walked to the door leading out to her back deck and was shocked to see what looked like over a half foot of snow covering her deck chairs and table. "Lauren, Phillip!" she called out in an excited voice. "Get down here, it's snowing!" She turned and walked to the end of the hall that led to the stairs and called out to them again.

Charlene didn't wait for her children to come downstairs; instead she rushed into the family room and opened the blinds so she could see the beautiful snow falling outside. "This is unbelievable!" she said as she watched the fluffy white flakes descend from the sky. She turned on the TV and took a seat on the couch, sitting in rapt attention as she listened to the announcer give updates about the unexpected snowstorm that had roared through most of the southern states that afternoon, bringing travel and holiday activities to a halt. It was an emergency situation because none of the weather models had forecasted the storm, which was supposed to dump close to a foot of snow in some areas by early morning. As it stood, Amber would get at least nine inches of the white stuff, if not more.

Charlene looked up when she saw Lauren enter the room. "Can you believe this?" she asked her daughter. "I knew it was cloudy outside when I lay down for my nap earlier this afternoon, but I had no idea we'd get snow. Amber hardly ever gets snow, and certainly not this early in the season."

"I know," Lauren replied. "If I'd known I'd get snowed in and stuck in the house, I would've stayed in Baltimore."

Charlene stared into her daughter's eyes, which were laced with unmistakable frustration and disappointment at the fact that she was being forced to stay home. The exhilaration Charlene had felt just moments ago was snuffed out by Lauren's comment. *What have I done to make her resent me so much?* she wondered.

There had been a time, not too long ago, when Lauren had considered Charlene her best friend. But now Charlene barely recognized her baby girl, either physically or emotionally. The neatly dressed, levelheaded, respectful, high-achieving daughter she'd raised had been replaced by a disheveled, irrational, rude dropout with an enormous chip on her shoulder. And despite Lauren's claims of being fine, Charlene knew there was something very wrong with her, and she planned to get to the bottom of it.

"Lauren, you've made it clear that you don't want

to be here, yet a few hours ago you said you wanted to move back here because you'd dropped out of school. Which is it?"

"I didn't drop out, I withdrew," Lauren snapped.

"Same thing," Charlene snapped back at her. "If you wanted to move back here, then why are you saying that you wish you'd stayed in Baltimore?"

Lauren was silent, and her lack of a sarcastic comeback let Charlene know that she'd struck a nerve in her rebellious daughter. "Nothing you've said has made any sense to me. I want to understand you, really I do. But it's hard to talk to you because you have your guard up, as if you have to protect yourself from me. Baby, I'm your mother, and all I want to do is help you."

Suddenly, Lauren broke into tears. "I'm pregnant."

Charlene tilted her head in confusion. She thought she just heard her daughter say she was pregnant, but Lauren was sobbing so hard that Charlene wasn't sure. "What did you say?"

"I'm pregnant, Mom. That's why I withdrew from my classes and why I wanted to come home. I lied when I said Hakeem wanted me to stay in Baltimore with him, and honestly, he's the one who suggested I come back home because he made it clear that he doesn't want me or our baby in his life."

Lauren stood in the middle of the family room and cried as if she'd fallen off her bike and skinned her knee. Charlene's heart ached for her, and she wished she could make everything better with a kiss and freshly baked cookies the way she used to when Lauren was a little girl. But those days were long gone, and Charlene knew she had to stand in the reality that was right in front of her. Lauren was a grown woman who was about to walk down a rocky road, and she needed a mother's strength, love, and guidance to help her along the path.

"How far along are you?" Charlene asked.

"Three months."

Although Lauren was no longer a small child, she would always be Charlene's baby girl. Charlene rose from where was sitting and walked over to her daughter, wrapped her in her arms, and rocked her back and forth. "It's gonna be all right, baby. Everything's gonna be all right."

Charlene sat across from Lauren at the breakfast table as they sipped from their second cups of double hot chocolate that Charlene had made from a recipe her mother had handed down to her. She glanced out the window, noticing that the wind had picked up, causing the heavy snow that was falling to completely blanket everything in sight. For a brief moment, the picturesque scene made her forget about all her troubles because everything seemed so perfect. She was sitting inside her beautiful home, safe and warm, sharing quality time with her daughter during the holidays. But unfortunately, that surface portrait belied the complications bubbling underneath.

Charlene had spent the last hour listening to her daughter tell her the truth about what had been the real cause for her steady decline over the last two years. And just as Charlene had suspected, all roads led back to the terrible revelation when Lauren discovered she'd been dating her half brother. But the part that Charlene had been in the dark about and was shocked to learn was the truth behind why Lauren had brought the boy home in the first place. She'd been pregnant then, too.

When she'd met Jeffery, a handsome young man in one of her premed classes, he'd been her first real boyfriend and eventually, her first sexual experience. She'd been in love and so had he. One night they slipped up, losing themselves in the heat of passion, and two months later she learned she was pregnant.

Lauren and Jeffery had every intention of keeping the baby, getting married, and both continuing on with medical school while they juggled raising their child. But their youthful, idealistic dreams were vanquished when she'd brought him home to meet her family. After the "who are your people?" quiz, the truth was revealed, a young love was shattered, a decades-old marriage was destroyed, and Lauren's downward spiral had begun.

"After we returned to school, Jeffery and I talked and decided it was best that I had an abortion," Lauren said in a solemn voice. "He told me he would be by my side, but on the morning of the procedure he was nowhere to be found. A friend of mine ended up driving me to the clinic and then took me back to my dorm. I tried calling Jeffery but he wouldn't pick up his phone, and two weeks later I found out that he'd transferred to Auburn. I haven't heard from him since."

"Lauren, I wish you had come to me," Charlene said as she reached for her daughter's hand. "You shouldn't have gone through that alone. I would've helped you, baby."

A tear fell from Lauren's eye. "I was so embarrassed and ashamed, and I didn't know what to do. It's one thing to fall for the wrong guy, but to fall for your own brother, and then get pregnant by him?"

"Baby, nothing that happened was your fault. There's no way you could've known . . . that's on your father."

Lauren nodded. "I know, and I'll never forgive Dad for that. But what was my fault was the fact that I was careless and ended up pregnant." She paused and took another sip of her hot chocolate. She looked at her mother as her voice began to tremble. "You'd think I would've learned about how to pick the right guy and protect myself. But I fell for a loser, and now I'm pregnant—again. I know you're disappointed in me, and so am I."

Charlene wanted to break down and cry because she hated hearing the pain in Lauren's voice, but she knew that Lauren needed a steady hand to guide her fragile heart. "I'll always be proud of you," Charlene said. "I'm proud of you right now, in this moment, because even though you've made some mistakes— which we all do—you're going to move forward and do great things. You're still young and you have your whole life in front of you. Living here with me will cut your expenses, and once you have the baby, next fall you can enroll in med school at the University of Alabama, and life will keep on moving right along."

"You make it sound so easy."

Charlene shook her head. "Baby, don't mistake my optimism for fantasy. It won't be a walk in the park, but it also won't be as bad as you think. You've got support, a roof over your head, and people who love you. You and my grandchild are going to be just fine."

A long moment passed between them. They both looked out the window, each thinking about a future that was full of uncertainty. Finally, Lauren spoke.

"I love you, Mom."

Charlene smiled. "I love you, too, baby."

"And I'm really loving this double hot chocolate," Lauren said as she took another sip. "If I'm not careful, I'll be working on my third cup."

"There's more on the stove, so help yourself. I made a huge pot because I thought your brother would be down here by now. He loves my hot chocolate almost as much as you do."

Lauren shook her head. "Phillip's not here."

"What?"

"He's not here."

"Where is he?"

"He left a couple of hours ago while you were still asleep. I told him not to go out in the middle of a snowstorm, but he was determined."

"Where did he go?"

Lauren pursed her lips. "Where do you think?"

"I don't know, that's why I'm asking you." But in all truth, Charlene knew exactly where her hot-blooded, woman-chasing son was. "He went to see a woman, didn't he?"

"You know it."

Charlene looked out the window, picked up her phone, and dialed Phillip's number.

"His cell is dead. He didn't have his charger, and because he has an iPhone he couldn't use your charger or mine."

Charlene shook her head. "I can't believe that boy got behind the wheel in the middle of the worst snowstorm the Southeast has seen in over fifty years."

"Some men have done a lot worse."

"But he has no means of communication," Charlene said with frustration. "It's dark outside, what if his car gets stuck and he's stranded . . . risking his life just to see a woman?"

"Like I told him, she must be one bad chick."

Charlene looked out the window and prayed that her son was all right.

Chapter 25

DONETTA

When Donetta left Phillip the first message, she hadn't been too concerned that her call had gone straight to voice mail. She'd known that he'd been in the middle of some sort of family drama when they'd briefly spoken earlier, so she'd kept her message short and simple, asking him to call her when he got a moment. But after several hours went by and she still hadn't heard from him, she'd begun to worry. She left him another message, this time more detailed, letting him know she was worried and that she hoped everything with him and his family was okay. She knew that when he listened to the message he would hear the desperation in her voice, because despite trying to hide it, that was exactly how she'd felt, desperate and vulnerable. She longed to hear from him and be with him. The feeling had both excited and frightened her.

Geneva had texted her an hour ago to see how her conversation with Phillip had gone.

Geneva: Hey girl, how did it go? Is everything all right?

Donetta: Left him a message but haven't heard back ☹. Will let you know when I do.

Geneva: Okay, don't worry, everything will work out. I'm praying for you.

Donetta was glad she had Geneva in her corner, because no matter what Phillip's reaction might be, Donetta knew that her best friend would be there to either rejoice with her or wipe her tears.

She'd remained perched by her phone and her television all afternoon, watching news coverage of the unexpected record snowfall hitting Amber, and anticipating Phillip's call. Now it was dark outside, and she finally decided to stop moping because it wouldn't make Phillip dial her number any sooner. "I need to cheer myself up," she'd said, "and I need to turn lemons into a lemonade martini." She walked into her kitchen, pulled a lemon from her crisper and vodka from her wine refrigerator, and within a few minutes, she was sipping a delicious drink.

She was off from work for the next six days, which meant she could relax. She had a refrigerator and a pantry full of food, which meant she could eat good meals. And she had a huge supply of firewood, which meant she was going to be nice and cozy whether it was Phillip or her fireplace keeping her warm. She walked back to her living room and looked around. She needed something to do to occupy her mind and time. "This is a perfect time to pamper myself."

Donetta took a long, hot shower, washed her hair, and gave herself a facial that made her glow with radiance. She smoothed sweetly scented body butter over her skin, layered it with one of her Victoria's Secret perfume mists, and then slipped on a brightly colored silk negligee and matching robe. "I might not have a man who I can look good for, but I can damn sure look good for myself," she said as she peered into the mirror and applied her cocoa-tinted lip gloss to her perfect pout. She ran her hands through her wavy, freshly air-dried hair, looked into the mirror again, and blew herself a kiss. "Girl, you look fabulous, you know that?"

Donetta walked into her kitchen and started taking out ingredients to make a savory pot roast with potatoes, carrots, and onions. After she finished prepping the dish, she put it in the oven to let it slow-roast, and then took out a pack of noodles to boil once the roast was close to being done. She opened a bottle of red wine, poured herself a glass, and went into her living room to relax in front of her cozy fireplace.

She was about to switch the channel on her TV from the weather to HGTV, when her doorbell rang. "Who in the world could that be?"

Donetta looked through her living room window and didn't see a car out front that would indicate she had a visitor. As a matter of fact, her street was blanketed with snow from one end to the other and there wasn't a vehicle in sight, save for a few of her neighbors' who'd opted to leave their cars parked in their driveways, rather than their garages. But as she looked closer, with the help of the streetlights, she saw a set of tracks through her front yard leading up to her door. She thought it must be one of her neighbors stopping by to either check on her or borrow some food staples to help them while they were snowed in.

Donetta walked to her door, looked through the peephole, and couldn't believe her eyes. She opened her front door so quickly she nearly knocked herself over. "Phillip, what are you doing here?"

"It's nice to see you, too," he said as he panted and huffed. "Can I come in?"

Donetta moved to the side and let him in, along with a rush of arctic-like air. His jeans were soaked from the waist down, and his shoes were covered in snow. He removed the bag he'd strapped across his body and let it fall to the floor. He was shivering, and his teeth were chattering.

"How did you get here?" Donetta asked. "I've been watching the news and they said the roads are impassable."

Phillip peeled out of his coat and let it fall to the floor alongside his bag. "Yeah, they're right. I had to leave my car parked off the exit leading to your neighborhood."

Donetta blinked. "That's about two miles away."

"Tell me about it. It's a good thing I work out every day, because it was a rough walk getting here. Some of the snow drifts were taller than me, and I fell in one. It was hell crawling out of that thing, that's why I'm wet from head to toe."

"Oh no. Come on, you need to get warmed up."

Donetta and Phillip walked into her living room and stood in front of her fireplace.

"You have no idea how good this feels," Phillip said. "It took me over an hour to get here from the time I left my car. For a minute I thought I was in real trouble because it's freezing and the wind and heavy snow made it hard to see. But I knew if I could make it here before it got completely dark, I'd be okay."

Donetta nodded. She was glad he'd made it to her house safely, but she wanted to know what had happened to him earlier. "Why didn't you call me? I left you two messages."

"I'm sorry, Donetta." He took a few steps, moving closer to her, and reached for her hand. "I took a nap and slept longer than I thought I would."

"Your hands feel like ice cubes," she said with gentle concern. "You're freezing."

He squeezed her palm. "I'm sure your touch will warm me up in no time."

She blushed hard and shook her head. "You're a smooth talker."

"I'm an honest man. You bring out the best in me."

His sexy voice and endearing words made her smile. "Okay, Mr. Honesty. Tell me why you didn't call me back after your nap."

"By the time I woke up five inches had already fallen. I tried to call you, but my battery had died and I forgot to pack my phone charger. My mom and sister have Androids, so there was no way for me to charge my phone. I would've called you from my sister's phone, but I couldn't remember your cell number."

Donetta's voice became soft with relief. "Oh."

"You didn't think I was avoiding you on purpose, did you?"

"I didn't know what to think. I left you two messages, and each time my call went straight to voice mail, so . . ."

Phillip pulled her close and wrapped his arms

around her waist. He held her tightly and gently kissed her lips. "I walked through a snowstorm to get to you. That should tell you all you need to know."

Donetta enjoyed the way his cool lips felt pressed against her warm ones. After they shared a long, sensual kiss she looked into his eyes. "I missed you," she whispered.

"I missed you, too." Phillip inhaled deeply. "You smell good." He let his eyes roam her body, and he smiled. "Look at you, snowed in and looking all sexy." He touched her hair, letting his thick fingers glide across her silky waves. "I like your hair like this."

"Thanks, I washed it."

His eyes landed on the glass of wine sitting on a crystal-studded coaster atop the coffee table. "I can see you've been having a good afternoon."

"I figured since I was going to be alone, I might as well make the most of my evening." She paused for a moment, then looked into his eyes again. "I treat myself well, Phillip, and I know how to have a good time all by myself. I've learned that I'm the only one who's gonna take care of me."

"It doesn't have to be that way, you know?"

"What do you mean?"

"Don't you think it would be nice to have a companion, a mate . . . um, maybe even a husband, to help take care of you?"

Donetta's heart started beating fast. *Husband* was the only word that rang in her ears. Although she'd tried to remain hopeful over the years, one bad relationship after another had soured her faith on finding love, let alone a husband. Now here it was, a handsome man standing in front of her had just hinted of a commitment—which would've been a dream come true, except for the larger-than-life detail that Phillip didn't know about her background. Donetta wondered if he would still be as interested once he found out everything there was to know about who she really was.

"Are you okay?" Phillip asked, drawing her even closer to him.

"Yes, I'm fine."

"You don't sound convincing. We haven't known each other long, but I already know you well enough to see that you're not. What's wrong, baby?"

She wanted to melt when he called her that. So many things had gone wrong in her life, but this whirlwind romance felt right, and for now she was determined to enjoy every second of it. So instead of fretting and stressing, she decided to live in the moment that was right in front of her. "You're right. I have something on my mind that I need to tell you."

"I'm listening."

"I think you need to get out of those wet clothes and let me take care of you first."

"Now you're talking."

Phillip followed Donetta into her bedroom and undressed while she turned the bronze-colored faucet on her soaker tub. She poured a combination of fragrant sea salts, vanilla-scented bath foam, eucalyptus Epsom salt, and lavender bath oil under the running water. The combination of scents were light, with a hint of musky amber that smelled deliciously inviting. While the water continued to run, Donetta lit several pillar candles scattered throughout the room, and the end result was a warm, sensuous spa-like retreat that was fit for a photo spread in any home décor magazine.

Phillip walked into the bathroom wearing nothing but a smile, and Donetta had to literally contain herself. *Damn, this man is fine!* She looked at Phillip's sculpted body and thought his broad chest, well-defined abs, muscular arms, and toned legs were a delight to her eyes. His Adonis-like body was complemented by his ruggedly handsome face, which made his outside package even more alluring. But as Donetta watched him walk into the room with a casual air, she knew that it was what lay inside Phillip that made him so attractive, and in fact, beautiful. He was unpretentious, without an arrogant bone in his body. He was open and honest, making it easy to place her trust in him. He was gentle and kind with a caring spirit. And he was intelligent, with a desire to learn new things. Donetta smiled inside when she thought about how good she felt in this moment.

"Wow," Phillip said. He was standing in glorious nakedness with his legs spread hips-width apart and his long arms dangling by his side. He looked around the room, taking in the décor, candles, and scent. "You really know how to decorate and set a mood."

"Thank you. It's one of my passions."

"I can see. This is like walking into a spa. Are you going to soak in those bubbles while I shower?"

Donetta shook her head. "No, I took a long, hot shower before you got here. These suds are for you."

"Me? I haven't taken a bubble bath since I was ten."

"Trust me, once you sink down into this tub, you won't want to come out."

Phillip walked over to Donetta and kissed her on her forehead. "Thanks, baby."

She watched him as he carefully lifted one leg into the tub and then the other. Slowly, he eased his body down, submerging himself in the white bubbles. When he closed his eyes, leaned back, and let out a relaxing groan, Donetta knew he was enjoying himself. "I'll be right back," she said.

When she returned, she was carrying two glasses in one hand and a bottle of wine in the other. She poured Phillip a glass and handed it to him. "Here, I think you'll like this."

Phillip reached for the glass and took a sip. "Thanks, this is good, and this bubble bath is incredible." He placed his glass on the edge of the large tub and reclined again. "What did you put in the water?"

"It's my secret potion."

"This is well worth a two-mile walk in the snow. If I'd known bubble baths felt this good, I would've been taking them a long time ago."

Donetta smiled. "I've loved taking bubble baths since I was a small child. They're so pampering and relaxing. A couple of years ago I was in Atlanta for a hair convention, and on my last night in town I decided to treat myself. I checked into the Ritz-Carlton and ordered champagne and room service. I saw that they had a bath butler service so I ordered it. Let me tell you, that changed my world. It was the most luxurious, soothing bath I'd ever had. I felt like a queen after I got out of that tub. I asked the lady who drew my bath to tell me exactly what she put in it, and I've been luxuriating in style ever since."

"Donetta, this is the most relaxed I've felt in a long time." Phillip opened his eyes and smiled. "Thank you for this."

"It's the least I can do for someone who walked through a snowstorm for me." She winked and walked over to the small slipper chair beside the tub and took a seat. She had to sit carefully because she was still sore.

"You could've stayed in the comfort of your home with your family, but instead you braved the weather and risked your life on the dangerous roads, just to see me. Why?"

"I was thinking the same thing while I was climbing out of that damn snow drift," Phillip said with a laugh as Donetta joined him. He looked at her, and his voice became low and serious. "All I could think about was how much I wanted to see you, to just be in your presence."

Donetta felt as though she was half-dreaming. The self-help books she'd read, and even a few customers she knew, had said that this kind of thing was possible—that you could meet someone and instantly know they were the one. While she couldn't say that what she now felt for Phillip had been instant, what she absolutely knew was that this was the first time in her life that she'd felt genuinely respected and cared for by a man. As Donetta stared back into Phillip's deep brown eyes, her heart couldn't deny that what she was feeling was love.

Donetta and Phillip talked by wine and candlelight, laughing and sharing more insights into each other's lives. They discussed their likes and dislikes, and she discovered they had more in common than she'd initially thought. She could tell that Phillip was surprised when she told him that she liked sports, and that she could name all the professional teams along with their stats. And she was surprised when she learned that he was a fan of HGTV, and even liked some of the same shows that she did. Then they moved on to more serious subjects, like social issues, and what they wanted for their future, especially in a relationship. This was when Donetta knew she needed to reiterate her point from last night and remind him about what she wanted, flat-out. Even though he'd hinted about a relationship, she wanted to make her position unequivocally clear, and that if he didn't want the same thing, she wouldn't waste her time or his. "I'd like to get married someday," she said plainly.

"Does 'someday' mean soon, as in 'my biological clock is ticking and I need a husband and a baby'? Or 'someday' as in 'when the right man comes along we'll take our time and see how it goes'?"

Donetta shifted a bit in her seat at the sound of ticking clocks and babies, neither of which applied to her biological makeup, so she addressed what she felt comfortable saying. "'Someday' means when I find the man I want to spend the rest of my days with, and he feels the same about me. But let me be clear, once that happens, there's no way in hell I intend to wait till infinity with the promise of marriage."

Phillip raised his brow. "How long is too long? Would you give him an ultimatum if he didn't propose to you on the timeline you have in mind?"

"An ultimatum implies a demand, and I'd never want someone to make a commitment to me unless they wanted to of their own free will."

"Ahh, free will rears its head again. That's big with you."

She nodded. "It sure is. It's something we exercise every day, whether we know it or not. Everything is in our power to either do, or not do. At this point in my life, I know what I want, and I don't believe in wasting time. Patience is a virtue, but so is discernment."

"Discernment of knowing how long is too long?" Phillip questioned.

"I don't want to get hung up on time, but yes.

When you apply the wisdom of your intuition to discover what is essential and true, with contemplative
vigilance, you gain clarity of the soul."

"Damn, that's deep."

"It should be, I got it off the Internet."

They shared a long hearty laugh. Donetta loved
how easy it was to talk about sensitive subjects with
Phillip, who didn't judge or debate. He questioned
what he didn't know, which showed his willingness to
learn, and he stood firm in what he believed, which
demonstrated his integrity. She was becoming more
and more confident that once she told him her full
story, he would be accepting.

"I'd like to get married someday, too," Phillip said.
"And I pretty much agree with everything you said
about when the right person comes along."

Donetta couldn't hide the smile that had formed
deep in her insides and had spread to her lips. "Great
minds think alike."

"I definitely want kids," Phillip said. "I'd like the
chance to be a better father to my child than mine was
to me."

"I can't have children," Donetta said quietly. There
was a brief pause filled with silence that hovered over
them.

Phillip cleared his throat. "Does it have anything
to do with your bleeding this morning?"

"Yes, it does . . . and it's, um, complicated."

She could tell that Phillip was thinking, and she
was scared to ask him what was on his mind. He leaned
forward, drank the last sip of his wine, and spoke.
"There are lots of children on adoption lists who need
loving homes. Family doesn't mean blood, it means

love, and as long as I have a partner I can build love with, I'm cool."

"So it doesn't matter to you if you don't plant your biological seed?"

"What matters to me is that I can raise a son or daughter, maybe both, with love. I don't even speak to my biological father, and I'm closer to my college mentor than I've ever been to the man I'm connected to only through DNA. So no, it's not a big deal."

Donetta noticed that every time Phillip spoke of his father, it was with disdain, and she wondered what kind of terrible thing the man had done to make Phillip dislike him so much. Unlike him, she hadn't grown up with her parents because they'd both abandoned her when she was a child, and she'd never been close enough to either of them to feel like or dislike. She made a mental note that she wanted to talk more with Phillip about his family. As a matter of fact, she just realized that she knew what he did for a living, where he lived, and what his favorite color was, but she didn't even know his last name. She was about to ask when he leaned forward in the tub and stood up.

"This bath has been great, but the water's getting cold." He reached for the towel Donetta had draped on the side of the tub. "Let's continue this conversation over that delicious-smelling roast that's been calling my name since I walked through the door."

Chapter 26

PHILLIP

Phillip was full, not only from the fork-tender, perfectly seasoned pot roast and noodles that Donetta had cooked and he'd eagerly devoured, but from the satisfying knowledge of realizing that he'd somehow found "the one" without even looking for her.

As he sat next to Donetta at her dining room table, which was decorated with cream-colored candles, elegant plates, and shiny stemware, he once again thought about his mother's words, and how she'd talked about having someone to come home to. He knew that coming home to a beautiful, independent, kindhearted woman who could cook, decorate a house into a home, and completely satisfy him in bed, was something he now desired. He'd had a lot of women over the years, and he'd sown more oats than Quaker. And now he was ready to take everything in his life to another level.

"This meal was delicious," Phillip said. "Who taught you how to cook like this?"

"Thank you. My grandmother used let me help her in the kitchen, and because I love to eat, I learned real fast about what to do to make food taste good."

"Is there anything you can't do well?"

Donetta put her hand to her head, as if she was in deep thought. "The list is way too long to name."

"I find that hard to believe."

"Flattery will get you anything you want from me." She laughed and set her cloth napkin on the table. "I really am glad you enjoyed your meal, and I'm especially glad that you're here."

"Me too."

"I hope you won't get sick of me, because from the looks of it, you're gonna be here awhile."

Phillip looked out of the dining room window at the snow that was still falling just as heavily as it had been when he'd been walking in it. "Let's turn on the news and see what they're saying now."

They sat close together on her couch, with his arm wrapped around her shoulder, as they listened to the weather announcer tell them of the reports of ten inches in some areas of Amber, with snow drifts of up to several feet. His thoughts drew his mind to his mother, and the fact that he needed to call her because she was probably worried about him. "I need to call my mother and let her know I didn't end up in a ditch or one of those snowdrifts," he said.

"Your phone should be charged by now."

Phillip stood and walked over to the accent table where his phone had been charging since shortly after he'd arrived. When he pressed the button to bring his screen to life it remained black. He plugged it back in again, but nothing happened. "My phone's still dead."

Donetta walked over to where he was standing. "Let me take a look and see what's wrong." She jiggled the cord and then plugged it in again, just as Phillip had done. But the screen was still black, and each time she pushed the On button nothing happened.

"There must be something wrong with your charger." He unplugged and then plugged it in again, but the result was the same.

"I haven't used it in ages," Donetta said, "because after I switched from Apple to Android, I really had no need to."

"Can I use your phone?"

"Sure." Donetta walked over to the coffee table and handed it to him.

"Thanks." Phillip dialed his mother's cell phone and watched Donetta walk over to the fireplace. She lifted two logs—one at a time—and gently placed them in the fire. He was aroused by the visual image of her smooth, mocha-colored skin draped in brightly colored lingerie. She'd just made a manual task look sexy, and it convinced him that despite her earlier claim, there was nothing she didn't do well. He continued to watch her, enjoying the way her body swayed as she stoked the fire with the poker. He was lost in the moment, until he heard his mother's voice on the other end.

"Hello?"

"Hey, Mom, it's me." He walked over to the couch and took a seat because he knew he might be in for a mild interrogation.

"Phillip?"

"I've only been gone a few hours and already you've forgotten my voice," he teased. "Of course it's me."

"Well, I wasn't sure. The caller ID said unavailable, and I usually don't bother answering those calls because most of the time it's a telemarketer. But because your sister told me about your phone battery, and that you decided to risk your life for . . . um, well, I just had a feeling it might be you."

Phillip knew she'd caught herself just shy of saying he was out chasing a piece of ass, but her genteel manners would never allow her to mouth something so bold. But even though she'd exercised her typical diplomacy, he could tell by his mother's tone that she wasn't pleased. "Yeah, I didn't pack my charger. I'm at my friend's house and I'm using her phone." He looked over at Donetta, who was now straightening the magazines in the basket next to the couch. He could tell she was trying to appear as if she wasn't listening, but he knew she was taking in every syllable he uttered.

"Your friend has a blocked number?"

"I guess so."

"Hmmmm."

He shifted in his seat. "You were asleep when I left, otherwise I would've let you know I was going out."

"You could've woken me up, Phillip."

"You had a rough day yesterday and a rough night. Plus after the blowup this afternoon, I figured you needed your sleep. How are you feeling?"

She sighed. "I'm better now that I know you're alive."

"Yes, Mom. I'm fine. It's just snow."

"Just snow?" she balked. "Have you been watching the news?"

"I've been out in it."

"Then you know it's the worst snowstorm we've had in fifty years. They've been reporting accidents all afternoon. I didn't know if you'd been injured. I've been worried sick."

"No need to worry, I'm fine."

"Where are you, son?"

He looked over at Donetta, who had now taken a seat on the opposite end of the couch and was thumbing through an *Essence* magazine. "I told you, I'm at my friend's house. We just finished dinner and it was delicious. She can throw down." He knew for sure that she was listening because she smiled.

"Umm-hmm . . . I bet she can."

"So, you guys are okay?"

"We're fine. Your sister's upstairs in the shower, and I'm in the kitchen taking out some of the food you bought last night so I can start cooking our Thanksgiving meal."

"That's right, tomorrow's Turkey Day."

"Sure is. We'll be here celebrating and you'll be with whomever you're with, wherever you are. Are you even in town?"

"Yes, I'm in Amber, Mom."

"I'm not trying to get in your business, I just want to make sure you're all right."

"I'm better than all right. I'm great." He winked at Donetta, and she smiled again.

"I guess you'll be spending the holiday with her?" his mother asked, even though the answer was obvious.

"Looks like it." Phillip looked out the living room

window at the snow that was continuing to fall. "I barely got here when there was about seven or eight inches on the ground, and now that there's nearly a foot out there, I doubt if I'll be able to get out for at least another day or two."

She sighed again. "Well, okay. As long as you're safe, and as you said, you're great, that's all that matters."

"I'll call you tomorrow to check in on you guys. You know, I have to make sure that you and that bullheaded sister of mine are all right. By the way, how is she?"

His mother's sigh grew heavier. "It's a long story. I'll tell you when you come home."

"Mom, what's wrong?" Phillip leaned forward to the edge of the couch and rubbed his chin. His mother's voice sounded painfully distressed, and he knew whatever was going on couldn't be good. He could see that Donetta felt the same thing because she'd stopped pretending to read her magazine and was staring at him.

"I'll tell you when you come home," his mother said again. "It's too much to get into over the phone."

"You can't say something like that and then not tell me. If she's in trouble or something has happened, I need to know."

"Lauren's pregnant. That's why she dropped out of school."

Phillip closed his eyes and shook his head. "Is that clown she mentioned the father?"

"Yes, but they're not together anymore."

"When did this happen? This afternoon she said he was the only one who understood her."

"She lied. The short part of this long story is that once he found out she was pregnant, he told her she was on her own. But she's not, and she and I have already started planning what her next move is going to be."

Phillip exhaled deeply. He knew that the road Lauren was getting ready to travel wouldn't be easy, but if anyone could take a bad situation and turn it into something good, it was his mother, and for that reason he felt a little relief.

"Phillip, are you still there?" his mother asked.

"Yeah, I'm here."

"Are you okay?"

"Yeah, I'm okay, just thinking."

"That's all I've been doing all evening. Like I said, we'll talk more about it when you come home."

"Definitely."

"Speaking of you coming home, am I going to get a chance to meet this one?"

This one! His mother's words stung, but Phillip knew she was well within her rights to phrase her question the way she did. He looked over at Donetta and smiled, knowing she wasn't *this one*, she was "the one." She was the first woman he wasn't skeptical about introducing to his mother, and, in fact, he was excited about it because he knew they'd hit it off. "I'm not sure. The weather's going to make it a challenge. But if not now, definitely in the near future."

"Really?"

"Yes, really," he said with confidence.

"I have so many questions. But we'll table them until I see you."

"Okay. Love you, Mom, and I'll call you tomorrow."

After Phillip hung up, he set Donetta's phone on the coffee table and let out a deep breath.

"I couldn't help but hear," Donetta said. "Is your sister okay?"

"She's pregnant."

"I guess that's not a good thing, huh?"

Phillip turned to her. "She dropped out of school, and the father of her baby dumped her."

Donetta shook her head. "Wow, I'm sorry to hear that."

"My mom's putting up a strong face, but I know she's so disappointed. My sister had a full scholarship to med school, and now it's down the drain, not to mention she's got to face being a single parent."

"Your sister was in med school?"

Phillip nodded. "Johns Hopkins." He looked into Donetta's eyes and knew something was wrong. "Are you okay?"

Donetta put her hand to her mouth. "Is your sister's name Lauren?"

"Yes, how did you know that?" Now Phillip looked just as startled as Donetta was. "Do you know my sister?"

"No, but I think I know your mother." Slowly, she set her magazine on the table and swallowed hard. "Is your mom Councilwoman Harris?"

Phillip nodded. "Yes, I don't advertise it because when people find out, they always want me to ask her for favors for one thing or another."

"Sweet baby Jesus in heaven. I can't believe this! I just can't believe this!"

"You're starting to make me nervous," Phillip said with concern. "What's the deal between you and my mom?"

Donetta rose from the couch and started pacing back and forth in front of the fireplace. "I can't believe

I didn't put two and two together before now. You live in DC, you're a lawyer, you obviously come from money, and you're home for the holidays. Why didn't I realize who you were before now?"

Phillip stood to his feet and walked over to Donetta. He reached for her hand, but she pulled away and it jarred him. "Who I am is obviously a problem for you, so tell me why—"

"It's not who you are, it's who I am . . . or at least, who I used to be."

"What are you talking about?"

She took a deep breath. "Let's have a seat. We need to talk."

Chapter 27

GENEVA

Geneva's day had started off with a nightmare before the crack of dawn, followed by a fistfight between her husband and his brother shortly after breakfast, which ushered in a stressful afternoon because not only had it started snowing, Joe had told his parents he was thinking about pressing assault charges against Samuel. Herbert and Sarah had spent over an hour on the phone trying to convince their oldest son not to press charges against his little brother. And although that minor catastrophe had been averted, it had been stressful nonetheless.

Now it was nighttime, and the house was calm. Geneva had just put Gabrielle down ten minutes ago, and her in-laws had been in bed for an hour. Samuel was taking a shower, preparing to end his day, and

Geneva was in the kitchen. Although all she wanted to do was go upstairs, lie down in her bed, and sleep through the holiday, she knew she couldn't do that, and, if anything, she needed to do just the opposite. Her happy family holiday had morphed into antics fit for reality TV, and Geneva knew she needed to turn things around. So she began to do the one thing she knew was guaranteed to uplift everyone: She began to cook.

She knew she had to work fast, while they still had electricity. The wicked snowstorm that had snuck up on the area had not only caused dozens of accidents in Amber and left thousands of holiday travelers stranded in airports throughout the Southeast, it had left entire neighborhoods dark from widespread power outages. As it stood, the lights in Geneva's kitchen had been flickering on and off for the last thirty minutes and she knew she couldn't afford to waste time because she might find herself in the dark, too.

Geneva worked quickly as she cleaned and chopped a sink full of collard greens, washed and peeled a bag of sweet potatoes, and put the perfectly brined, twenty-pound turkey in the oven. She was cracking the eggs to make her specialty five-flavor pound cake when she heard Samuel enter the kitchen.

"It smells delicious in here," Samuel said as he walked up Geneva, stood behind her, and wrapped his arms around her waist. "Can I lick the bowl once you finish?"

"You're worse than a child," she teased.

"I take that as a yes."

"Of course. How's your hand feeling?"

Samuel stood back and stretched the fingers on his swollen hand. "It's okay," he said as he shook his head. "This will heal quicker than the rift between Joe and me."

"Honey, I'm so sorry about what happened."

"It's not your fault, and as a matter of fact, he should actually be thanking you because if it hadn't been for the fact that I didn't want to upset you, I would've called him out about what he did when I first found out. And to think, he was going to try to have me arrested today. Every time I think about it . . ."

The only other person Geneva had ever seen Samuel show this kind of frustration toward had been Johnny, and she knew that in order to be thrown into the same category as her deceitful late husband, the person had to be a real snake. "Hopefully Joe's in his hotel room thinking about the mistakes he's made and how he can make them right."

"You can't be serious."

"Yes, as a matter of fact I am. For all you know, Joe might develop a conscience and apologize to you before he leaves town."

"Do you really believe he'll do that? Remember, we're talking about my brother."

"I don't believe in Joe, but I do believe in the power of redemption, and I have hope."

Samuel smiled and kissed Geneva's cheek. "That's why I love you. You always try to find the best in people."

"You never know, honey. Sometimes people can change in ways you'd never imagine."

He shrugged his shoulders. "I guess it can happen, but you're talking about changing someone's mind-set, which means changing their attitude."

"It can happen."

Samuel shook his head. "It usually takes something really drastic to make a person change, like experienc-

ing a life-altering event, or something that's nearly cat-
astrophic, and even that might not be enough."

Geneva thought about what he'd just said, and she
had to admit he had a very good point. Johnny had
been a perfect example of that. He'd lost his marriage,
his relationship with his best friend, and his real estate
business, and even then he'd still been up to the same
old tricks. It wasn't until the very end, when he was
about to lose his life, that Johnny had tried to put forth
a change. As Geneva thought about Johnny, it made
her remember her dream.

She shook her head and shivered as her mind took
her back to the image of Johnny's dead body lying on
the kitchen floor, and his real killer—a shadowy figure
draped in black—calmly walking from the scene and
out the kitchen door. She closed her eyes and tried to
push the image out of her mind, but she couldn't. It
was as vivid and real as if she was standing right there.
Then, out of the blue, a new detail came to her that she
hadn't paid attention to in her dream. As the killer
walked away, Geneva had noticed that the woman was
wearing a hat. She couldn't tell what kind of hat it was,
just that it was small and black. Geneva tried to concentrate so the image would come in clearer, but just as
soon as the vision had come to her, it was gone.
Geneva was so startled her knees became wobbly.

"Baby, are you okay?" Samuel reached for her el-
bow and slowly led her over to the bar stool. "The stress
from yesterday and the chaos from today has taken its
toll on you," he said. "Now you're cooking, but baby,
you need to relax." He walked over to the refrigerator
and poured her a glass of water. "Here, drink this."

Geneva took small sips, trying to make sense of

what had just happened and what she'd seen. "Could it be real?" she whispered aloud.

"Could what be real?"

"Samuel, I'm not imagining things, I was there."

"Baby, you're not making sense. Are you all right?"

"No, I'm not. There's something I need to tell you."

The cake batter that Geneva had been mixing sat untouched as she began to tell Samuel about the dream she'd had, and then about the vision that had just come to her and nearly knocked her off her feet. "It can't be a dream because I'm fully awake," she said. "I don't know how or why this is happening, but I do know it's real."

Samuel was quiet, and Geneva could tell he was processing every word she was saying. If there was one thing she knew about her husband, it was that he never made a judgment about something until thoroughly thinking it over, and once he did, the questions would begin. "What do you think about what I just told you?" she asked. "I know I've been under some stress, but what I saw was real."

Samuel rubbed his hand over his closely cropped hair and cleared his throat. "I believe that everything you saw is quite possible."

"You do?"

"Yes, I do. The mind, and particularly the subconscious, is very powerful. There's lots of mysterious, otherworldly things that happen that can't be explained. Just because we don't have a rational or scientific answer for something, it doesn't discount that it's possible. I don't remember, but did you have any dreams like this after Johnny's murder?"

"No, I didn't. The nightmare I just told you about was the first time."

"Maybe the fact that there's possible evidence that may prove Vivana's innocence, is the reason this is happening to you."

What Samuel had just said made complete sense to her, and she believed his theory was on point. Geneva was amazed by how calm Samuel's reaction was. She knew he was levelheaded and introspective, but what she'd just told him would be hard for anyone to believe, let alone rationalize into the probability that it was real. She had to ask him. "Honey, how can you be so calm about what I just told you?"

"Because I've heard about things like this happening before."

"You have?"

Samuel nodded. "My first job in elementary education was as a teacher at a private school in DC. There was a very nice woman who worked there named Emily Baldwin, who was originally from the South. She and I became good friends, and her husband and I used to golf together on the weekends. Anyway, there was a student whom we both taught who exhibited what could only be categorized as 'otherworldly' behavior. He'd do things that were completely unexplainable. One morning he told a girl in the class that she needed to be careful because she was going to fall and hurt herself during recess. Sure enough, the girl fell off the monkey bars and broke her arm."

Geneva scratched her head. "That sounds a lot like the power of suggestive thinking. You know, when you say or suggest something and it happens."

"That's what I thought, until it happened over and over again. It bothered me so much that I talked to Emily about it, and she told me something I'd never heard before. She said the boy had what people in the South call the 'gift'."

"What's that?"

"It's basically the ability to see things before they happen. But the gift can manifest itself in different ways. Some people can see into the future, some can read minds, and some can have out-of-body experiences, where they can go outside of themselves and see things as they happen, whether it's in the past or the present. I think the latter is what happened to you."

Just then the lights flickered again. Geneva looked into Samuel's eyes and could see that he was gravely serious. "Do you think I have the 'gift'?"

Samuel hunched his shoulders. "I don't know. It could just be an isolated episode, but whatever is happening to you, it's real."

"When I saw Johnny sitting on the living room couch, drinking, I could actually smell the liquor in his glass, and when I saw his body lying on the floor . . ." Geneva's voice trailed off into a faint whisper. "I could see the blood oozing out of his body. It was just as real as the conversation I'm having with you right now."

"I believe you. The level of detail you were able to tell me about the things you saw let me know that you were there. Somehow, someway, there's an unexplained, maybe even supernatural energy that's trying to lead you to who really killed Johnny."

"And that makes sense, because my dream happened right at the time Vivana and her lawyer said there's new evidence."

"Right, and my guess is that whatever evidence they have isn't concrete—otherwise, a crafty, well-seasoned lawyer like Leslie Sachs would've put it all out there and Vivana would be out of prison by now, preparing for Thanksgiving dinner like we're doing."

The wheels were turning in Geneva's mind. She hadn't thought about what Samuel had just said, but it was very plausible. "I'm willing to bet that something I saw in my dream is the key to proving Vivana's innocence, and I know what it is."

"The blue box that held the pictures, video discs, and burner phone." Samuel said.

"Yes, and the black hat I just saw."

"Do you think you should contact Leslie Sachs?"

"Yes, but before I talk to her I'm going to call Councilwoman Harris, because I want legal guidance, just to cover my back in case things turn upside down and they try to pin something on me."

Samuel nodded. "I agree with you. Charlene Harris is a fair and honest woman, and she'll guide you through whatever you need to do. Having her as a friend is a definite advantage."

The lights flickered again and made Geneva jump. "I'm going to call her before it gets too late, and before the electricity goes out." Geneva dialed Charlene Harris's number and the woman picked up on the second ring.

"Hi, Geneva," Charlene said.

"Hi. I'm so sorry to bother you so late, and right before the holiday."

"Nonsense. You're never a bother, dear. Besides, the only thing I'm doing is sitting in my family room, and I just lit a candle."

"You lost power?"

"About ten minutes ago. I was in the middle of cooking, too."

"The lights have been flickering here, so I guess we might be next."

"I hope not, but keep your candles and flashlight handy, and I hope you have a wood-burning fireplace," Charlene said.

"We don't," Geneva responded with disappointment, thinking about how cold it would get if their electricity went out.

"Well, you, Samuel, and Gabrielle need to wrap up in blankets so you can keep warm. As a matter of fact, I need to put another log on the fire because it's going to get cold in here, and Lauren will probably be downstairs any minute because she's more cold-natured than I am."

Geneva walked to the closet down the hall and removed a flashlight and candles. "I guess Phillip can load up the firewood so you two can stay warm."

Charlene sighed. "Don't get me started about him."

"Is there something wrong with Phillip?"

"Nothing that a cold shower can't cure."

Geneva knew exactly what Charlene was talking about because she knew from conversations with Charlene that Phillip was a ladies' man. "Does this involve a woman?"

"Bingo!" she said with frustration. "That son of mine left out of here a few hours ago in the middle of this ridiculous snowstorm just to see some woman."

"Wow, she must be very special."

"That's what Lauren said. And the crazy thing about it is that he just met the girl."

"Really?"

"Yes, last night he went to Sebastian's to get us dinner, and then to the grocery store after that. The next thing I knew he was back out the door and I didn't see him again until this morning when he picked Lauren up from the airport, and now he's gone again. At least he stocked the house with food from the grocery list I texted him last night. Otherwise we'd be in real trouble."

Geneva set the flashlight and candles on the kitchen counter and slowly sat on the bar stool in a daze. She started thinking about her conversation last night with Donetta, and how she'd been at Sebastian's and there had been a good-looking man there who'd stared at her, and then had appeared in the grocery store. She'd even helped him find groceries from a list his mother had texted him. Donetta's Phillip was Charlene's son!

"Is everything all right?" Charlene asked. "I know for you to call this late at night right before the holidays you must have something on your mind."

Geneva knew she had to pull herself together so she could talk to Charlene about her dream, and then right after that she planned to call Donetta to warn her.

Chapter 28

CHARLENE

Charlene sat motionless on her couch, watching the flame flicker back and forth on the candle she'd lit as she listened to Geneva tell a story so real it gave her flashbacks and chills at the same time. When Geneva's number had appeared across Charlene's phone screen, she'd known right away that the call wasn't going to yield anything good. Ever since Vivana's jailhouse interview yesterday, things had been turned upside down, and now they were about to do a backward flip.

"I know it sounds crazy," Geneva said, "but, Charlene, I promise you, what I'm saying is true. It was as if I was there and I saw everything happening just as it surely did the night Johnny was murdered, and I know without a doubt in my mind that Vivana didn't kill him."

"How can you be so sure?"

"Because I saw her."

Charlene's hands started shaking and her mouth turned so dry she began to cough.

"Are you okay?" Geneva asked.

"Um, yes. I'm fine. I had a tickle in my throat." Charlene was afraid to ask Geneva to continue, but Geneva resumed her story and Charlene's blood pressure began to rise.

"Like I said, I heard the sound of the gun, even though the killer used a silencer. When I was finally able to walk into the kitchen, I saw Johnny's body lying on the ground, and it was awful, just awful."

Charlene didn't know if Geneva was trying to play mind games or if the woman was experiencing a mental collapse brought on by stress, but one thing was sure, and that was the fact that Charlene was more nervous right now than when Shartell had sent her the cryptic text. Charlene quickly tried to think about what Geneva's angle might be, but she drew a blank. Geneva wasn't the type of person who played games. She was kindhearted and honest. She was a woman of integrity whom Charlene had great respect for. But right now that woman of integrity had Charlene petrified. As she listened to Geneva on the other end of the phone, Charlene knew she couldn't sit in the dark, cold and afraid. If Geneva had hard-core evidence against her, she needed to know. "Not to be too blunt, but why are you calling me with this information?" She held her breath.

"Because I want to get your legal advice before I contact Leslie Sachs, first thing Monday morning."

If Geneva knew that Charlene was the real killer, Charlene wondered why Geneva didn't just come right out and say it? Why toy with her nerves by threatening to go to Vivana's lawyer. She knew the only way to find the answers to her questions was to ask. "Who killed Johnny?"

"I don't know."

"But you said you saw the killer."

"I did, but she was hidden by a large shadow. I know she was slim, she was wearing all black, and she had on a black hat."

Charlene thought she was going to pass out. She'd dressed in all black when she'd left the drug-laced cupcake on Vivana's doorstep. But a few hours later when she was preparing to go kill Johnny, she'd decided to tuck her asymmetrically cut bob under a small black fedora.

"Wait," Geneva said. "It just came to me. The killer was wearing a fedora."

Charlene closed her eyes as her stomach turned in knots. *How in the hell does she know this?* Charlene's slim frame had been dressed in all black, she'd been wearing a fedora, and the center light in Johnny's kitchen had been dimmed, which had cast a shadow over the room.

"Charlene, are you still there?"

"Yes, I'm still here."

"I don't think the new evidence that Leslie Sachs has is concrete; otherwise, she would've already presented it and Vivana would be free. I think she staged the interview to draw out the real killer in hopes she'll slip up. The way she looked into the camera during the interview, it was almost as if she was talking directly to the killer, trying to send her a message. I wouldn't be surprised if she knows who it is."

Charlene knew that Geneva was right, because she'd felt as though Leslie had looked through the camera yesterday afternoon and positively identified her as the killer. And now Charlene knew for sure why Leslie wanted to have coffee with her Monday morning. The shrewd attorney wanted her to slip up. Leslie would most likely engage her in a conversation about the trial, and ask questions that would tie in to whatever new evidence she'd uncovered, in hopes that Charlene would make a mistake and incriminate herself.

"I know this sounds crazy," Geneva continued, "but I believe I had the dream for a reason, and I believe that the details I saw, along with whatever Ms. Sachs has, will prove Vivana's innocence. And although the thought of Vivana roaming free scares the daylights out of me, the thought that a cold-blooded killer got away with murder while an innocent woman sits in jail, is something I can't live with."

Charlene knew she couldn't let Geneva talk to Leslie, at least not before she did. "Geneva, I'll meet with Leslie first thing Monday morning and I'll talk to her myself."

"You will?"

"Yes, and as a matter of fact I'll ask her to meet me for coffee, that way she and I can have an informal chat. We used to work together many years ago, so I'm sure that, in addition to the fact that I'm an elected city official and a concerned resident, will warrant a meeting."

"You would do that for me?"

"Of course I will."

"I'm so, so very thankful for all your help."

"Don't mention it."

"There's one other detail I need to tell you . . . oh no . . . hold on, Charlene," Geneva said.

Charlene could hear Geneva talking to her husband in the background.

"Our lights just went out," Geneva said in a quick panic. "I'll call you back tomorrow."

"But Geneva . . ." Before Charlene could ask Geneva what she wanted to tell her, the phone went dead, and Geneva was gone.

If Charlene thought she was worried before, she was disturbed now. Not only was Leslie hot on her trail, Geneva was, too. A thousand things were going through Charlene's mind. "What have I gotten myself into?" she whispered to herself. She looked up when she saw a bright light coming her way.

"I got out of the shower just in time," Lauren said as she entered the room, guided by the flashlight app on her phone. "I was upstairs getting things together so we can camp out by the fire." She was holding a set of blankets and sheets under one arm and pillows under the other.

Charlene watched as her daughter placed the blankets and pillows on the floor and then walked over to the fireplace. She placed several logs inside, moved them around with the poker, and made sure the fire was ready to blaze.

"I'll be right back, Mom."

Charlene moved from the couch to the floor and made a pallet of the sheets and blankets. She looked at the fire that had begun to roar, and she smiled. Just a few minutes ago she'd been worried out of her mind, and now she felt as happy as could be, because her daughter seemed like her old self, and it occurred to her how quickly life could change in the blink of an eye.

"Here we go," Lauren said as she returned with a

bowl of popcorn. "We had cocoa, which is my favorite, and now we'll have popcorn, which is yours. It's from a bag, but it'll have to do for now until the lights come back on and we can use the microwave."

Charlene looked at her daughter, dressed in her flannel pajamas with her hair tied up in a bright yellow scarf. "Awww, thank you, baby."

"You're welcome. It's the least I can do for the way I've acted. I'm sorry, Mom."

"Baby, there's no need to apologize."

"Yes, there is. You've been nothing but good to me, and you loved me unconditionally, even when I purposely did things that I knew would hurt you. But that never stopped you from being there whenever I needed you. Like now, even though I've messed up royally, and I know you're disappointed in me, you told me right away that I'm welcome to stay here as long as I need to. You're going to help me with the baby, and with medical school. That's more than anyone else would ever do for me."

"Lauren, I'll do anything, and I mean anything, to protect my family and make sure you have what you need."

"I know that, and I appreciate you so much." Lauren's voice trembled, and tears began to fall from her eyes. "Ever since we had that talk while we sipped your cocoa, I've felt so much better. It's like a burden was lifted off my shoulders, and I'm no longer scared of what the future's going to hold because I know that as long as I have my mama by my side, there's nothing I can't achieve. I just hope that I can be half the mother to my child that you are to me. I love you, Mom."

Charlene's heart was bursting with love. She reached for her daughter and rocked her in her arms the way she used to when Lauren was a child. This holiday had started off with gloom and doom, but right now all Charlene felt was gratitude at the fact that she had her daughter back. And as she held her baby girl, who was on the road to having a child of her own, Charlene knew she had to protect her family at all costs. She could no longer be afraid, and she couldn't hover in fear. Just as she'd taken measures to rid the world of scum like Johnny Mayfield, she was equally determined to make sure the truth about what she'd done never saw the light of day—and she was prepared to do anything she had to in order to guarantee that happened, by any means necessary.

Chapter 29

DONETTA

Donetta and Phillip sat in silence on opposite ends of the couch because Donetta had told him it would be necessary for what she was about to say.

"Who did you used to be?" Phillip asked, repeating her last statement. "I'm thinking it must be pretty bad if you don't want to be near me?"

"I think it's the other way around. It's you who might not want to be near me."

"You're starting to worry me. You're a straight shooter who isn't afraid to speak her mind. So tell me what's so bad that we need to sit a mile apart in order for you to tell me."

Donetta took a deep breath and looked into Phillip's eyes. It was a heartbreaking moment, because she realized in those brief seconds that she loved this man, and that she was also in jeopardy of losing him. She hadn't wanted to tell him under these circumstances, but now her hand had been forced. She'd always stood true about who she was, and now she knew she needed to share it with Phillip. "I'm a trans woman."

Just as a long pause had hung in the air when she'd told him that she couldn't have children, it returned, and now it was hovering in the space between them. Phillip tilted his head and chuckled lightheartedly. "That's a good one, Donetta. You got me with that one," he said as his laughter subsided. "Now that you've played a cruel joke on me that almost gave me a heart attack, please tell me what's really going on."

Donetta didn't blink or flinch. "I told you, I'm a trans woman."

"This is no longer funny. Stop playing around and tell me what's up."

Donetta looked deeply into Phillip's eyes. "I'm going to tell you my truth, and some of the things I'm going to say are going to startle you, and might even make you angry . . . but I hope you'll fully listen and hear me."

"Donetta, this is really starting to upset me." Phillip eased his body to the edge of the couch as he'd done when he'd been talking to his mother. "Are you involved in drugs?"

"No, I'm not!"

"Then what the hell are you into?"

"I told you. I'm trans."

Phillip looked deep into her eyes. "You're serious, aren't you?"

"Yes, I was born Donald Eric Pierce."

"Wait a minute. You're a dude?"

"No, I'm a woman, and as far back as I can remember, I've always known that. Even though I was born into a body that didn't match who I am, I've never, ever questioned that I'm female."

Phillip shook his head and raised his voice. "This is fuckin' unbelievable. This is some bullshit!"

For the first time since their conversation had started, Donetta began to feel afraid. "If you think you're going to become violent, I want you to know that I'm fully capable of defending myself, and I have weapons in this house that I can use against you."

Phillip stared at her. "What the fuck are you talking about? First you tell me you're a dude, and now you're threatening me?"

"I'm a woman, and I'm not threatening you. I'm just making you aware."

"Fuck!" He placed his head in his hands. "I can't believe this . . . we had sex!"

Donetta felt a stab at her heart. "And it was a beautiful experience. And Phillip, you can clearly see that I'm a woman."

Another pause loomed in the air, and Donetta could see that Phillip was thinking so hard that a crease had formed in the middle of his forehead. She prayed that she wouldn't have to use the pistol she kept under the couch, which she was glad was beneath the section where she was sitting. She didn't know what was going to happen next, but from the look on Phillip's face it wasn't going to be good.

"If you're a transgender woman, and you have a vagina, that means you had surgery?"

Donetta nodded. "A little over a year ago."

"Why didn't you fucking tell me you used to have a dick?"

"When was I supposed to tell you? In the produce

aisle at the grocery store? In the lounge at the prestigious Roosevelt Hotel?"

"How about somewhere in between the time I said hello to you and when we were in your bed!" Phillip yelled. He jumped up from the couch. "I can't believe this shit! You made me believe that you were an honest person. I thought you were special, but you're nothing but a liar. I don't even know who you are."

Donetta's heart started racing. Phillip didn't strike her as the type of man who would become violent, but life had taught her that anyone was capable of anything, especially once their emotions started running high, as Phillip's were now. She wanted to ask him to calm down, and to remind him that she would defend herself if she had to. But she was afraid to open her mouth, and her good common sense told her that she should keep it shut for now. She watched him as he stood as still as a statue and looked into the fireplace, as if he was transfixed. She desperately wanted him to say something. After what felt like an hour, he finally spoke.

"You tricked me," he said. "You knew that if you told me the truth from the jump that I wouldn't have anything to do with you, so you lied and manipulated me."

"That's not true. I never lied to you about who I am, not once. I'm sitting here being honest with you."

"Don't split hairs, you know exactly what the fuck I'm talking about."

"I planned to tell you, and the only reason why I didn't before now is because I didn't want to do it in person. But now that we're snowed in, I had no choice. And besides, your mother knows me."

Phillip glared at her and shook his head.

"My best friend and business partner, Geneva, does

your mother's hair. Your mother comes into the salon every week like clockwork. I just saw her yesterday."

Phillip crossed his arms over his chest. "This is unbelievable. I feel like I'm in the middle of a freakin' nightmare."

"I'm sorry that you think being with me is a nightmare," Donetta said, her voice full of hurt.

"Do you always go around doing shit like this? Tricking men into sleeping with you and then dropping the bomb on them?"

Donetta closed her eyes and shook her head. "I've been beaten and raped, and it happened because I told them in person. There's a rule of safety in the community that you should never tell someone in person because it can cost you your life. I'd planned to tell you over the phone after our date last night. But then you came over here and—"

"You could've told me on the phone when I invited you to the hotel, before it ever got this far."

"I wanted you to get to know me for who I am, and not some misinformed stereotype."

Phillip shook his head. "I can't believe I actually jumped in my car and raced over here."

"I'm still the same person you were laughing with last night and today. I'm the same person you shared your likes and dislikes with, and I'm still opinionated, strong-willed, and a deeply caring woman," Donetta said in a pleading tone. "I haven't changed one bit, Phillip. I am who I am, through and through."

"This is crazy. It's so fucked up I don't even know what to say."

"You can start by trying to understand where I'm coming from."

"Where you're coming from? How about how I

feel? Did it ever occur to you that the entire way you went about this was wrong?" He paused. "Oh wait, you knew you were wrong, and that's why you kept the truth from me."

"You act like I lured you over here and seduced you. You're the one who pursued me."

"Only because I thought you were a woman."

"I am a woman, damn it! And I've been a woman all my life. I've had to walk on eggshells since I was a child, trying to protect myself from other people's anger, rage, and hatred toward me all because of who I am. My father left our family when I was five years old because he hated me, and my mother abandoned me when I was in middle school for the same reason. I came home from school one afternoon and all her things were gone, except for a raggedy note that basically said she didn't want me in her life.

"I caught hell growing up and I had to fight and defend myself almost daily. By the time I graduated from high school I'd had both my arms broken and a total of forty stitches in different places on my body. I even contemplated suicide a few times because I felt so miserable. My grandmother, who raised me, was the only person, besides my best friend, Geneva, who has ever loved me unconditionally." Just then Donetta's cell phone rang loud with Geneva's ringtone. She knew that her friend was worried about her, and as irony would have it, she was probably calling to see if she'd had a chance to talk to Phillip. Donetta knew she'd have to call Geneva back at another time, with what she now knew was going to be bad news, so she continued on with what she was saying.

"Once my grandmother died, I knew I couldn't continue to live in fear or shame. I'm not saying this to make you feel sorry for me, I'm telling you because it's who I am. I've worked too damn hard and fought too many battles to go back to the sad life I used to live.

"I feel good about myself, and I'm not ashamed of who I am. I'm a good person, I'm kind, I'm generous, I'm smart, I'm hardworking, I'm loving, and I'm one of the most loyal people you'll ever meet. I'm not bragging on myself, I'm just telling you what's true. I think in the short amount of time that we've been together, you've been able to see those qualities." Donetta swallowed hard as tears began to form in her eyes. "I always trust my heart and my gut because they've never led me wrong. And that's why as crazy as it might sound, my heart and my gut are telling me that you're the one. I've never felt about anyone the way I feel about you. I love you, Phillip."

Phillip stared at her, but she couldn't read the expression on his face. Finally, he spoke.

"Where is your guest room?"

She answered him softly. "Down the hall, to your right."

Without saying a word, Phillip turned, walked down the hall, and slammed the door shut behind him. A minute later the lights flickered and the electricity went out. The house fell into blackness as Donetta sat on the couch and cried in the dark.

A few hours later, Donetta was curled up on the floor in front of the fireplace. She'd pulled her heavy comforter and sheets off her bed and had made a makeshift sleeping bag that she was nestled inside. She was thankful for her wood-burning fireplace. When she'd moved into her house a few years ago, she'd hired a contractor to customize her home to the specifications she liked. When she'd told him that she wanted a traditional fireplace over gas logs, he'd looked at her as if she'd told him she wanted to jump out of a moving car. And now, as the orange and red flames kept her nice and toasty without the need for electricity, she wondered if that contractor was freezing in his home without the use of his precious gas logs. She was pulled away from her thoughts when she heard Phillip cough again.

He'd been coughing for the last half hour, and it was getting worse by the minute. She knew he'd probably caught a cold from having walked two miles in the snow, and it didn't help that he was sleeping in a room at the back of the house that Donetta knew had to be freezing. This certainly wasn't how she'd envisioned her evening was going to be. She'd started out with high hopes, and as she and Phillip had dined on the delicious meal she'd made, she'd been happy with the excitement of being snowed in with him. But now she was anything but happy, and her spirits hadn't been this low since her grandmother had passed away.

Donetta wanted to cry every time she thought about the way Phillip had looked at her with disdain after she'd opened up to him. The fact that he'd rather freeze in the guest room than be near her where it was warm, all because he didn't want to be in the same room with her, made her feel even worse. But she knew she couldn't continue to cry or give in to feelings of guilt or pity for herself. It would be hard, but she knew she'd survive this, and in years to come when she looked back on this moment, she'd be able to say that it served to make her stronger.

Ten minutes later, Phillip's cough was progressing, to the point that he sounded as if he was in distress. Donetta knew she had to do something. "He may not want to see me," she mumbled as she unbundled herself from the comforter, "but this is my house, and I'm going into that room whether he wants me to or not." She walked back to the guest room and knocked on the door. She waited, but there was no response, only coughing. She knocked again and was met with the same silence. "This is ridiculous," she said with frustration. Donetta pushed the door open and walked in. "Get up, you need to come to the living room where it's warm."

"I'm fine where I am," Phillip said through two loud coughs. He sounded weak, and his voice was stuffy with congestion.

Donetta shook her head. "It's so cold back here I can see my breath. You've caught a cold, Phillip, and you don't need to be back here in this room. It's freezing."

"I said I'm fine."

Even though it was dark, Donetta could clearly see him through the light that was streaming in from the window. He looked tired, and it was obvious that he wasn't fine. "You sound like you're gonna cough up a lung."

"It's nothing a little rest won't cure, so get out of here and leave me alone."

Donetta was tired of trying to persuade him. She walked over to the bed and quickly snatched the covers away from his body.

Phillip sat up and coughed as if someone had kicked him in his throat. "What the hell's wrong with you?"

"I should be asking your stupid ass the same thing,"

she said matter-of-factly, with her hand on her hip. She could see that she'd gotten his attention. "You're back here about to catch pneumonia when you should be in the living room where it's warm, right in front of the fire." He was quiet, and she could tell that as stubborn as he was trying to be, he knew she was right. "I'm not taking no for an answer," she said. "You can either walk out to the living room on your own, or I can drag you down the hall. I might be dainty, but I'm strong."

Slowly, Phillip rose from the bed and shuffled down the hallway. Donetta opened her makeshift sleeping bag. "Get in." She could tell that Phillip felt horrible because he didn't put up any resistance. He buried himself under the heavy comforter and pulled it up to his neck.

Donetta walked into the kitchen and rifled through her cabinets. She came back carrying several bottles, along with a glass of orange juice and a thermometer. She sat down beside Phillip and crossed her legs to make herself comfortable. "Open your mouth." She slid the digital thermometer under his tongue, which took no time to beep, letting her know that he had a temperature and it was high. She removed it from his mouth. "Your temp is a hundred and three," she said with concern in her voice. She knew this was the result of his two-mile walk to reach her. Donetta's heart ached when she thought about the desire that had fueled Phillip's determination to see her, and the fact that it was now gone, only to be replaced by anger and disdain for her. But she pushed her feelings aside because right now he was sick, and he needed her.

"Here, take a sip of this," Donetta said as she handed him the glass of orange juice. Next, she gave him a capful of NyQuil Severe Cold medicine, followed by a cherry-flavored Hall's cough drop. She returned to the kitchen when she heard her teakettle whistling on the stove. A few minutes later she held a cup to his mouth that was filled with chamomile tea and mixed with natural brown sugar, organic honey, a freshly squeezed lemon, and a strong dose of alcohol.

"The cough drop and the honey will help soothe your cough," she said. "The NyQuil will help relieve your cold symptoms, the chamomile will relax your body so you can go to sleep, and the booze will do the rest."

After Phillip finished drinking the tea, Donetta handed him another cough drop, which he took willingly. She walked down the hall to her large linen closet and pulled out an old patchwork quilt and several sheets. She returned to the living room, placed them on the floor, and then walked over to her stash of firewood. She put a few more logs on top of the ones that were already burning, which would ensure that the room would be warm throughout the night. She made another makeshift sleeping bag on the floor, a few feet away from where Phillip was lying, but close enough to the fire to stay warm while keeping an eye on him in case he awoke and needed anything.

Donetta looked over at Phillip, who had stopped coughing and appeared to be fast asleep. Even in sickness, and despite the harsh way he'd treated her and the things he'd said, she still thought he was beautiful, and she still loved him.

As she continued to stare at him, bundled up beneath her comforter, she couldn't help but feel happy and sad at the same time. She was sad to have lost Phillip before she'd had the chance to ever really have him, and she was happy because she'd found love, even if it had been only for a brief moment. Donetta knew it was something a lot of people would never experience, but she had, and for that blessing she was grateful.

"Good night, Phillip. I love you," she whispered. After a few minutes she drifted off to sleep.

Chapter 30

PHILLIP

The sun was on the verge of making its appearance, as everything remained quiet and still in the predawn morning. The snow had stopped falling and had left a beautiful scene fit for a postcard. Phillip had been awake for the last hour, thinking, contemplating, and trying to make sense of the situation he was in. His head was pounding, and he didn't know if it was from the fever that had gripped his body, or if it was because of everything that had taken place last night.

He looked over at Donetta, who was lying a few feet away from him, bundled beneath an intricate patchwork quilt. She was sleeping on her side, facing him, and she looked as if she was awake with her eyes closed. As much as he struggled with the thoughts that were running through his head, he had to admit that

Donetta was breathtakingly beautiful—and that truth disturbed him and left him feeling confused.

Phillip didn't want to be attracted to her. He wanted to despise her for what she'd done to him. And more than anything, he wanted to think of "her" as "him," so it would make his feelings easier to define. But the truth was that when he looked at Donetta, all he saw was a beautiful, vulnerable woman. He let out a low, deep breath as he replayed last night's conversation in his mind.

After he'd stomped away and shut himself off in Donetta's guest room, he'd lain for hours in the quiet darkness, alone with his thoughts. He'd felt deceived because, although Donetta hadn't told a lie in the traditional sense, he'd felt her omission of who she was was tantamount to straight-up deception. After thoroughly processing what she'd said about her reasons for not telling him face-to-face, he understood the very real physical threat of violence and possible death that she'd cited. But he also felt she should have told him about being trans before they'd slept together, which had now brought about a set of issues he'd never even thought about before.

Phillip was wrestling with the internal struggle about how he—a heterosexual, alpha male—could still be attracted to Donetta after finding out she'd been born male. He felt that his mind and heart had conspired to play a cruel game, because even though he knew Donetta's background, all he could see when he looked at her was a beautiful woman. She smelled sweet like a woman. Her body was soft and curvaceous in all the right places like a woman. She had a sexy walk and feminine flair like a woman. When they'd made love, she'd felt like a woman. And that last part was one of the hardest realities for him to come to grips with.

Phillip wanted to laugh at the irony that out of all the women he'd been with in his life, the one whom he found the most interesting, sexy, desirable, and best in bed, had been born just like him. The thought was something he didn't know how to assign feelings to.

Phillip looked at the fire that was now burning low. He remembered that Donetta had stacked it full of wood so it would burn through the rest of the night and keep them warm. He slowly climbed from underneath his heavy blanket, careful not to make any noise, and went over to the firewood stacked inside a large basket. He put four logs into the fireplace, making sure they were positioned to yield a roaring flame, and then climbed back under his warm blanket without so much as a sound.

As he covered himself up to his neck, he looked at Donetta, wrapped in her quilt, and it occurred to him that she'd given him the heavier of the two blankets. She could have easily given him the thinner of the two, or, left him in the guest room altogether, but she hadn't. He thought about how she'd barged into the room where he'd been lying wide awake, called him stupid, and told him that if he didn't come into the living room on his own, she'd drag him there.

That was one of the things beyond Donetta's physical appearance that had attracted him to her. She was feisty and unafraid, and that made her a natural survivor. He also thought about how she'd taken care of him by giving him medicine and had even held a hot cup of tea to his mouth as he'd sipped. He'd been too weak to put up a fight, but again, as much as he didn't want to admit his real feelings, the honest truth was that he'd enjoyed the way she'd taken care of him. Then finally, he remembered how she'd thought he was asleep and she'd told him she loved him. He was glad she didn't know he'd been wide awake, because he hadn't known what to say or do.

Phillip took a deep breath and sneezed. His throat felt raw, his head hurt, and his body was sore. Just as he was about to turn on his other side, Donetta's eyes flew open.

"Are you okay? How do you feel?" she asked, full of concern.

She didn't have an ounce of grogginess in her voice, and he was amazed that she'd woken up without a struggle. She was clearly the morning person that he wasn't, because if not for his alarm clock, he'd oversleep every day. She sat up as straight as an arrow and fluffed her hair. He could see that she'd changed at some point last night from the brightly colored lingerie she'd been wearing, into a pink thermal pajama set. She gathered her covers around her. "How do you feel this morning?" she asked again.

He looked away from her and closed his eyes.

"Listen, Phillip, I know you don't want to hold a conversation with me, and that's fine. But I'm trying to help you, so you need to tell me how you're feeling so I'll know what to give you. Now, I'm going to ask you again, how do you feel?"

"Not so good." He rubbed his sleeve against the mucus that had started to run from his nose after he'd sneezed.

Donetta peeled out from under her thin quilt and stood to her feet. She turned around and walked to the kitchen, and Phillip couldn't help but notice the perfect curve of her hips, the roundness of her behind, and the sexy way her small waist brought attention to her slender frame. Everything about her stimulated his senses, even in his sickly state.

Donetta returned with a fresh cup of orange juice and a box of Kleenex. "I put some water in the kettle for your tea," she said as she handed him the box of tissues. She picked up the thermometer. "You know the drill."

Phillip blew his nose and then opened his mouth. He watched her out of the corner of his eye as he held the thermometer under his tongue. She was looking out the window, and he could see that a smile had begun to form on her face. He turned toward the window to see what was holding her attention, and he saw that the sun was beginning to rise. They sat in silence, watching one of nature's most beautiful gifts. He was a person who was always on the go, living in the city, always navigating at a fast pace. This was the first time he'd ever watched the sun rise, and it was nothing less than amazing. The thermometer beeped, but neither of them moved. They remained still, appreciating the moment.

"This is how you know there's a God," Donetta said softly. "Only He can create something so beautiful."

Phillip heard sadness in her voice, and he knew it was because of the turn that their relationship had taken. He knew she wanted him to talk to her, but he couldn't bring himself to engage her because he didn't know what to say, and he felt drained from fever and body aches. Donetta looked at him and removed the thermometer from his mouth.

"You're down one degree, to a hundred and two," Donetta said. "That's still high, but not as bad as last night." She handed him the glass of orange juice and he took it willingly, followed by a capful of NyQuil. And just as she'd done last night, she rose when she heard the kettle whistle, and she returned with a hot cup of tea. This time he sipped it on his own as she sat and watched him. The last thing he remembered was a slight smile on her face before he closed his eyes and fell asleep.

Phillip awoke from the worst nightmare he'd ever had, and his chest heaved up and down as he thought about the chilling details. He and Donetta had been sitting in front of the fireplace sharing a passionate kiss, wrapped in a warm embrace. He'd held her so tightly that he could feel the pull in his biceps. Then he released her slowly, looked into her eyes, and smiled. "I love you, Donetta," he had said. She'd repeated the same back to him, and then, without warning, he quickly wrapped his large hands around her throat. He pressed his fingers at the base of her larynx with so much force she could barely gasp. He watched the light leave her eyes and the life drain from her body until she became limp with death. He released her neck, she fell to the floor, and he awoke in a terrified sweat.

Phillip could only attribute his dream to his high fever, and the intense conversation he'd had with Donetta last night when she revealed that she'd been physically assaulted. Phillip knew there was no way he could ever harm Donetta, because even though he'd been angry with her last night, he'd been even angrier at the thought that she'd been hurt at the hands of men. His nightmare had been awful, but it was a dream. He knew that Donetta's nightmare had happened when she'd been awake, and it was reality. The thought made him sick inside, and he wished he could dream a happy ending to everything that had happened since last night.

Phillip's mouth felt so dry that his throat hurt. He blinked his eyes slowly and looked around the room to find Donetta sitting on her couch, wrapped in her quilt, reading a book. She immediately put her book down when she heard him stir.

"You're awake," she said. "You've been asleep for the past six hours."

He couldn't believe he'd been asleep that long because it felt as though he'd just closed his eyes a few minutes ago. He reached for a tissue, blew his nose, and then sneezed. Like clockwork, Donetta descended upon him again with juice, a thermometer, and this time a bowl of chicken noodle soup. "Good news," she said. "Your fever is down to one hundred." She wiped the thermometer with alcohol and handed him the bowl of soup. He didn't have an appetite, but she told him that if he didn't eat it she was going to shove it down his throat. He shook his head at her pure grit, which was something he actually admired.

"It's Thanksgiving Day, and I know your mom would love to hear from you." She handed him her phone and then walked to her bedroom.

Phillip dialed his mother's cell phone, and she picked up on the first ring.

"Phillip, is this you?"

He sat up and cleared his throat. "Happy Thanksgiving, Mom." His voice surprised even him, so he knew his mother was going to be alarmed.

"You sound awful," his mother said. "Do you have a cold?"

"Yeah," he said through extreme congestion. "I guess I caught it out there in the snow."

"Awww, baby, I'm sorry. Are you running a fever?"

"Yeah, it's one hundred."

"Oh no."

"That's actually pretty good, because last night it was a hundred and three." He looked over at the fire and could see that Donetta had placed more logs inside. She'd also left a pack of Ritz Crackers and a bag of cough drops next to him. Even while he'd been sleeping, she'd been taking care of him.

"I guess that's good news," his mother said. "What kind of medicine are you taking?"

"NyQuil and lots of juice, tea, and cough drops."

"Make sure you put some honey and lemon in your tea. That will help."

"She did."

He could hear the pause in his mother's voice. "So . . . she's taking care of you?"

"Yes, she is." He wanted to change the subject before his mother asked too many questions. "How are you and Lauren?"

"We're great," she said. "I couldn't make the Thanksgiving feast that I'd wanted to because of the power outage, but Lauren and I made turkey sandwiches from the deli meat I had in the fridge, along with the chips you bought the other night, and it tasted like a gourmet meal."

Phillip was glad to hear that his mother sounded like her old self. "That sounds good."

"Have you felt up to eating anything?"

He blew his nose. "Yes, I ate a bowl of chicken noodle soup."

"When you were a little boy, every time you got sick I'd fix you chicken noodle soup and you'd feel so much better."

He blew his nose again. "Even though I sound bad, I actually feel better, so I guess the chicken noodle soup is still doing the job after all these years."

"Yes, it sure is, son. Is the electricity still on where you are?"

Phillip looked around the house. The bright sun that had beamed in the sky this morning was now gone, and it was overcast and dark again. Donetta had lit two pillar candles that were sitting on the coffee table, and combined with the fire, they gave the room a warm glow. "No, we lost power late last night. But she has a wood-burning fireplace like yours, so we've been warm. And, Mom, this woman has more candles than anyone I've ever seen."

"More than me?"

"Believe it or not, she does. And they're in different scents, too."

"I absolutely love scented candles."

"Well, you'd have a field day over here." *What the hell am I doing?!* Phillip had to catch himself. He was talking about Donetta with the same excitement in his voice that he'd had before last night, and he had to remind himself that there was a world of difference between then and now.

"I can't wait to meet her," his mother said enthusiastically.

Phillip quickly changed the subject again. "When do you think the snowplows will start coming through the neighborhoods?"

"It'll be a while."

"How long is 'a while'?" Phillip knew he couldn't

stay at Donetta's much longer. He needed to get out of her house so he could think and regroup.

"At least another day, maybe even two. City services are shut down for the holidays, and the few snowplows we have are only in operation for emergency situations. I had a city council conference call meeting this morning, and my colleagues and I agreed that the situation is so bad we're going to have to overspend our budget getting additional plows into the city, simply because of the sheer volume of snow we received."

Phillip stood up and walked over to the window. Even though it was overcast the snow was so bright it was blinding, and as he looked up and down the street, there were no signs that anyone had ventured outside their houses. "I guess you're right. My flight leaves out Sunday morning, so hopefully I'll be able to make it."

"I hope so. If not, it sounds like you're in good hands where you are, and that makes me feel so much better." Happiness filled her voice. "Lauren and I are safe and warm, and even though you're battling a cold, you're being nursed back to health by someone who obviously cares for you. Son, I haven't met this young woman, but I can tell she's special by the sound in your voice. When you find someone who makes you feel good, and who will stand by your side and take care of you, that's a blessing."

Phillip thought about what his mother had just said and he had to agree. "Yes, it is."

He and his mother talked a few minutes longer before she handed the phone to Lauren, who wished him a happy Thanksgiving and then proceeded to tease him about catching a cold from walking through a snowstorm in order to see a woman. Even though she'd given him a hard time, she'd said she was glad that he was happy. After he hung up the phone he felt tired, just from talking.

Phillip returned to his warm blanket by the fire. Donetta was still in her bedroom, giving him the privacy he needed for his phone call, which he appreciated. But an hour later she hadn't yet come back into the room, and as he lay by the warm fire in the stillness of her cozy living room, he realized that he missed her.

Chapter 31

DONETTA

Donetta was a light sleeper, so when she heard the knock on her bedroom door she rubbed her eyes and blinked. The room was completely dark, save for the moonlight peeping in through the blinds she'd left open at her window. She was lying in her bed, curled into a tight ball under four bedsheets, two robes, thick socks, a pair of gloves, and a fur-lined toboggan atop her head. And even though she was cocooned under several layers of coverings and clothing, she was still cold. She'd left the warmth of the cozy fire in the living room and had gone to her bedroom so Phillip could freely talk to his mother.

There was another hard set of knocks, followed by the strained sound of Phillip's voice. "Donetta, are you awake?"

"Yes," she answered.

Phillip slowly walked into the room holding a candle to light his way. He was still dressed in the navy lounge pants and long-sleeved gray T-shirt he'd been wearing since last night. He stood at the edge of her bed and stared at her.

"What do you want?" she asked.

"You've been back here a long time so I came to check on you."

"What time is it?"

"Seven o'clock."

"What?" She sat up and squinted. Donetta hadn't slept a wink last night because she'd been worried about Phillip's health and heartbroken over the way things had turned out between them. When she'd finally lain down earlier today, sleep had welcomed her. But now it was nighttime again, it was freezing, and her stomach had just begun to growl. Even though she was cold and hungry, she wanted to know how Phillip was feeling. He still sounded congested, but he looked as if he was beginning to rebound. "How are you feeling?" she asked.

"I'm better, but I'm afraid you're going to get sick like I did if you stay back here."

She'd been expecting Phillip to answer her in the same angry, uncaring tone he'd been using since last night. But to her surprise his response was actually polite and thoughtful, and it surprised her to the point that she didn't know what to say.

"Let's go back to the living room where it's warm," he said in a gentle tone. He extended his arm for her to walk in front of him as he escorted her out of the room.

Donetta wondered if his fever had risen so high that he was having some kind of brain malfunction. "Are you sure you're all right?" she asked as they walked out to the living room.

"Yes, like I said, I'm much better . . . thanks to you."

Now Donetta knew there was definitely something wrong with Phillip. Although it was apparent that he was physically better, as was evidenced by the strength of his movements and the healthy hue that had returned to his caramel-colored skin, his mental health was now in question. He'd changed from salt to sugar in the course of an afternoon. Donetta remembered her grandmother used to say that if a man had an abrupt change in attitude, it was because he had something up his sleeve. "Do you still have a fever?" she asked.

"Yeah, it's still one hundred, but that's no biggie. I took more medicine a few hours ago, and that's helped a lot."

When they reached the living room Phillip led Donetta over to the fireplace. He picked up the heavy blanket he'd been lying under and draped it around Donetta's shoulders. He looked at her and smiled. "I'll be back in a second."

Donetta stood still, frozen with panic. *Oh Lord, he's gonna try to kill me!* she thought. She'd heard about situations like this, where a spouse or disgruntled lover played nice, all the while plotting to kill their mate. Before she'd gone to sleep, Phillip's attitude had been as tart as vinegar, and now he was cotton-candy sweet, all in the matter of one afternoon. She didn't trust his sudden kindness, and she knew she needed to protect herself. She walked over to the couch and sat on the cushion underneath which she kept her pistol hidden. Just then, Phillip came back into the room carrying two plates.

"Why're you sitting over there?" he asked.

She cleared her throat. "The couch is more comfortable than the floor."

"But it's warmer by the fire."

"I'll take my chances," she said with a definite edge in her voice.

He looked as if he wanted to say something, but instead he remained silent. He took a seat next to her and held the two plates in his lap. "I made us sandwiches," he said with a smile. "And this is actually what my mom and sister had for lunch and dinner tonight."

"You talked to your mother again?" she asked.

"Yes, I did."

Now Donetta was really worried, and she was sure that whatever he and his mother had talked about had everything to do with his sudden change of heart. Charlene Harris was a lawyer by vocation and a politician by way of natural charisma. She was a woman who knew the ins and outs of the law, and she sat on powerful boards and committees that made the city run. Donetta's mind raced as she thought about what Phillip and his mother could be up to, and then it came to her. They could be setting up a murder scene to make it look as though Phillip was defending himself against a trans woman who tried to attack him after being rejected. Donetta remembered how the calm, kindhearted councilwoman had beaten her ex-husband with a baseball bat a couple of years ago, giving him injuries so serious he'd had to go to the hospital.

Lord, please help me, Donetta prayed silently. She

nearly jumped when she heard Phillip's voice, breaking her thoughts.

"I know you said you don't like mayo, so I only put mustard on yours."

Donetta looked at the sandwich as if he'd just served her poison between two slices of bread. "I'm not hungry."

"I heard your stomach growl when we were in your bedroom."

She rolled her eyes and then glared at him. "I'm not eating that sandwich."

"Donetta, are you all right?"

"Are you?"

She saw a look on Phillip's face that resembled hurt, but she knew it had to be part of his act. She'd fought men who were more streetwise and definitely meaner than Phillip in her day, so she wasn't about to let his gentle mood and fake charm fool her. She was at a physical disadvantage against his size and strength, but she hadn't met a man alive who could outfight a bullet. She hated that it had come to this, but she scooted to the edge of the couch so she could easily retrieve the gun if she had to.

Phillip placed the two plates on the coffee table and cleared his throat. "I don't blame you for being angry, because I was angry, too."

"I'm not angry, I'm cautious."

He stared into her eyes, and she could see that he knew exactly what she meant. The hurt look that had come across his face a few minutes ago returned, and from where she sat it appeared genuine. Donetta was emotional, nervous, and confused about what was happening. At this point all she could do was trust that

God would see her through whatever was about to happen next.

"Donetta, I hope you don't think I would try to hurt you," Phillip said.

"Right now I don't know what to think. Before I went to sleep you were avoiding all eye contact with me, as if you were going to turn into stone if you looked my way. You barely said a word when I talked to you, and when you did decide to speak, you were short and harsh. But now you're staring into my eyes, making nice, and fixing me food that God only knows what you put in it. So, hell yeah, I'm afraid that you might hurt me . . . you wouldn't be the first."

"I would never lay a hand on you."

"And you want me to just take your word for it?"

He let out a deep sigh. "Yes, because right now that's all I have."

He sounded sincere, with his gentle tone and kind eyes, but Donetta still wasn't fully convinced. The mental stress of trying to figure out Phillip's angle was beginning to wear on her, and the fact that she hadn't eaten since last night had begun to make her feel lightheaded. She was tired and she didn't want to be held hostage by her fears. She knew she needed to get everything out in the open and play her hand as it was dealt. She faced him and stared into his eyes.

"What did you and your mother talk about?" she asked. "You called her a second time, and now your entire attitude has changed. So what's up?"

Phillip chuckled and shook his head. "That's one of the things I like about you, Donetta. You're smart and you get right to the point."

"Thank you, but that still doesn't answer my question."

"I told her about you."

"About me, as in what kind of person I am? Or about me, as in, her name is Donetta Pierce?"

Phillip stared back at her with an intensity that matched hers. "After you went to your bedroom, I thought you were going to come back out here after my phone call with my mom ended, but you didn't. While you were gone, it gave me a lot of time to think about all the feelings and emotions going on inside of me. I couldn't make sense of some of the thoughts running through my mind, so I called my mother because she's literally the smartest and most compassionate person I know.

"I told her everything, which was a first for me. I've always kept my relationships to myself, and it's the only part of my life that my mom and I don't discuss in detail. Like I told you, I've been with a lot of women, and even though I've always been honest and up front in my relationships, my lifestyle has bothered my mother. She's a woman who was cheated on throughout her marriage, and I guess she's afraid that one day I might hurt someone like she was hurt, or that someone might get mad and hurt me . . . like she did my dad, which I'm sure you probably heard about."

Donetta nodded. "News travels fast."

"Especially bad news. Anyway, my mom allowed me to vent without interruption, which is a skill we lawyers have to master. After I cussed and fussed, she asked me a lot of questions, mainly about how I felt about you before you told me that you're trans. She helped me work through some things, not everything, but what we talked about was significant." He paused and smiled. "She has a lot of respect for you, Donetta. She likes you—a lot."

"She does?" Donetta was in shock about nearly everything Phillip had said, and especially about his mother having respect for her and liking her. Donetta knew that Charlene was one of Geneva's most loyal clients and that the two had become close ever since Charlene had generously offered to help Geneva with legal advice and emotional support after Johnny had been murdered. Donetta knew that Charlene had always been courteous to her, as she was with most everyone, but she didn't know that the councilwoman respected and liked her.

"Yes, she does," Phillip continued. "My mother's a very open-minded person, and she doesn't judge. But when it comes to her children she's very partial, so she naturally had some concerns, which she'd have about anyone I started dating. But she knows you."

"Even though she comes into the salon every week, I've never had a one-on-one conversation with her."

"Maybe not, but she said—not to my surprise— that you're quite the conversationalist and you have strong-willed opinions about everything."

Donetta began to relax and actually smiled. "Yeah, that's me."

"She thinks you're smart, beautiful, funny, and a stylish dresser."

"Coming from your mother, that's a great compliment, and I can say the same thing about her. As a matter of fact, I'd love to raid her closet," Donetta teased.

"It's amazing to me how women always size each other up when it comes to looks and clothes."

Donetta noticed that Phillip was talking to her as if he fully accepted her for who she was. And even though she'd prayed he would, she knew there was no way his emotions could ping-pong back and forth so quickly without there being underlying fears, anger, and emotions that still needed to be addressed. She always believed in attacking situations head-on, but this was one time when she decided it was best to take things slow.

"I know this has been hard for you," Donetta said, "and I'm truly, truly sorry that I told you the way I did . . . when I did. But, Phillip, I wasn't trying to deceive you, and I hope you believe me when I say that."

"I do. And you're right, it's been hard on me, but I now understand that it's been hard on you, too. After I talked with my mom, I used your phone to find out more about trans people because it's a world I know absolutely nothing about. After surfing the net and reading blogs and listening to women tell their stories in YouTube videos, I was able to get a glimpse into what you've had to live your entire life. Not once have I ever questioned my manhood, so again, it's foreign to me, but I want to understand, and if we're going to do this, I need to."

Donetta looked at Phillip and smiled. When they'd first started their conversation she'd thought he was trying to kill her, and now he was saying he actually wanted to be with her. She knew she should feel surprised and shocked, but she didn't because if there was one lesson she'd learned over the last two days it was that absolutely anything was possible. "I have so much to share with you," she said, "and I'm sure you have a lot to share with me, too."

"We'll learn together."

The next two hours flew by like two minutes as Donetta and Phillip talked, and began a journey to a place neither of them had ever been before. They confided, confessed, and consoled. At some points she cried, and at all times he listened. They agreed that a long dis-

tance relationship would be tough, and that they would
take turns traveling to see each other, every other week.
Phillip told her that he would attend her support group
meetings when he was in town. And even though he'd
said it didn't bother him, she'd told him that she would
continue to work on toning down her cursing, which
she'd already curtailed over the last two days.

As the night drew on and the temperature dropped,
Phillip put more wood on the fire and they returned to
their spots in front of the fireplace. Donetta was over-
joyed that Phillip had fed her soul, but now she needed
to feed her stomach. She eyed the sandwich still sitting
on her plate that had gone untouched for the last two
hours.

"Are you okay?" Phillip asked.

"No, I'm so damn hungry I could eat paper right
now."

She and Phillip shared their first laugh together
since the night before, and it felt better to Donetta than
the warmth coming from the fire.

"Let's dig in," Phillip said. "I think you'll like it. I
make a hell of a sandwich."

"I can't wait to find out!"

Just as Donetta was about to stand up and reach for
her plate, Phillip pulled her into him and delivered the
softest, most gentle kiss to her lips, another first they'd
shared since last night. He held her close to his chest
with a tight hold that nearly made Donetta lose her
breath. Slowly, he looked into her eyes and smiled.

"I love you, Donetta."

"I love you, too."

They shared another passionate kiss, this time longer
than the first, and then they devoured their sandwiches
by the light of the fire.

Chapter 32

GENEVA

Even though Geneva had been snowbound like most of the residents in Amber, the last three days had flown by in a flurry of activity at her house. After their lights had gone out a few days ago, she and Samuel had come to appreciate what a valuable commodity electricity was, especially given that they had a baby and houseguests to deal with. Geneva's main concern had been how to keep Gabrielle warm and fed, and Samuel's main focus had been keeping his wife worry-free, his child safe, and his parents comfortable.

Geneva had also been worried about Donetta. After the power outage had caused her to cut her conversation short with Charlene Harris on Thanksgiving Eve, Geneva had pulled herself together and called Donetta to tell her that Phillip was Charlene's son. But her call had gone to Donetta's voice mail, so she'd left her friend a message, telling Donetta what she'd learned. Geneva had figured out from her conversation with Charlene that Phillip was already at Donetta's house, snowed in, and she prayed that if Donetta decided to tell him about her background, that it had gone well.

Geneva had worried that entire night, and all Thanksgiving Day, because she hadn't heard a word from Donetta. But she'd breathed with relief later that night when Donetta had called her and explained the roller-coaster ride that she and Phillip had taken. Geneva had been happy when she'd heard the excitement in her friend's voice.

"We're officially a couple," Donetta had said. "It's not picture perfect and we've got hurdles to overcome, but it's a beginning."

"No relationship is perfect," Geneva replied. "The main thing is that you were able to tell him the truth and he's accepted it. Honesty is the bedrock of any relationship, and now that you've established that, you can work through the rest."

"You're right, and I have to credit his mother for raising him to be the type of person he is."

Geneva admired the councilwoman even more knowing that Charlene had given Donetta and Phillip her blessing. Donetta had talked to Charlene by phone, and Charlene had told her that while she had certain concerns about Donetta and Phillip's relationship, as any caring parent would, she would nonetheless support them as a couple in any way that she could.

Geneva had wanted to call Charlene back to tell her about the blue box that Johnny had had the night he'd been murdered, but she decided against it because the woman had been dealing with more pressing issues. As an elected official, Charlene had to manage and respond to the concerns and complaints of frustrated, snowbound residents. She'd been providing support for her daughter—whom Geneva had learned from Donetta—had dropped out of medical school, was pregnant, and would be back in Amber living under Charlene's roof. And all that was on top of learning the news that her playboy son had been reformed by a trans woman. When Geneva added all those things together, she knew that her story about a blue box in a dream about a dead man could wait a few days until things calmed down in Charlene's life.

Now it was Monday morning, and Geneva and Samuel were at the airport. His parent's early morning flight was still running on time, and Samuel was inside the terminal, making sure they got their bags checked and tickets assigned, while Geneva sat in the parking deck inside their SUV, feeding Gabrielle her breakfast. She didn't know if Joe was at the airport or stuck in his hotel room because they hadn't heard from him since he'd left the house, and after the havoc he'd caused, no news seemed like good news. No one worried about Joe because if there was one thing he was good at, it was looking after himself above anyone else.

Geneva thought about how ironic it was that Phillip and her in-laws were scheduled to leave on the same flight. When she'd talked to Donetta last night and had learned that his Sunday morning flight had been rescheduled to today, she'd told Samuel's parents, who'd said they would make sure to be on the lookout for him at their gate so they could introduce themselves. As Geneva held Gabrielle while she fed her a bottle, she wondered if Phillip would actually make it to the airport at all.

Donetta's neighborhood had been hard hit, and snowplows had been scarce. Donetta had called Geneva this morning and told her that she'd kissed Phillip good-bye on her steps as she'd watched him make his way through the snow in the early morning darkness en route to his car, which was still parked off her exit. Donetta had also told her that Phillip didn't have the use of his cell phone, and Geneva said she'd already told her in-laws he was on their flight and they'd let him use their phone so he could call her and let her know he was safe.

Geneva smiled as she looked at her baby and thought about the fact that no matter how complicated situations could become, having people in your life whom you loved and who loved you back, made everything worthwhile. After all the emotions she'd experienced over this holiday, she was thankful that she'd had her family and that she'd come so far—and that made her think of Johnny.

Geneva burped Gabrielle and put her back in her car seat as she drifted off to sleep. "I guess I should call Charlene now and finish telling her about the blue box that the real killer took after she murdered Johnny." She hit speed-dial on her cell phone.

Chapter 33

CHARLENE

Charlene was glad she'd survived the holiday weekend, which had been no small feat considering the onslaught of drama she'd dealt with. Her fellow city council colleagues had nearly buckled under the pressures that had resulted from the massive snowstorm, but Charlene had looked at it as child's play when compared to the real chaos that had been brewing in her personal life.

Charlene had been driven to drink and even take sleeping pills as she'd tried to deal with the stress of Vivana's claim of new evidence. She'd tipped the scales of stress after she'd e-mailed Shartell, asking the gossiper to contact her because she had a juicy scoop for her, only to sit by her computer without receiving a reply. That was when Charlene knew for sure that Shartell was probably already at work on a story about who really killed Johnny Mayfield. Then, if that hadn't been bad enough, Geneva had called her on Thanksgiving Eve and told her about a dream that Charlene knew had to be real because she'd lived it. Geneva had abruptly hung up when her lights had gone out and had never called back, which Charlene hadn't been too concerned about because she'd had bigger concerns.

For Charlene, the threat of life in prison took a back-seat to the happiness of her children. Lauren and Phillip had each come to a pivotal crossroads in their lives over the weekend, and Charlene had had to put her own issues to the side to help them get through it.

Charlene had spent each day and night talking with Lauren about her and her unborn child's future, and slowly, the reliable, focused, and determined young woman whom Charlene had raised, started to return. Because Lauren had packed everything she owned and brought it home on the plane, there was no need for her to return to Baltimore, so Charlene had helped her get settled in for the long haul. She'd even called her good friend and OBGYN, Dr. Valerie Bell, and scheduled an appointment for Lauren on Monday morning, right after her meeting with Leslie Sachs.

Charlene had actually become more concerned about Phillip than she'd been about Lauren. Her daughter would be under the same roof with her every day, and she'd be able to keep a watchful eye on her so she could help when needed. But Phillip lived a plane ride away and had become involved in a relationship that would force him to come up against hurdles of discrimination that neither his nor Charlene's legal background would be able to protect him from. But even with that challenge, Charlene found comfort that her son was in love with someone who possessed good character and a kind heart, and for that she was grateful.

Now it was Monday morning and she was about to have one of the most important meetings of her life, and although Charlene was tired, she was ready for battle. Because she didn't know how the roads would be once she got out and she didn't want to run the risk of going back and forth in the snow, she decided to have Lauren ride with her and stay in the car with the engine running while she met with Leslie. Then after what she knew was going to be a short but intense conversation, she'd head over to Dr. Bell's office to make sure her grandchild was progressing nicely.

"Are you okay, Mom?" Lauren asked from the passenger seat. "You look tired."

"I'm fine, baby," Charlene replied. "I just have a lot on my mind, but I know that everything will all work out."

"I really appreciate everything you're doing for me, Mom."

Charlene smiled. "That's what mothers do, as you'll soon see."

Charlene came up to a four-way intersection. As she looked in all directions, she tried to anticipate some of Leslie's questions. She turned down the street that led to Leslie's house and felt her stomach jump. Leslie had called her an hour ago and asked Charlene to come to her house instead of the coffee shop.

"Are you able to get out of your neighborhood?" Leslie had asked after she'd labored through the niceties of post-holiday greetings.

"Yes, my street is passable. How about yours?"

"My street is fine, however, there's a five-foot snowdrift blocking my garage," Leslie had said. "But that's not the issue."

"What do you mean?"

"My garage is on the side of my house where the snow hasn't been plowed, so I can't get out."

"Would you like to reschedule for later in the week? The weather won't be an issue then."

"No," Leslie had said in a definitive tone. "Charlene, the matter I'd like to discuss with you regarding the new evidence I've uncovered in the Mayfield murder case is of particular concern to you, for legal reasons, and as you know I can't discuss it over the phone. Can you come to my house at the scheduled time?"

Charlene had known since last week that Leslie was going to try to trap her in a web, and now she'd confirmed it when she pulled up to Leslie's house and saw that the woman's garage was in plain view, and the huge snowdrift that Leslie spoke of had been shoveled to the side. Charlene even saw tire tracks leading from where Leslie had obviously driven her car out.

"Mom," Lauren said with a quizzical look on her face, "I thought you said you needed to meet Ms. Sachs at her house because she couldn't get out, but look." Lauren pointed her finger toward Leslie's garage. "The snow is gone and her garage is clear."

Charlene measured her breathing in an effort to remain calm because she didn't want Lauren to know how she really felt. "I see. I guess she must have gotten some help from one of her neighbors." She unbuckled her seatbelt and reached in the back seat for her handbag. "This shouldn't take long . . . ten minutes, tops, and then we'll head over to Dr. Bell's office."

Instead of being a nervous wreck as she'd been last week, Charlene was steady as a rock as she walked up to Leslie's door. She had her game face on and she was prepared to hit every ball Leslie threw her way. She rang the bell and waited.

"So glad you made it safely, Charlene," Leslie said as she opened the door. "Please come in."

Charlene entered, and intentionally stepped over Leslie's monogrammed doormat, purposely neglecting to wipe her feet. She smiled with satisfaction as she watched Leslie's eye twitch when she saw the mess that Charlene's dirt-covered boots left in her wake. "Looks like the situation with your garage got taken care of."

Leslie nodded. "Oh, that. Yes, one of my kind neighbors came over right after I called you and offered to shovel it for me."

Charlene knew that Leslie had just told her a lie, but she also knew that this conversation was going to be about lies and deceit, so she didn't waste her time debating the obvious.

"Let's talk in my study." Leslie pointed to her right and led the way. "I love being at the front of my house," she said. "I'm all about easy access."

Leslie sat behind her desk as Charlene took a seat in the ultra-plush chair in front of her. The chair was so inviting and comfortable that Charlene almost forgot that she was on guard. This was one of Leslie's tactics, making people feel comfortable as she went in for the kill. Charlene looked around Leslie's office, which looked more like a glammed-out walk-in closet than a home office. Now Charlene understood why the TV camera had zoomed in so closely on her during her Saturday morning interview. They hadn't wanted to include the shoes, handbags, and jewelry Leslie had displayed in her built-ins throughout the space.

"I know this isn't what you expected," Leslie said with a grin. "But like I said, I like easy access, and since I spend more time working in here than in any other room in the house, I can work late, fall asleep on my couch, and then get dressed and head out to the garage, which you can see is easily accessible, snow-drift and all."

"What new evidence do you have?" Charlene asked, getting straight to the point.

Leslie grinned. "You know that one of the first things we learned in law school was never to ask a question in court that we didn't know the answer to," she said slyly. "Well, we're not in court, but I think you already know the answer, and you know that Vivana Jackson is innocent of the murder of Johnny Mayfield."

Charlene crossed her legs and flipped her foot so the dirty snow on her boot could drip on Leslie's pristine cream-colored rug. "And how would I know that?"

Leslie didn't flinch. "Because you killed him."

"You must be out of your mind."

Leslie shook her head. "Cut it out, Charlene. I didn't call you over here to play games."

"You most certainly did, Leslie. Otherwise you would've gotten in your car and driven to the coffee shop the same way you did before I got here." Charlene's eyes narrowed in on the scone and cup of coffee on Leslie's desk. She'd frequented the Whole Bean

Café enough to know they were the only coffee shop in the city that served their one-of-a-kind, homemade lemon-poppyseed-blueberry scones. Charlene knew that Leslie was meticulous and careful, and that she'd left the food there on purpose.

"Admit that you killed Johnny Mayfield."

"As I said, you must be out of your mind."

Just then Charlene's phone rang. She'd talked to Phillip earlier that morning when he'd called her before he left Donetta's house. He'd told her that Geneva's in-laws were on his flight, and that he'd use their phone to call her once he reached his gate. Charlene pulled out her phone, intending to make sure Phillip had made it there safely and then shut Leslie down before walking back out the door. "Excuse me. I need to take this call from my son."

But when Charlene looked at her screen, it was Geneva's name and number that appeared. Charlene had told Geneva that she was going to meet with Leslie this morning, so she knew Geneva was probably calling to make sure. The last thing Charlene needed was for Geneva to take it upon herself to contact Leslie, so she answered her call. "I'm in the middle of something, I'll call you back."

"Are you meeting with Leslie Sachs?"

"Yes."

"Thank you so much, Charlene. I can't tell you how grateful I am to you," Geneva said with gratitude in her voice. "I won't keep you, I just wanted to tell you one more detail I remembered from my dream that I think is proof that Vivana didn't kill Johnny."

Charlene's heart started beating fast, but she remained as cool as a fan. "Okay."

Geneva spoke quickly. "Right before Johnny was

murdered in the kitchen, he'd been sitting on the couch in the living room looking through a decorative blue box, like the kind you get at craft stores, and it was filled with photos, plus a few DVDs and a burner phone. He was still holding the box in his hand when he walked into the kitchen. When I finally walked into the room the killer was leaving, and I noticed the blue box was gone. Whoever killed Johnny has that blue box, because it contained the evidence."

Charlene immediately regretted that she'd answered Geneva's call, because she'd been thrown off her game once again, and this time Charlene didn't know whether she could recover. Geneva had been accurate in all that she'd told Charlene up to now. After Charlene had killed Johnny, she'd looked around the kitchen to make sure she hadn't left any evidence behind before fleeing the scene. She was certain there hadn't been a decorative blue box anywhere in the room, since that was something she couldn't have missed. "Thanks so much, I'll call you back," she said in a strictly-business tone. Charlene slid her finger across the phone and hung up on Geneva as she tried to refocus. When she looked up, Leslie was staring into her eyes with a maniacal expression on her face.

"Your phone call almost caught me off guard," Leslie said. "But lucky for me I added some extra time into my plan to account for any unforeseen mishaps that might arise."

"What are you talking about?"

Leslie looked at her watch. "The camera crew will be here shortly, and once they call the police this entire messy ordeal will be over." Leslie pulled a gun from her desk drawer, aimed it at Charlene, and smiled.

"What the hell is wrong with you? Why're you pulling a gun on me?" Charlene said in terror.

"Because I'm going to kill you."

"Leslie, put the gun away," Charlene said, mustering what little calm she had left. Slowly, she looked out the corner of her eye to see if she could run in a zigzag motion past Leslie's collection of clothes and shoes so that the crazy woman wouldn't have a straight line of fire. But something caught Charlene's eye that made her blood suddenly run cold. Sitting off to the side on Leslie's shelf was a decorative blue box, right next a pair of red heels. Charlene's mind immediately went to what Geneva had told her, and then to Leslie's Saturday morning interview.

Charlene had memorized every word that Leslie had said and every movement she'd made during her interview in an attempt to gain some insight into what the cunning woman might have been planning. Charlene remembered that at one point during the interview when Leslie had talked about the new evidence, she'd looked off-camera to the side, as if something had caught her attention. Now Charlene knew that Leslie had been looking at the blue box, and she'd probably been gloating because she had the evidence right there in the room. But Charlene couldn't figure out how that box had come into Leslie's possession. Charlene jumped when she heard Leslie bang the butt of the gun against her desk.

Leslie smiled and began to twirl the pistol in her hand, showing that she was adept with the weapon. She changed her smile to a smirk as she set the gun down on her desk, making sure to rest her hand atop the handle. "Bravo, Councilwoman Harris. I see the wheels turning, and you're trying to figure out how the blue box ended up on my shelf after you carelessly forgot to take it with you after you shot Johnny."

Charlene remained silent and still.

"It must have been pure torture for you, knowing that you left such a crucial piece of evidence behind that contained a video of you and Johnny getting it on. I can only imagine how scared and frantic you felt, especially after I sent you that text."

Charlene shifted her weight in her seat.

"I would've given anything to see the look on your face when you read it," Leslie said with another wide smirk. "I bet you stayed up day and night trying to figure out who sent it. But I've got to hand it to you, Charlene. You didn't respond, or panic and make a stupid move like most people would've."

Charlene shook her head at the thought that Leslie had been behind the text all along. But at the moment, that revelation was a moot point that didn't make a difference. Charlene no longer cared about how Leslie had ended up with the blue box, or that she herself had overlooked it that fateful night. The only thing Charlene now regretted was that she wouldn't be around to see her children through the challenges that lay ahead. And as she stared at Leslie's gun, she knew how Johnny must have felt when he realized he was going to die.

"I really wish I didn't have to kill you, Charlene," Leslie said. "I actually liked you, and I used to think you were one of the few people I'd ever met whom I considered to be on my intellectual level. But sadly, I realized you weren't on the night of Johnny's murder—because you left the blue box behind. Lucky for me, I came in right behind you and found it."

Charlene broke her silence. "What? This is crazy!"

"No," Leslie said with a smile, "it's genius and smart, but not crazy. Johnny had been blackmailing me just like he'd done all those other women. I'd been watching him for months, plotting my move. Once I read about what happened to Geneva in the police blotter, I knew I had to stop him, just like I did that pig who raped me when I was a naïve young associate. As fate would have it, though, our brilliant minds thought alike and we planned to kill Johnny on the same night. You got there before I did and handled the tricky part for me by shooting him. After I watched you casually saunter out the door, I went in behind you and recovered the evidence that's sitting on my shelf."

"I never saw that blue box," Charlene said quietly, admitting guilt for the first time.

"I almost missed it, too. I guess when Johnny was fixing his drink, he was so wasted that he put it in the cabinet along with the liquor. I knew he'd been drinking, so I looked to see if he'd left anything near his booze, and bingo!"

"Why are you doing this, Leslie? You're an eyewitness to the murder I committed and you have the evidence. Why go through all this trouble, and why kill me? Why didn't you just go to the authorities the next day?"

Leslie laughed, pleased with herself. "What fun would that have been? I decided to toy with you so I could study the way you went about covering your tracks. You actually taught me a thing or two that I can use, and pretending to be Geneva's friend . . . that was classic."

"It wasn't an act. She's a good woman, and I'm

sorry I put her through hell." Charlene shook her head and swallowed hard.

"Whatever, Charlene." Leslie sighed, as if she was growing bored.

"You'll never get away with this, Leslie. How're you going to explain killing me?"

"I've gotten away with at least ten murders since I killed that bastard over thirty years ago, and I'll simply add you to the list. Once I shoot you, the news crew I called yesterday will arrive under the pretext that they're going to do a breaking news interview of me unveiling the evidence. But what they're going to find is the body of a respected city council member I had to kill in self-defense because I'd uncovered your sex tape . . . in that little blue box." Leslie paused. "Of course, you know I took mine out."

Charlene shook her head again. "You're sick."

"Maybe so, but no one will think that except you, and it won't matter because you'll be dead. I'll be a hero, I'll write a book, and I'll be the most celebrated criminal defense attorney in the country."

Charlene looked over at the blue box and closed her eyes.

"If you hadn't been moving so slowly that night I might not have seen you," Leslie said, as she picked up the gun. "But I have to admit I was surprised. I didn't think you had it in you, Charlene. You walked out of there without a care in the world, as if you were taking a stroll in the park. You've got guts."

Charlene's eyes narrowed in on Leslie's. "What are you talking about? I ran out of Johnny's house like I was being chased."

Leslie laughed. "Most people come clean and confess their wrongs right before they die, so they can leave this world with a clear conscience. But you're going to lie to the end. Like I said, you've got guts."

"I'm not lying. I was so frantic after what I'd done that I ran out the door at full speed and I didn't stop until I got to my car."

"That's impossible," Leslie said.

The sound of Lauren's voice startled them both. "No, it's not!"

Charlene and Leslie turned their heads to find Lauren standing in the middle of the doorway. Charlene was so shocked she couldn't move and Leslie was equally taken by surprise. Slowly, Lauren entered the room as Leslie grabbed her gun and rose from behind her desk. Charlene felt a rising sense of panic. She wasn't sure how much Lauren had heard, but it didn't matter because she'd seen the gun in Leslie's hand, and now that meant Leslie was going to have to kill Lauren, too.

"Charlene, you really should've kept your daughter out of this. Now the police are going to have a double homicide on their hands."

Charlene rushed from her chair and stood in front of her daughter. "Leslie, please don't do this. Lauren didn't do anything, so let her go. I'll confess to everything, just please don't hurt my baby."

"You don't have to confess to anything, Mom," Lauren said in a calm voice. "You didn't race out of Johnny's house that night because you're not the one who killed him. I did."

Charlene and Leslie both looked at Lauren with shock and disbelief.

"What are you talking about?" Charlene said, feeling as though she was getting ready to lose what little balance she had left.

"Johnny had to pay for what he'd done, so I went to his house to kill him. When I got there he'd already been shot, but he was still alive. I didn't know who beat me there and pulled the trigger, but I knew I needed to finish him off. I walked over to where he was lying on the floor and I could see that he was trying to talk . . . to ask me to help him. But he couldn't really speak. That's when I bent down over him and covered his nose and mouth until he stopped breathing.

Charlene's eyes grew wide and her hand flew to her mouth. "Lauren, what are you saying?"

"She's saying she killed that son of a bitch," Leslie said with a laugh. "Now it makes sense why the coroner's report said he died of suffocation on his own blood as a result of being shot. This just keeps getting better. A mother-daughter tag-team murder duo."

Lauren lowered her head. "I'm sorry, Mom."

They all jumped when they heard a door slam outside and voices coming from the front yard. The news crew had just arrived and they were taking their equipment out of their van.

Leslie walked toward Charlene and Lauren. "I hate to break up this touching confession but I've got a job to do before News Channel 7 knocks on that door." She aimed her gun directly at Charlene and pulled the trigger.

Pooooowwww!

"Urrgghhh!" Charlene groaned. The hot, burning sensation of Leslie's bullet was painful, but it didn't stop her because she knew she had to save Lauren. She gritted her teeth and lunged forward, grabbing Leslie by her wrist as they both fell to the floor. In a quick move Charlene managed to wrestle the gun from Leslie's hand, aim it toward her neck, and shoot her in the throat.

Lauren raced to her mother's side. "Oh God, Oh God!" she said in a panic as she dropped to the floor beside Charlene.

Charlene's jacket was covered in Leslie's blood, and the woman's gurgling became erratic as she fought to breathe.

Ding, Dong. Knock, Knock!

"Is everything okay in there?" One of the cameramen had heard the shots as they were unloading their news van and rushed to the door. "We heard shots. We just called the police."

Charlene managed to roll over on her side, and when she did, blood oozed from her abdomen.

"Mom!" Lauren cried. "Oh God! Please don't die. Please don't die."

Charlene had faced many difficult situations in her life, and with each one she'd developed a plan and moved forward with solving the problem. She knew that this moment was no different, and she had to think quickly. She was losing blood, her head felt light, and she knew it would be only a matter of minutes before she lost consciousness. "I'm okay," Charlene said as she breathed hard, trying to calm Lauren. "Baby, I need you to focus and listen to everything I'm about to say."

Lauren began to cry and that's when Charlene knew she was going to have to get tough with her daughter. "Listen to me, dammit!" Charlene hissed, as she labored to speak. "The police are going to be here any minute. Don't say a word, do you hear me?"

Lauren continued to cry, and was now rocking

back and forth, nearly hysterical. Charlene grabbed her daughter's hand and squeezed. "Look at me, Lauren," she said in a tone that finally got her daughter's attention. "Don't say anything, to anyone, under any circumstances. Not even your brother. They'll think you're in shock, and that will buy you some time. But don't say a word. Do you understand?"

Lauren nodded.

"Repeat what I said."

"I won't say a word, Mom."

"Good, I'll handle everything."

The last thing Charlene remembered hearing before she lost consciousness was her daughter's soft cries and the sound of sirens blaring from the police squad cars outside.

Charlene blinked slowly as she opened her eyes in her dimly-lit room. She looked down at the tubes extending from her nose and arms and realized she was in the hospital.

"Thank God, you're awake," Lauren said. She rose from her chair beside Charlene's bed and went to her side. "We've been so worried about you, Mom."

Charlene smiled, but it quickly faded when she saw that Lauren was wearing a hospital gown and robe. "Are you . . ." she coughed as she tried to speak. "Are you all right?"

"I'm fine, Mom."

Charlene's voice was now a raspy whisper. "Why're you wearing a hospital gown?"

"They admitted me right after the shooting. I haven't spoken a word to anyone since that day, not even to Phillip. And like you said, they think I'm in shock so they admitted me. They've been probing me every day but I haven't said a word."

Charlene closed her eyes and took a deep breath. "How many days have passed?"

"Three."

Just then a nurse walked into the room. "You're awake!" she said with enthusiasm. She looked at Lauren. "I know you're happy to see your mother's eyes open, aren't you?"

Lauren looked at the nurse with a blank stare, and remained silent.

Charlene swallowed and grimaced with pain. It felt as though sandpaper was lodged in her throat. She tried to speak again, but this time she could barely talk. "My stomach hurts, and my throat is . . ." she couldn't finish her sentence.

The nurse immediately started taking Charlene's vitals. "That's to be expected, Ms. Harris. You suffered a gunshot to your abdomen, but you were lucky because it missed your intestines, and the bullet came out right through your back. And your throat is sore because we had to intubate you. We took the tracheal intubation out this morning and the scratchiness will go away in a day or so."

Charlene let out a deep breath as her words sputtered out. "Am I going to be all right?"

"Shhh," the nurse said. "Try not to speak. You need to save your strength. I'm going to get you some pain meds and let the doctor know that you're awake."

Once the nurse was out of the room Lauren spoke up. "The doctor said you're going to make a full recovery. But we don't have much time because the staff has been instructed to contact the police as soon as you regain consciousness."

Charlene knew that Lauren had figured out that they needed to get their stories in sync. Although it was hard for her to speak, Charlene whispered quickly. "You got out of the car because you had to use the bathroom. You rang the doorbell and when no one answered you came inside, thinking something might be wrong. You stood outside Leslie's study and listened as she confessed to coming into Johnny's house after I'd shot him. He was still alive so she covered his mouth and nose until he stopped breathing, then she took the blue box and . . ." Charlene stopped when she realized that Leslie had left everyone's tapes in the box except her own, and that was the crucial piece of evidence that would tie Leslie to Johnny and corroborate her motive.

"Don't worry," Lauren said. "Once the police found the blue box they searched Leslie's house and they found it hidden inside one of her legal books."

Charlene nodded and continued. "Leslie was planning to kill me and let me take the fall for Johnny's murder, got it?"

Lauren nodded. "I mean, yes." She shook her head. "I've gotten so used to not talking. I'm still in silent mode."

"Good, stay that way until I give my statement." Charlene was glad that Lauren had kept quiet, which relieved some of her worries. But she couldn't fully relax, because she knew she had to finish talking before her voice gave out or the police came. "The rest of the story will be exactly what Leslie said about her being a hero and a celebrated attorney." Charlene braced herself for the pain as she cleared her throat again. "The police will probably be here any minute, so repeat everything to me as quickly as you can. Don't add or take away from anything I said."

Charlene watched the door as she listened carefully to her daughter recite her account of what happened the day of the shooting. She was amazed by how smoothly Lauren systematically rattled off each detail, just as she'd been instructed, no more and no less. Charlene knew that if Lauren ever had to take the witness stand she'd nail her testimony. "Very good," Charlene said. Under any other circumstance, Charlene would have been proud of how Lauren had just performed, but her pride grew dim because she realized that most killers were efficient when it came to details.

"Mom, I'm so sorry about all this. I know you're wondering how I got mixed up with Johnny and why I killed him. It's a long story, and I'll tell you when you get out."

Charlene shook her head. "I shot him, but Leslie killed him. Leslie Sachs is the killer."

Lauren nodded. "Okay."

"It's good to see you awake, Ms. Harris," the doctor said as he entered the room. Charlene reached for Lauren's hand as they watched two police detectives walk in on the heels of the doctor.

A week after being admitted to the hospital, Charlene was released. Her injuries had been serious, but she'd miraculously bounced back. "She's got the heart of a fighter," her doctor had said. The truth was Charlene wasn't fighting for herself, she was fighting for her children, and she knew in order to do that she had to stay alive.

Charlene had smiled with gratitude when Phillip

and Lauren drove her home and then got her settled into her bed. "It's good to be home again," she said.

Phillip nodded. "You've been through a lot, Mom. Get some rest."

Charlene looked up when she saw Lauren enter her bedroom carrying a glass of water.

"Here, Mom," Lauren said. "I thought you might be thirsty."

"Thanks," Charlene said.

Lauren turned to her brother. "I'm going to stay in here with Mom until she falls asleep."

"Okay, if either of you needs anything I'll be down the hall."

They waited until they were sure Phillip was out of earshot before they began to speak. Lauren sat on the edge of her mother's bed and held her hand. "I'm going to tell you what happened, and how I got involved with Johnny."

Charlene nodded and lay in quiet shock as Lauren divulged the details of what had led her to become a killer.

"I was at a very low point in my life after everything that happened with Jeffery," Lauren said. "I was hurt and humiliated, but I couldn't tell anyone I was pregnant because I was also embarrassed and ashamed. While I was at the clinic where I had the abortion I met a nurse named Candace, who volunteered there on weekends. We instantly bonded and she told me that I could call her if I ever needed anything. After I returned to school I kept in contact with her. We talked several times a week and she helped me through some dark days. I don't know what I would've done without her.

"One night I called her and I could tell she'd been crying. Candace was strong, like you, Mom, and she wasn't the type to shed tears easily. She'd had a really bad argument with Bernard, who was her fiancé. He'd been in a downward spiral for months after losing his job, and it was all because of his best friend, Johnny Mayfield. Johnny had come to Bernard's job talking junk about Candace. One thing led to another and they ended up fighting right there in Bernard's office. A few days later Bernard was fired and a few months after that his finances fell apart, and that's when the arguments, along with Bernard's heavy drinking started.

"A week later, Candace called me, and she was distraught. She'd gone over to Bernard's house and found him passed out drunk with a naked woman lying beside him. Candace called off the wedding and gave Bernard his ring back. I called Candace the next day to check on her and she was crying again, this time because Johnny had caused his estranged wife to miscarry in a bad fall. Candace had said that she'd been a really nice woman, and that losing her baby had devastated her."

Charlene sat up and cleared her throat. "That woman was my stylist, Geneva."

Lauren nodded. "Yes, I know that now."

"That man hurt a lot of people."

There was a silent pause, and Lauren wiped away a tear. "After losing a baby of my own, all because of a tangled web caused by a liar and a cheat, I lost it, and I wanted to rid the world of men like Dad and Johnny. I couldn't find it in my heart to kill my own father, but I didn't think twice about killing Johnny."

Charlene bristled at the fact that her daughter had found it so easy to kill someone, but then again, Charlene knew that she'd done the same thing. She took a sip of her water and cleared her throat. "So you'd never met him? You just knew about him through your friend, Candace?"

"Yes, after our conversation I googled Johnny and found out everything I needed to know about him. A week later I rented a car and drove to Amber to kill him."

"My Lord," Charlene said, thinking about how she'd spent a week plotting how she would kill the same man whom her daughter had also targeted.

"I parked several blocks from his house and walked to his back door. It was ajar so I let myself in, and you know the rest."

Charlene nodded. "What are the odds of both of us trying to kill the same man on the same night?"

"Beyond that, throw in the fact that Leslie Sachs crept up to kill him, too, just in time to see me leave. I guess because at the time you and I were the same size, and because we look so much alike, she thought I was you."

"Plus . . ." Charlene hesitated, but then decided to speak her truth. "I'm sure that after Leslie went through the blue box searching for her tape, and then stumbled across mine, she matched things up and started plotting. This feels like a bad dream."

Lauren let out a heavy sigh. "It's been a nightmare, Mom. From the moment I stood over Johnny's dead body my life started slipping away, and I didn't care about anything anymore. It was as if my life was moving in slow motion."

"That's why you walked slowly out of the house, as if you didn't have a care in the world." Charlene said with new understanding.

"Yes, and it's also why I gained all the weight and changed who I was. I wanted to distance myself from the person who'd killed a baby and murdered a man. The last two years have been hell. When I came home last week I was angry and afraid, but you showed me that I was still worthy, and that meant the world to me." Lauren smiled, and then became serious. "Then, while we were snowed in I watched a replay of Leslie Sach's interview online and I felt like everything was going to fall apart all over again. I didn't know what to do.

"But miraculously, you scheduled a doctor's appointment for me on the same day you went to meet with Leslie . . ."

Charlene nodded. "If you hadn't been there, I wouldn't be here right now."

"I remember growing up you used to always tell Phillip and me that everything always works out the way it's supposed to, and not a minute before or after its proper time. You were right, Mom, it does."

The two women looked at each other for a long time, each thinking silent thoughts about what the future might hold.

EPILOGUE

Two Years Later

Charlene Harris had been forced to resign from the Amber City Council and was sentenced to one year in jail on aggravated assault charges stemming from the fact that she'd shot, but not killed, Johnny Mayfield. Charlene had gotten lucky, though, because the judge had reduced her sentence to time served, and she was free to help care for her new granddaughter while her daughter, Lauren, attended medical school at ASU. Charlene also enjoyed visiting DC and spending time with her new grandson, whom her son, Phillip, and his wife, Donetta, had adopted after they'd gotten married last year. She did all this in between her adjunct professorship at the university law school, where she taught

Criminal Defense 101, or as it had been aptly nick-named: How To Get Away With Murder.

As for Geneva, the calm, mild-mannered hairstylist and business owner became a *New York Times* and international best-selling author after penning her memoir which detailed her life and times with the man behind one of the most infamous and deadly webs of murder the country had ever seen.

Even Shartell and Joe ended up smelling the roses. After Samuel had thrown Joe out of his and Geneva's house, Joe had immediately called Shartell and told her that he had another juicy story that he could give her if she came by his hotel. In reality, the only thing Joe had was loneliness, which turned into horniness once Shartell got there and was snowed in with him. They'd been holed up in his room through the snow-storm, and that was why Joe hadn't called his family and Shartell hadn't responded to Charlene's e-mail. Eventually they moved to California together and opened a detective agency that specialized in catching cheating spouses.

There was one person who faded into the back-ground, and that was Vivana Jackson. After she was re-leased from prison, she'd tried to sell her story for a book deal, like the one Geneva had gotten. But Vivana had been such an unmarketable and despised figure that her would-be publisher walked away from the deal after she cursed out the CEO, along with the entire ed-itorial staff, during negotiations. It didn't help that she'd made public threats to each of them and then was arrested, spending three months in jail for the offense before moving back to the rural South Carolina town where she'd been born.

But there was one other person who'd faded into the background even deeper than Vivana Jackson, and that was Leslie Sachs. The gunshot wound to her throat had left her a quadriplegic in a vegetative state. After Charlene and Lauren Harris gave their sworn statements, detectives combed through every detail of Leslie's life and all of her grimy criminal activities came to light, including the other murders she'd committed over the years. Now she spent her days in a nursing facility run by the Alabama Department of Corrections. The only person holding on to hope that Leslie would regain consciousness was her sister, Camille Sachs. Camille had never believed Charlene and Lauren's story, and she prayed each day that Leslie would open her eyes so the real truth could come to light.